And then he kissed her.

Faith felt the sweetness pour into her with so much force that she would have melted down the horse's flanks had his arm not been holding her secure. The kiss was so wonderful and so unlike anything she'd ever experienced that all she could do was surrender to the tantalizing lure of his masterful lips against her untutored own. Her virgin mouth answered him hesitantly at first; enjoying the tastes and textures, letting herself be swept away by the swell of pleasure until her shyness took flight and was replaced by an age-old knowing of the woman awakening inside. His lips brushed against her cheek and she shimmered in response as they traveled up her jaw before settling possessively against her mouth once more. She couldn't breathe or think. The sensations sparked by this interlude were creating a storm.

"Nick," she rasped in a strangled voice. "We must stop," but she didn't want him to. He was gifting her with short, heated presses of his lips, punctuating them with lazy strokes of his flame-tipped tongue against her mouth's parted corners, and she had to stop this or die.

"Please," she pleaded and drew away. She was breathless. Trying to find herself in the haze around her, she looked up into his handsome face and saw the glitter of his eyes in the moonlight.

Romances by **Beverly Jenkins**

BEVERLY JENKINS

MIDNIGHT

AVON

An Imprint of HarperCollinsPublishers

This is a work of fiction. Names, characters, places, and incidents are products of the author's imagination or are used fictitiously and are not to be construed as real. Any resemblance to actual events, locales, organizations, or persons, living or dead, is entirely coincidental.

AVON BOOKS
An Imprint of HarperCollins*Publishers*
195 Broadway
New York, NY 10007

First Avon Books paperback printing: November 2010

Avon Trademark Reg. U.S. Pat. Off. and in Other Countries, Marca Registrada, Hecho en U.S.A.
HarperCollins® is a registered trademark of HarperCollins Publishers.

Printed in the U.S.A.

10 9 8 7 6 5 4 3

For Carrie Miller

MIDNIGHT

MIDNIGHT

Prologue

Boston
December 1774

Primus Grey waited in the dark behind his print shop for his contact to arrive. Although she'd passed him secret information about the British before, he was the only member of the Sons of Liberty to know her true identity. To the others she was known only as Lady Midnight, the code name he'd bestowed upon her in honor of the time she usually appeared. Quiet as a shadow and silent as the moonlight, she never tarried longer than the time it took to pass along whatever news she had to relay, and then she was gone. More than once, he'd been asked by the Sons to trail her in an attempt to learn who she might be, but in truth, he preferred they not know. In the world of spies, the less they knew about her, the less likely she could be betrayed.

A bit past midnight, she arrived. "Good evening, Mr. Grey."

"M'lady. What news have you?"

"Your name has come to the attention of General Gage. You should leave Boston immediately if you do not wish to hang for treason. I'm so sorry."

He froze.

"Godspeed, Mr. Grey."

Filled with alarm, he watched her fade into the darkness before hurrying back inside to gather what personal belongings he could, but it was too late. A pounding on the door made him look up.

A voice shouted, "Primus Grey!" The knocking grew louder.

Fighting to keep his voice even, he called out, "Who's there?"

"Representatives of the King."

He drew in a deep breath and walked over to open the door.

There were six of them, all wearing the red coats of the British Army. It was a cold night and he could see the steam from their breaths in the dim light of the torch above his door. The sharp tips of their bayonets glittered ominously in the moonlight. "What do you want with me?"

"You are under arrest."

"And the charge?"

"Treason for aiding the rebels against the King."

His chin rose. "Let me lock my shop."

They allowed him to do so, and once it was done, they surrounded him. Word of their mission must have spread because a crowd of angry citizens began to gather. Primus couldn't tell how many strong they were, but by the lights of the torches lining the shops and homes on the narrow winding street, they appeared sizable. Calls and curses began to rain down on the soldiers. Snowballs flew at their heads. The citizens of Boston had grown weary of the presence of the King's four thousand troops who'd been stationed in and around the city for the sole purpose of putting down the growing rebellion.

"Let him go!" a male voice rang out.

"Bloody lobster backs!" cried out another.

Rocks and snowballs flew, some hitting the soldiers, who quickly responded by taking up a defensive position around their prisoner. More people began to arrive, adding their voices and rocks to the fray. The officer in charge raised his weapon and sent out a warning shot. The people moved back. British soldiers had fired on a similar crowd back in March 1770, and when the smoke cleared, men lay dead, including Crispus Attucks, a mariner of mixed African and Nantucket blood. In the five years since, the incident had become known as the Boston Massacre, and stood as one of the most grievous marks against the policies of the hated King George III and his equally despised Parliament.

Apparently no one wanted to die that night. The crowd continued to hurl curses, snowballs, and chunks of ice, but the soldiers were allowed to leave with their prisoner.

Chapter 1

Boston
March 1775

Faith Kingston stirred the venison stew in the big black pot hanging above the fire in her father's inn. There weren't many people inside, just a few of his loyalist friends, but he was expecting General Gage and his officers for supper shortly.

"Is the stew ready, Faith?" he asked, entering the main room. Stuart Kingston was a portly man and his face bore the dark kiss of his Jamaican heritage. He'd been in the cellar preparing the room for Gage and the others.

"It will be in time, Father, don't worry."

"Not many inns can boast of feeding the general, Faith. It is quite a boon for us."

Even though she didn't agree, she nodded. Her dislike of the crown and its occupying troops mirrored that of the rebels, but she kept her views to herself. Her father was a staunch loyalist. In his eyes, all the repressive laws, taxes, and soldiers were necessary to bring the rebellious colonies back under the King's rule.

Moments later, the inn's door opened. Cold March air swept into the main room, bringing with it the general and his aides. Without a word, the six officers retired to the cellar, and Faith hurried to ladle the stew into a smaller vessel so she could serve them. As far as she knew, the general was never charged for his meals, and his lack of greeting always rankled her. Whether the discourtesy offended her father was unknown, but she was offended enough for the both of them.

"Hurry, Faith," he implored her, "and don't let them find fault with your serving."

At her entrance into the cellar room the six men looked up and all conversation ceased. The silence held while she ladled the rich stew into their bowls, and not one of them offered the slightest acknowledgment of her presence or thanked her for her service. She set what remained of the stew in the center of the table. Offering a terse curtsy, she withdrew as silently as she'd come. However, she didn't immediately return upstairs. Instead, she quietly entered the small room next door where the inn's extra wood was kept in order to listen to what they might say. It was widely assumed that once the weather broke for good, and the Concord Road leading to Boston became more passable, Gage would be sending troops to root out the weapons the Sons of Liberty were amassing in anticipation of armed confrontation. There'd already been one such confrontation back in February. Troops sent to nearby Salem to confiscate suspected weapons caches had been met and opposed by a group of minutemen led by Colonel Thomas Pickering. No shots were fired during the tense standoff, and after a compromise the British were allowed to conduct their search. However, the rebels' cannons, shot, and guns had already been safely hidden away, so the redcoats marched back to their Boston barracks empty-handed.

This evening Gage and his men were indeed discussing the rebels and sneering at the minutemen's military readiness and capabilities.

"They're so raw and undisciplined, the cowards will probably throw down their muskets and run in the face of our superior skill and numbers."

"Hear! Hear!" the aides cheered.

Faith held on to her temper. The colonial minutemen might not equal the British force in numbers or skill but their hearts and determination were strong, factors Gage would do well not to underestimate.

Gage added, "And to make certain we put the fear of God and the Empire in them, I've made a request for more men. They should arrive by May, along with Generals Howe, Clinton, and Burgoyne."

Faith knew this was something the Sons would be interested in knowing. That more soldiers would be added to the occupying force was not good news. With that, she left her hiding place and quickly returned above stairs.

Her father was in the kitchen looking worried when she entered. She knew he was concerned that she might have offended the general in some way, so she told him reassuringly, "All's well, Father. I brought no dishonor to your name."

"See that you don't," he pronounced, and exited.

Faith shook her head at his attitude. All her life she'd done her best to be a respectful and dutiful daughter. She rose every morning before dawn to start the morning fires, served him breakfast promptly at six, and spent the rest of the day cooking, cleaning, mending, and taking care of all else needing attending to, yet it never seemed enough. Her mother, Morna, had died during a pox outbreak in 1757, leaving the eight-year-old Faith to be raised by a father who'd provided for her and made sure she was educated, but offered very little in the way of gentleness or affection. She was now twenty-six years old and felt no more loved than she had at age eight. She shrugged off the melancholy and turned her mind and hands to rolling out more biscuits.

Nicholas Grey was weary after the long ride from New York to Boston. A smuggler and a mercenary by trade, he'd fought with the French and the native tribes against the British during the French and Indian War, and he wasn't sure what kind of reception he'd receive from his loyalist father. Primus hadn't approved of Nick going against the King, and they hadn't seen each other in over a decade. Regardless of the reception, the urge to see his father had set him on this weeks-long journey to return to his home to see how the old man fared, in hopes of reconciling their differences.

When he arrived at the large wooden farmhouse where'd he been born, no lights could be seen shining from inside. Because of the late hour, he assumed his father was sleeping, so he drove the wagon around to the back of the property to the barn. Using his flint, Nick lit the oil lamp that hung by the barn door so he could see his way in. Finding the interior empty gave him pause. Where were his father's horse and other animals? It never occurred to him that Primus might not be there or that the land might now have a new owner. At the moment, however, his weary horses didn't care about the mystery and neither did he; all he needed was rest after the long cold trip, so he bedded the horses down, walked out to the pump to get water, and then knocked on the back door. No response. He tried the latch and the door swung open.

The inside was cold and dark. Waving the lantern around, he walked through the large kitchen and into the front parlor with its familiar furnishings. Memories of growing up flooded back. The large portrait of his late mother, Adeline, still hung above the mantel on the fireplace. Although she'd died giving him birth, he'd always imagined her smiling down on him with maternal love. As he looked up at her now, the sense was still strong. He left the parlor and walked to the staircase that led to the bedrooms on the second floor.

"Primus!" he called out. "The prodigal has returned!" But the echoing words went unanswered.

"He isn't here, Nick."

Nicholas turned, and in the lantern light saw his old friend and neighbor Artemis Clegg standing on the door's threshold. "Arte?"

"How are you, Nick?"

Nick set the lantern on the floor and the two men greeted each other with a strong, welcoming embrace. Arte lived on a farm directly across the road. He was considerably shorter than Nick's own six-foot-plus height, and they'd been friends since childhood.

Arte said, "I saw the light and came over to investigate. It's good to have you back."

"It's good to be back. Where's the old man?"

Artemis didn't respond for a long moment and Nick waited.

He finally spoke. "The British arrested him a few days after Christmas."

"What for?"

"Treason. Accused him of aiding the rebels."

"There has to be a mistake. Primus would never go against the King. Where's he being held?"

"He died three weeks ago on a British brig anchored off the harbor. Pneumonia."

The news put a weakness in Nicholas's knees that almost dropped him to the floor. The terrible sick feeling inside was unlike any he'd ever experienced before. *Dead?*

Artemis said gently, "Come with me over to the house. Bekkah can feed you while I tell you what I know."

Nick couldn't move.

"Come," Arte beckoned.

Reeling, Nicholas followed Arte out into the night.

Seated in the dining room of Artemis's home, Nicholas ate while Arte began the tale.

"I'd heard rumors that your father was a member of the Sons of Liberty, but it wasn't something he and I ever discussed. Some men are playing their affiliation close to the vest, and with good reason. Men have been hung, tarred and feathered, their homes broken into by the soldiers, then looted and burned."

Nick set his bowl aside and stared grimly into the shadows thrown off by the fire in the grate. That the staunchly loyalist Primus had even allied himself with the rebels against the crown was as surprising to hear of as his death. "How did the British find out about him?"

Arte shrugged. "I don't know. I was only allowed to speak with him privately for a few minutes before he was taken to the brig, and he told me that he'd been warned to leave Boston by the person he knew as Lady Midnight only moments before his arrest."

"Lady Midnight? Who is she?"

"Rumor has it that she's a spy for the rebels, but no one knows her true identity."

"Sounds more like an actress or a harlot," Nick noted, having had ample experience with both.

"True, but she's reportedly passed along information to John Hancock and Sam Adams, too."

"But if the soldiers arrived right after her warning, is it possible that she's working for the British?"

"Yes. There are so-called double agents, and she had to have gotten the information about Primus's arrest from somewhere or someone."

Nick left the riddle of Lady Midnight for a moment and thought about the war rumors sweeping the colonies. "It's said there will be a fight."

"I believe it's inevitable. Boston is leading the opposition and we are prepared to meet arms with arms, but only if England fires first."

"You say *we*. Do you consider yourself a rebel as well?"

"I do and proudly."

Nicholas considered Artemis a most unlikely candidate for a soldier. While they were growing up together, Nicholas had dreamt of seeing the world, but all Arte wanted to do was marry Bekkah Davis and tend his father's orchards in peace.

Artemis continued, "We could certainly use a man of your experience. Many veterans of the war with France have thrown in with us and they've been a godsend. The majority of the minutemen are farmers and merchants. We know nothing of weapons, tactics, or marching but we're drilling daily in preparation."

Nick had no plans to get involved, at least not at the present. His mind was on his father. "Did the British confiscate our land?"

"Yes. The sale occurred last week. I purchased it, though, hoping you'd come back to claim it someday."

For the first time that night, Nick's heart warmed. "Thank you, friend."

"I don't know how you're sitting coin wise, but if you need to buy it back a piece at a time, I'm amenable."

Nick shook his head. "I have enough to pay you in full." The years he'd spent smuggling weapons, trapping, and playing guide to the French, British, and Americans looking for new territory to own in spite of the tribes' prior claim, had made him a very wealthy man.

"When it is convenient," Arte reassured him.

Nick nodded even as the mystery surrounding his father's arrest reclaimed his thoughts. Solving the conundrum might be next to impossible, but he vowed it would be solved, even if it took the rest of his life. His father was due that respect from his only son. It came to him then that maybe he would join the rebels, if only to be able to access information that might help him accomplish his goal, but he kept the plans to himself for the present. He wanted to wait until he knew more about the British and the rebels before making a final decision. "Has he been buried?"

"Yes. Bekkah and I paid for the headstone. We laid him to rest next to your mother at Copp's Hill."

Nick was grateful. After being separated for so long in life, Primus and Adeline were now together again in death. "Thank you," he said genuinely. "I'll repay you for the headstone as well."

"I'm sorry for your loss, and mine. He was father to us both."

Just as Arte's late father, Josiah, had influenced Nicholas's early life, Primus had played a similar role in Arte's by taking them fishing and teaching them to hunt. Nick and his father hadn't always seen eye to eye, but Primus had walked the earth as a sterling example of an upstanding and educated free Black man. No longer. Nick wondered how things might have fared between father and son had he returned sooner, but speculating in hindsight served no purpose. Nick had hated the British for many years, and now, because of his father's ignominious death, that hate increased tenfold. "Who amongst the Blacks here do you think I might speak with about the arrest? Maybe someone within the rebel ranks."

"Prince Hall," Arte responded without hesitation.

"I don't know him."

"He moved to the city while you were away. Maybe been here ten years. Came with nothing but worked hard and is very well respected. He often spoke at anti-slavery rallies alongside your father. Unlike some, Hall clearly supports the rebels."

"So he may know how deeply my father was involved."

"I can't say, but he'd be someone to speak with about it. Your father trusted him." Arte peered over at the weary Nick as if trying to see what he might be thinking, then added, "You look dead on your feet. We have room if you want to sleep here tonight. Your house has to be freezing after being empty these past few months."

"Thank you. I accept."

"It's good to have you back, Nick."

Nick nodded. "Thanks for all you've done."

"It's what a man does for his friend."

The following morning, Nick thanked Arte and his wife, Bekkah, for their hospitality, and after promising to stop back later, he went home, saddled his horse, and rode into Boston to visit his father's grave.

The city of Boston was named after a town in England's Lincolnshire County. Colonial Boston was the capital of the Massachusetts Bay Colony. Following the end of the Seven Years' War in 1763, it stood as the wealthiest and most influential city in the colonies. Its deep harbor and favorable geographic placement also made it the busiest colonial seaport; a remarkable accomplishment considering the city was founded by one man.

From his days at school, Nick knew that the man was William Blackston or Blaxton, depending on which records were consulted, and in 1625 he had lived alone on the open grassy plain known to present-day citizens as the Boston Commons. When other Europeans arrived in 1636, they purchased hundreds of acres of land from him, which no doubt surprised the native population, who'd had no idea Blackston owned the land they and their ancestors had lived on for centuries.

They city was much more built up than it had been during Nick's youth. The winding narrow streets were now filled with a bevy of taverns, shops, and homes; some were familiar, others not. He saw soldiers everywhere. Their bloodred uniforms made them stand out like wounds against the drab earth tones worn by the citizens, and according to Arte, Gage's troops were considered just that.

While riding Nick avoided eye contact with those he passed and skirted the soldiers as best he could. He had no desire to call attention to himself. Having spent most of his adult life among cutthroats, smugglers, pirates and other ne'er-do-wells, he prized anonymity. Copp's Hill Burying Ground was on the north end of the city where the small but thriving free Black community had established itself.

He and his father had made yearly trips to Adeline's grave, so Nick had little difficulty finding it. The familiar weathered headstone with its angel wings framing Adeline's name, years of birth and death, stood next to a brand-new stone that bore Primus's name. It was stark and devoid of ornamentation, but rose from the earth with a pride that denoted the man interred beneath. Nick's heart tightened in his chest. Grief tinted with anger filled him in much the same way that the brisk wind of the cold spring day filled the air. Guilt plagued him as well, and again he wondered if Primus's fate would have been different had he returned home sooner. He set the thoughts aside and said aloud,

"I'm sorry, Father. Sorry for the years we spent apart. Sorry for the rift between us. Sorry that I'll never see you again."

The only reply was the wind. Nick looked out over the peaceful burial ground and fought to keep his emotions in check. He could not bring his father back to life but he vowed to find the person responsible for betraying him, and afterwards, maybe he could find peace.

Nick bade his parents a solemn and silent farewell, and after mounting his horse rode off to pay a visit to Prince Hall.

Nick found him at his home above the leather shop he owned, and after he introduced himself, the two men spent an hour or so discussing the events unfolding in Boston. As Artemis had said, Prince was open about his support for the rebels, mainly because he and the nation's other Blacks, both loyalist and non, were hoping the end of slavery would be one of the issues dealt with should the colonists prevail. In the discussion concerning his father, Prince had an interesting theory.

"I'm not one to pass along rumors, or to malign the innocent, but it is said that Stuart Kingston reports what he hears to the British. General Gage and his officers meet regularly at his inn, and Kingston refuses to support the ongoing boycott of crown goods that most residents have embraced. Do you know him?"

"Yes. He and my father were enemies when I was younger."

"I've only known him a few years. Vain as a peacock

and as bullheaded as King George. I knew Kingston and your father didn't get along, but to betray him? To turn him in to the British? It's unconscionable if the rumors are true."

Nicholas agreed and also wondered if the rumors were true.

"And I will tell you this. Even though Kingston and I are Masons and lodge brothers, I can't bring myself to trust him."

Nicholas was grateful for Prince's honesty, but he was admittedly surprised to hear that his father and Kingston had continued their feuding. Nick had no idea why the two had been at odds for so many years. It was not something his father had ever discussed, but had Kingston hated him enough to turn him in to the British? "What do you know about Lady Midnight?"

Hall paused and studied Nicholas silently before asking, "Why?"

Nicholas told him what Primus had revealed to Artemis after his arrest.

"I'd not heard of her visit to him that night, nor do I know her identity."

Nick studied him in turn. "And my being a stranger, you wouldn't tell me if you did, would you?"

Hall smiled. "I can tell you are Primus's son. That's the type of pointed question he'd ask. So my response is: I've told you what I know."

"An answer my father would have heartily approved of, I'm sure." Nick found that he liked Hall.

"These are serious times. One must be careful. You are Primus's son, and by all rights my trust in you should be strong, but the war has divided many families against each other. Even Ben Franklin's son has been found spying on him for the crown. We've learned not to take anything or anyone for granted."

"A wise policy."

"However, Kingston is sponsoring a small feast for our newly established Masons' lodge. Would you like to come along as my guest?"

"I would. Seeing him again might help me gauge how true the rumors might be about his involvement."

"Good. We'll leave shortly."

Chapter 2

Faith was running from pillar to post getting everything ready for the afternoon's gathering. After her usual predawn chores, she'd spent the day cooking the hens, preparing the winter vegetables, and making the bread her father and his friends would consume at the meal. Two long trestle tables had been moved into the cellar room to accommodate the attendees. Her father and fourteen other free Black men had been initiated into the mysterious organization known as the Masons, and a reception honoring their achievement was going to be held at the inn. Early afternoon had been chosen as the time for the affair in response to the presence of the British troops. No one, not even the loyalists, wanted to travel after dark and maybe be subjected to the redcoats' patrols. The newly commissioned Masons had been sworn in by a Masonic lodge within the British forces, and according to her father, he and his friends were the first Blacks to be inducted anywhere in the world. Although Faith didn't care for the soldiers, not even she was able to fault them for this singular first.

Faith had no idea what being a member entailed. It was an esoteric organization that on the surface supported charitable works but underneath was filled with mysterious rituals and lore. She did know that being a Mason made her father tremendously proud, especially being one of the first men of the race to ever be accepted, and she was happy for him.

As she set out plates and cutlery, she wondered if Primus Grey would have been a part of the historic group had he lived. Her heart still grieved at his passing. Although her father had never gotten along with Primus, Faith missed him as a friend and as a presence in the community. He'd been one of the area's most respected free Blacks, and always did his part to better conditions for people of color in and around Boston, whether they be Black, mulatto, or a member of the native tribes. Primus, and other men like Prince Hall, had regularly petitioned colonial governor Hutchinson to ban the importation of slavery, and had presented numerous other petitions directed at lifting some of the more noxious codes and restrictions aimed at the race. Granted, they'd been only moderately successful, but because of their fervent agitation, the Massachusetts Bay Colony was inching towards equality in ways other colonies like those in the South were not.

However, due to someone's treachery, Primus had been ripped from their lives, first by the British and then by death. He'd deserved better.

Faith was awaiting the arrival of her neighbor, the widow Blythe Lawson, who made the best trifle in Boston. Blythe was a free Black woman who owned property both in and around Boston. Under the auspices of what the colonists were calling the Intolerable Acts, a cadre of British officers had taken over one of her boardinghouses, but due to the law didn't have to pay her any compensation. She hated the British, too.

She arrived a short while later. Dressed in a voluminous cape that bore signs of the rainy day, she entered on a gust of wind lugging a large Dutch oven that Faith assumed held the luncheon's dessert.

"Let me help you with that," Faith said, hastily moving to assist her.

The beautiful older woman gladly turned over the burden. "I have more on the wagon."

Faith set the oven holding the trifle in the kitchen, then went with her back out into the raw weather and returned bearing another oven and a pot of blanched winter vegetables.

Once everything was in the kitchen, she and Blythe stood in front of the big fire to warm up.

"Awful day," Blythe declared.

Faith agreed and rubbed her hands together to try and rid them of the chill.

Once the women were thawed out, Blythe removed her cloak, and Faith said quietly, "There are three new generals arriving, along with an influx of new soldiers."

Blythe looked up with surprise. "When?"

"By May."

Dismay showed on Blythe's light brown face before she calmed her features and remarked, "I'm certain someone will find that news of interest."

"I agree."

They said no more.

The guests began arriving at the appointed time. While she and Blythe moved about the cellar room placing platters of food on the tables, the fourteen men conversed. Stuart Kingston was in his element. He'd always enjoyed being the center of attention, and was moving through the gathering as if he were the only honoree. Even though he was attempting to take credit for being the person responsible for their induction, everyone knew that Prince Hall had been the engine.

He boasted self-importantly, "Had it not been for my close relationship with General Gage, the Masons might not have looked so favorably upon our petitions."

Faith saw the displeasure on the faces of some of the other men at his declaration and hoped her father did, too. For all his posturing, he wasn't well liked by his peers because he was often abrasive and unthinking. His unwavering support for the King was mirrored by other free Black loyalists, but none went so far as to publicly condemn the rebels' cause, especially if that cause resulted in the end of slavery.

Faith saw Prince Hall enter. With Primus's untimely

death, Hall would likely inherit the mantle of leadership for their community, and she expected him to lead well. She didn't know the man who'd entered with Hall, however, even though his face seemed somewhat familiar. Where Prince was slight and short, his companion was tall and well built. Dressed in the standard breeches, waistcoat, and snowy cravat of the day, he was extremely handsome, and the clothes looked well made, but she noted a decided coolness in his dark gaze as it slowly swept the room. When that gaze rested on hers, it stopped. For a timeless moment she felt herself ensnared, caught like prey before a hawk. When his eyes finally left hers and moved on, she exhaled, not realizing she'd been holding her breath.

From across the table, Blythe remarked quietly, "Handsome devil, isn't he?"

"Who is he?"

"Primus's son, Nicholas."

Surprised, Faith turned back to view him again. She now understood why his features seemed familiar. He favored his father a great deal. "I remember him vaguely."

"You were young when he last lived here. I'd say he's about a decade older."

"Primus never mentioned him, at least not to me."

"They had a falling out when Nicholas chose to support the French during the war."

Faith found that interesting. Also interesting was her

father's reaction. When Prince Hall introduced him, her father declared angrily, "Why would you think you'd be welcome here?"

She and Blythe shared a speaking look. Blythe sighed and shook her head.

Stuart continued, "Your father and I never shared more than two words. Neither of them friendly."

Grey answered, "I didn't realize your quarrel was with me also. I'll leave."

Apparently the censure on the faces of the other men made her father rethink his rude behavior because he said hastily, "You are correct, the rancor existed between Primus and me. Welcome to my establishment."

Faith breathed a sigh of relief. Blythe reacted by shaking her head once more. For many years Faith had wondered about the cause of the bad blood between her father and Primus, but because her father refused to discuss the matter, the answer remained unknown. For all her father's ire, Grey looked unmoved by the show of temper, leading her to wonder how the rest of the afternoon might play out. Knowing she had work to do, though, she left more food, and Blythe followed.

Seated beside Prince Hall at one of the tables, Nicholas silently observed the men around him while listening to their conversation. He knew only a few of them and planned to talk to them about his father's arrest, but for the moment it was Kingston he was most interested in. The vehement reaction to his arrival should have been expected considering the long-running feud. How the two men had gone from being the best of friends upon arriving in the colonies before Nick's birth, to anger and Kingston's alleged betrayal, was beyond him, but apparently the bad feelings lived on even in the face of Primus's death.

Nick remembered Kingston as being a blowhard, and that hadn't changed, either. All the man seemed able to talk about was himself and his so-called close and personal relationship with General Gage. No one seemed impressed, especially not Nicholas.

"According to the general, the rebels will be soundly defeated. Britain has conquered far more superior opposition." Pointing his tankard of ale for emphasis, he added smugly, "We all know what happened with the French and their savage allies."

Nicholas's jaw tightened. It was the savage behavior of the British that had caused him to turn his back on England and the crown.

Hall, who'd been listening silently, too, asked, "So you give the rebels no chance?"

"Mr. Hall, I know you've been misled to believe there is one, but seriously now. A motley band of farmers is not going to win the day."

"Suppose they do," asked George Middleton, one of Primus's old friends.

"There'll be chaos. Utter chaos. Who would govern? Hancock? Sam Adams? Esteemed men in their own minds but not in mine."

"Surely you support gradual emancipation though?" a man seated across the table asked.

Nicholas knew that the emancipation of the colonies' slaves was a hotly contested subject, especially in the South, where many of the men agitating for freedom from the British were in fact slaveholders.

"I am, but gradually."

A man seated across from Nicholas remarked, "There's been much ado over the Somerset decision. Maybe slavery will end during our lifetime."

Some of his fellows nodded in agreement but others remained skeptical.

The decision involved a slave named Somerset, who'd petitioned the British courts to overturn his life-long bondage. The 1772 case, known to the world as *Somerset v. Stewart*, caused a tremendous stir when Britain's highest justice, William Lord Mansfield, ruled that slavery was not only too odious to be defended, but that the air of England was too free for a slave to breathe. As a result, Mansfield ruled in Somerset's favor and debate continued to rage over how the ruling would be interpreted in light of all the slaves held by Englishmen. Blacks in the colonies both slave and free were following the debate closely.

"No man should be a slave," Stuart Kingston, a former slave himself, added, and it was the one thing the man uttered that Nicholas agreed with.

The woman Nicholas had seen earlier with Blythe Lawson entered the room to replenish some of the platters. She was a comely, raven-eyed beauty. She met his eyes briefly and went about her task. He wondered who she was.

The mystery surrounding her identity was soon solved when Kingston asked her, "What's for dessert, daughter?"

Nicholas was surprised. He remembered Kingston having a daughter but had little memory of her appearance other than that she was younger. Who knew such a toadlike man could be the father of someone so lovely?

"Trifle, courtesy of Blythe," she offered, smiling.

"Then let's have some."

As she left the room, Nicholas watched her exit and found her father's disapproving face on his when he turned back.

"She's not for you, Mr. Grey," Kingston stated.

"Nor am I for her, sir."

Someone coughed as if to hide his reaction to Nick's blunt reply.

Nick held Kingston's glowering glare easily until the man finally turned away.

The daughter soon returned carrying a tray holding plates of trifle. While she served, her father asked Nicholas, "So what brings you back to Boston, Mr. Grey?"

"This is my home, as you well know, and I'd hoped to see my father."

All of the men offered their condolences, and Nicholas accepted them graciously.

"Had he not been taken in by the rebels, he'd be alive today," Kingston pointed out.

"Had he not been betrayed, he'd be alive today," Nick countered. "But I will find the culprit."

Kingston dropped his spoon. After retrieving it with a self-deprecating grin, he asked, "How do you know he was betrayed? The British are smart enough to know who's aiding the rebels without a Judas."

Hall drawled, "You're right. Who needs a Judas when you can rely on spies and rumor?"

Kingston waved him off. "Hubris brought Primus down. Nothing more."

"Hubris?" Nick echoed coldly. Was it his imagination, or had Kingston appeared rattled a moment ago? He searched Kingston's face.

Faith wanted to tell her father to hush and eat his trifle. Everyone could see the danger in Grey's hard eyes, but Stuart was too busy being right to notice. Or maybe he simply didn't care. "Father, it's ungodly to disparage the dead."

"Go back to the kitchen, girl. This does not concern you."

Tight-lipped and embarrassed, she nodded and left him to the gathering storm.

Nicholas didn't care for the dismissive way he'd ordered his daughter out, but since he was not her champion nor had any plans to be, he returned to the topic at hand. "Kingston, whatever you may think of my father's so-called failings, I will find the Judas and deal with him."

"If there is one," Kingston said. "Were I you, I'd be more concerned with my own fate. Didn't you go over to the French during the war?"

"I did and with a clear conscience. I had no stomach for burning the lodgings of innocent Indians."

"No such thing as an innocent Indian."

Hall drawled dryly, "Kingston, I'd heard you were intolerant but having never personally witnessed it, I gave such talk the benefit of the doubt. However, you have more than confirmed the gossip."

He pointed his spoon Hall's way. "As if I care what you or anyone else thinks. Primus was arrested for treason, and it was his own doing."

The words put frost in Nicholas's veins and voice, "Pray that I do not find you out to be my father's betrayer, Mr. Kingston."

"More hubris. Be careful what you wish for, Nicholas."

Their eyes met and Nicholas knew the battle had begun. To keep himself from causing a scene, he moved his dessert aside and stood. "I'm going to pay my respects to Mistress Lawson and take my leave. The air in here is suddenly too foul to bear."

He turned to Prince Hall. "Hall, I will call on you in a couple of days if I may."

Hall nodded.

Nick met Kingston's eyes and received a gloating smile.

The angry Nicholas found Blythe and Kingston's daughter in the kitchen eating by the fire. When he entered, Blythe stood and opened her arms in welcome. "Nicholas, it's so good to see you after so many years."

He walked over to her and let himself be enfolded for a moment. "Good to see you as well. You are still the loveliest woman in the colonies."

"And you are still the most charming. I'm so sorry for your loss. Primus was a dear man and a friend."

"Not according to Kingston." He looked to Faith and said, "My apologies, but your father is a difficult man."

"I know, but I am sorry for your loss as well. Although I've never told my father, Primus always had a kind word for me."

"Thank you." Nicholas found himself enthralled by her dark beauty. The thick black hair was pulled back showing off the blemish-free skin of her small face.

Wearing a knowing smile, Blythe looked between them and asked innocently, "Have the two of you been introduced?"

They shook their heads.

"Nicholas Grey, this is Faith Kingston. Faith— Nicholas."

He bowed. "I'm honored."

"I am as well."

Once again Faith found herself held by his eyes, and once again it was difficult to draw in an even breath.

As their gazes held, Blythe asked, "How long will you be staying with us, Nicholas?"

He finally moved his attention away from Faith. "I'll know better once I find the person who betrayed my father. I owe that to his memory."

Faith silently agreed and was glad that she wasn't the one who'd tipped off the British. Nicholas Grey impressed her as being a dangerous man, and she saw little sense in questioning him about what he would do once he discovered the betrayer's identity; the answer lay in his cold eyes.

Nicholas thought about the role played by the mysterious Lady Midnight in Primus's arrest but decided against bringing her into the conversation. He didn't wish to embarrass the ladies by asking about someone who might possibly be an actress or a woman of the streets, nor did he wish to give Kingston's daughter something to tell her father about. She was an unparalleled beauty, but he didn't let that blind him to the fact that she could have General Gage's ear, too. "Ladies, I'll be taking my leave. Miss Kingston, it was a pleasure meeting you."

"For me as well, Mr. Grey. Again, my condolences on your loss."

He inclined his head in acknowledgment, and after saying good-bye to Blythe made his exit.

Blythe said, "I think he was taken by you, Faith."

"And I think he's a man of the world, who'd find a poor country girl like myself very lacking."

The smiling Blythe gave no reply as she went back to her trifle.

That evening, while alone in her bedroom at the back of the inn, Faith took out her stationery and began a letter. Using standard ink, she penned a list of some of the loyalist churches in the area. Once that was done, she opened her desk's drawer and withdrew a small tin that held a different sort of ink. Dipping a fresh quill in it, she filled in the empty spaces between the list of names with a message about the newly arriving soldiers, and then added the names of the three generals Gage had mentioned. As she blew on the paper to help the ink dry, the words about the soldiers and generals magically disappeared. The letter's recipient would be able to read it after passing the paper over a candle flame. Invisible ink was one of the many ways both sides of the intelligence-gathering community conducted their shadowy spying, or tradecraft as it was sometimes called. Other methods of discreet correspondence employed coded messages, and Faith used those also, but she wanted to be careful passing along this information. Primus had helped the rebels and paid for it with his life, and she didn't want to share his fate. He'd been the leader of a small spy cabal made up of Blacks both slave and free. The maids, coopers, servants, and washwomen under his command were in a unique position to see and hear things from their loyalist owners and clientele that other information gatherers might not be privy to. Primus had been their captain and would pass along whatever his people heard or saw to his contacts within the Sons of Liberty. She regretted not being able to get word to him sooner about Gage's interest. She'd only been told by her father earlier that afternoon. Had she known in a more timely fashion, he might still be alive. She ran hands over her weary eyes. She'd failed him and it was something she'd have to live with for the rest of her life.

A knock on her door made her hastily slip the letter and ink back into the drawer.

Her father called, "Faith! Are you sleeping?"

"No, Father. Please, come in." He opened the door, and by his sour face she could tell something was wrong. "Are you ill?"

"Yes, ill from having to entertain Nicholas Grey."

"He seemed respectable."

"As respectable as the son of a traitor can be. I don't want you to have anything to do with him, understand?"

"Certainly."

"I hear he's quite wealthy, and the simple-minded women around here will be thinking him a good catch, but you keep your distance. He's not the man for you."

"Yes, Father, but may I ask what started the quarrel between you and his father?"

"No, you may not."

She gave no visible reaction but inside she sighed. She loved her father, but as Nicholas had so correctly pointed out, Stuart Kingston was a difficult man.

He asked, "Have you given any more thought to Will Case's request?"

"Yes, and the answer is still, no."

"You could do worse, daughter."

"True, but why agree to marry a man I can't abide?"

"You're long past the age of being choosy, Faith. You should already be in your own home and raising children."

"By society's standards, yes, but by my own, I'll not have Will."

"And if I insist?"

"I'll give myself to the first peddler that comes down the road."

His eyes widened. "You would speak so disrespectfully to me!"

"Yes, so do not force this issue, please." And then she smiled a bit. "Think of the positives. Should I remain unmarried, you'll have me at your beck and call for the rest of your years."

"Precisely what I'm trying to avoid." He gauged her for a few silent moments. "You always were a headstrong child."

"And have grown into a headstrong woman. I wonder where that comes from."

He nodded. "Go to bed, Faith. I'll see you in the morning."

"Good night, Father. Sleep well."

Chapter 3

To make certain her father would be asleep and snoring, Faith waited an hour before preparing to leave the house. Once confident, she placed the coded letter into the hidden pocket sewn into the seam of one of her petticoats. She then wrapped herself in her long gray cape with its attached hood. Walking quietly over to the window, she slowly opened the shutters to keep them from squeaking and peered out into the darkness. There was no moon and that pleased her. She glanced back into the room to make certain everything was as it should be, then swung her legs and feet over the sill and dropped down to the soft soil a few inches below. Before taking a step, she cautiously listened for anything that might disturb her leaving. Hearing only the wind in the pines, she quickly set out.

Under the cover of the darkness, Nicholas, astride his stallion, watched Kingston's daughter climb out through the window and couldn't believe his eyes. What was she about? he wondered. He'd been silently observing the inn for the past two hours in order to see what kind of night visitors Kingston might have, if any. He didn't know what he'd expected to see but it didn't involve the man's daughter leaving the house like a thief.

His eyes sharp, he watched her take to the field behind the house. Once she was far enough away not to detect his presence, he set out behind her.

With Primus gone, Faith had no one to siphon her spy news through, so she had to make do with another channel, her friend Charity Trotter, who worked in town as a hired servant for one of the Sons of Liberty. Outside of Primus and Faith, no one knew else Charity was a spy. Not even her husband, Ingram. Although the three were lifelong friends, Ingram was a loyalist, and as such, couldn't be trusted. That saddened Faith for two reasons, one because she knew him to be a man of integrity and therefore he would have been an asset to the Sons of Liberty, and two, Ingram Trotter was the only man she'd ever loved.

By wagon the Trotter farm was only a short distance away, but on foot it took close to three-quarters of an hour. She moved as quickly as the damp ground allowed her. Her boots were going to be a muddy mess by the time she returned home, but at the moment she didn't care. Due to the incriminating information hidden in her petticoats she was more concerned with staying hidden from the British patrols on the Concord Road. By keeping to the orchards and fields behind the farms along the route, she could avoid them. To her dismay, it began to rain, and by the time she reached her destination her cloak was nearly soaked through.

She knocked on the plank door. Because of the late hour, she expected Ingram to answer the summons and he did, carrying a short candle resting in a boat to aid his vision. "Faith?"

"I know it's late, but this couldn't wait until tomorrow. I need eggs for the general's breakfast. Do you think Charity may have some I might purchase?"

He was only a bit taller than she, but his gentle nature and kind, hazel brown eyes more than made up for his lack of stature. "Come in and you can ask her. How have you been?"

She stepped inside and closed the door. "I'm well. And you and the family?"

"All faring well. Let me go and get her."

"Thank you. I'll stand here so as not to track mud all over her floors."

"She'll appreciate that. I'll be back in a moment."

As he left her, Faith glanced around the dimly lit parlor at the furniture and other appointments that made a place a home. Even though she and Charity were the best of friends, Faith couldn't help but wonder, what if this were her home? The baby Ingram and Charity had, hers? The love the two of them shared, their love? But the scenario was just a meaningless exercise in fantasy. To Ingram, Faith had been someone he'd climbed trees with, built snow forts with in the winter, and hunted tadpoles with in the spring. In his own way he did love her, but not as a sweetheart.

When he and Charity first began to court, it was difficult for Faith to listen to him express his deep feelings for Charity, and it was even more wrenching watching them marry because love wasn't something you could snuff out like a candle. It became clear to her during adolescence that he'd never love her the way she did him, so she'd never revealed her feelings. However, she doubted she'd ever meet another man who'd capture her heart the way he had.

Charity came out of the back, and upon seeing Faith, smiled. "You need eggs?"

"Yes."

Because they'd passed secrets before, Charity seemed to sense Faith's true reason for the late night visit. "I have some eggs out by the coop. I'll get them."

She returned shortly with a small basket holding half a dozen brown eggs, cushioned and covered by a thin white cloth. "Here you are." She passed Faith the basket, and in the same motion, Faith passed her the letter.

As a housekeeper and cook, one of Charity's duties was to collect her employer's mail. It was very easy for her to anonymously place Faith's coded letters in among the others before turning the envelopes over to him. Faith had sent him messages before, all signed with the number one hundred and thirteen, the code number for Lady Midnight, so that he would know they were from her hand. However, he didn't know that his housekeeper was spying on him for Primus. Anything the Sons of Liberty discussed that pertained to the Black community Primus had wanted to know, and Charity had been placed there specifically to aid in that endeavor as well. "Thank you for the eggs. If the general stops in, these will please him."

"And we must keep the general pleased, mustn't we?" she replied with a straight face, and a distinct sparkle of mischief in her brown eyes.

Ingram joined them just as the conversation ended. He was cradling their sleeping newborn son, Peter. He passed the child over to his mother. "How does the general seem?" he asked with interest, having heard their last few words.

"He's well, I suppose. He seems to enjoy the food."

"That's quite a boon to have him visit you regularly."

"That's what my father thinks," she replied, and smoothly changed the subject. "The baby's getting big." Because few people ventured out in the winter, she hadn't seen Peter in some time.

Both parents smiled down at their son with fondness and pride.

Ingram said, "Once the weather warms, he can start making himself familiar with his aunt Faith."

Faith nodded and told them both, "Thank you for your kindness this evening."

Ingram opened the door and stepped outside with her. "Be careful going back."

"I will." And she headed out into the rain.

Faith wasn't looking forward to slogging through the mud again, so she decided to walk the road on the journey home. Having passed her secret letter off to Charity, she had nothing on her person that would get her in trouble if she was stopped, and with the weather so foul, the patrols were probably warming themselves next to a tavern fire and lifting tankards of ale.

Halfway home, the rain stopped and she thanked the heavens. Up ahead she saw the Lucky Irish Tavern, which catered mainly to the British soldiers. As she approached, she could hear the sound of fiddlers sawing away inside and the loud voices of men singing a drinking song. Apparently they were having a good time. She hurried on.

A long stand of trees flanked the portion of the road she was now on. Suddenly a man astride a horse came out of the darkness. Frightened by the abrupt appearance her heart raced and she looked for a place to flee.

"Good evening, Miss Kingston."

Realizing she knew the voice, she stared at the man in surprise and pushed her hood back to get a better view of his face. "Mr. Grey?"

He drew the horse closer. "Yes, it is."

Relief filled her. "You frightened me."

"My apology. Do you often go walking at midnight, Miss Kingston?"

Faith's chin rose in response to the subtle accusation in his tone. "I had an errand to take care of."

Nicholas didn't believe her for a moment. He wondered if she'd been out making extra coin by lifting her skirts. It was an honest question, because wherever soldiers marched, loose women followed. However, she'd not given off the air of a strumpet when they were introduced earlier, but who knew the truth? The only certainty was that Kingston was unaware of his daughter's excursion, otherwise she would have left by the front door. "What type of errand involves you sneaking out of a window? One that you don't wish your father to know of, perhaps?"

Grabbing hold of her wits, she responded. "Yes. Because I've run out of eggs and he'd want to know why at breakfast in the morning."

"Eggs?" he echoed.

"Yes." And she showed him the basket. "In spite of what tales you may be begging to tell, I went to buy eggs. Am I to assume you were lurking in the trees?"

A lesser man might have wilted under her withering questioning, but Nick found her show of spine impressive. This was not the meek, dutiful young woman who'd been sent from the room like a child earlier in the day. "Yes, I was lurking in the trees."

"For what purpose?"

"To see what I could see."

"But you saw me instead."

Nicholas delayed his response in order to study her small face. In the now rising moon, her skin looked soft as brown velvet, and her lips, although tightly set, couldn't hide their well-formed lushness. Her nostrils appeared to be flaring and the black eyes assessing him so fearlessly were like a thunderstorm throwing lightning. He didn't know whether to smile or be afraid.

"Why were you watching the inn?"

"For answers to my father's death."

"And you think you will find them here?" Her skepticism was plain.

"Our fathers were enemies. One was a loyalist, the other a supporter of the rebels. Were our roles reversed, where would you begin?"

"Elsewhere. Especially on such insignificant evidence."

"You've a tart tongue."

"Honed from debating nonsense with men like you, Mr. Grey." And she stormed away.

Nicholas watched the subtle swing of her cape as she marched ahead. Drawn by her sassiness and the mystery she presented, he propelled his stallion forward to catch up to her.

Once he and his horse were in pace beside her, she asked stonily, "Don't you have a better place to be, Mr. Grey?"

"I'm content."

"I'm not, so be on your way."

"And leave you out here on the road alone? I'm a better gentleman than that."

"Anyone spying on me and my father is no gentleman at all, sir."

"I admit to many failings."

"Go away."

Nick smiled. "And probably miss out on the most

interesting encounter I've had in some time? I think not. I'll be escorting you home."

"That isn't necessary."

"View it as my penance for spying on you and your father."

He saw the sharp look she shot his way, and the pleasure he was deriving from this late night meeting increased. "Why isn't a beautiful woman like you married?"

"Do you always ask such rude questions?"

"Yes."

Faith stopped. "Are you bedeviling me on purpose because of your feelings about my father?"

"No, Miss Kingston, I'm bedeviling you because I find you quite interesting. Not many women can give as good as they get."

She didn't respond.

"You should take that as a compliment."

She walked off again.

Once he was beside her again, he said, "You haven't answered my question."

"I'm not married because I chose not to be," she responded without breaking stride.

"None of the males here measure up?"

"No, I'm the one lacking. I'm educated and opinionated. Men don't care for those qualities in a wife."

Nick pondered that. It was true that many men were drawn to simpering, simpleminded women. He'd never been one who was, however. "You could be rid of me quicker were you to join me on Hades' back and let us carry you home."

"No thank you. And what kind of name is that for a horse."

"It's where I found him."

"In Hades?" she asked skeptically.

"Yes. He was in the hold of a ship that had been set afire. We've been together since."

"And this ship was where?"

"Off the coast of Bengal."

"Bengal? India?"

"Yes."

"What were you doing there?"

"Taking part in a mutiny along with hundreds of others impressed by the King's navy."

That made Faith stop and search his face in the moonlight. She'd heard horrible stories about men being impressed. When the British Navy ran short of sailors, the captains ofttimes had men abducted to fill the rolls. They took them from the docks, taverns, and in some cases right off the streets. The unethical policy added more fuel to the incendiary atmosphere between the colonial citizens and the crown. "I'm sorry," was all she could think to say.

"No need to apologize. You didn't shanghai me. It was a way to see the world, even though I had no choice in the matter."

Faith began to see him in a new light. She'd called him worldly this afternoon and realized she'd been correct. "I have never traveled beyond Massachusetts. What's the world like?" she asked softly.

"Vicious and unfair, but filled with vistas so beautiful and wondrous your heart breaks trying to take it all in."

He met her eyes. Feeling something she couldn't name slide into her soul from within the depths of his gaze, Faith turned from him. "I must get home."

They covered the remaining distance in silence but Faith was very aware of his presence at her side.

They finally reached the inn. "Good night, Mr. Grey."

"Same to you, Miss Kingston."

"I would appreciate it if you would not tell my father about this."

"You have my word."

She held his eyes for a long moment, wondering about who he really was inside, then hurried towards the back of the inn. To learn that he was on a witch hunt targeting her father was almost as appalling as learning that he'd seen her sneak out of the house. Even if he didn't know the truth behind her errand, the idea that he'd been watching her and had trailed her was alarming. That he might do it again gave her yet one more thing to worry about besides the patrols of British soldiers, being unmasked as Lady Midnight, and being brought to trial and hanged for treason. Out of necessity she'd have to keep the startling encounter to herself. Revealing it to her father would not only add to his dislike of the Grey name but shed a suspicious light on her own actions, because he'd know the midnight trip for eggs had been unnecessary. So Grey's lurking would have to remain a secret, and any further contact with him had to be kept at a minimum. Not that she minded, because now that she knew his true colors, she planned to avoid him, but she also needed to find out as much about him as she discreetly could. The first rule of war was to know the enemy. Opening the shutters, she climbed back in.

Nicholas waited until she disappeared inside before he and Hades rode for home. Once there he climbed the stairs to his bedroom to settle in for the rest of the night. Since returning from New York, Nick kept expecting to see his father walk in, and he wondered how long it would be before the expectation faded. Days, weeks, years, never? Even now, as he sat in his fire-lit bedroom, he kept listening for Primus's footsteps on the stairs, only to remind himself that he'd never hear them again. The loss was still keen. After leaving the Masons' luncheon, he'd gone to visit some of his father's old friends. The few he'd been able to find expressed their condolences, and all were of a mind that Stuart Kingston was the Judas he sought, but how to prove it was the question. Thinking of Kingston brought back the encounter with his daughter. What a gorgeous and fiery beauty she was, but as her father so rudely pointed out, Faith wasn't for him. The facts that she was Kingston's daughter and that she was more than likely a virgin were two marks against her. Nick preferred his women experienced enough to expect nothing more than the pleasure he could bring in bed, and virgins, especially virgins of good family, would want more.

Faith aside, what he needed now was someone who'd heard or seen Stuart Kingston betray his father. Primus wouldn't want Nick to confront the man with only rumors at his back. He needed facts, which meant he had to find Lady Midnight in order to get to the truth.

With that in mind, Nicholas decided to reestablish himself in the community. He'd go to gatherings, rallies, and maybe even church if need be. Every smuggler knew that the more innocently one acted, the more information one could obtain.

Nicholas spent the next few days establishing his father's home as his own. Having to pack up his father's things was more emotional than he'd imagined. Touching his hunting rifle brought back memories as had boxing up the clothing he'd planned to donate to the local charities. For a while he had to walk away and sit outside until the sadness became more manageable. Thanks to Artemis's foresight, the large house with its orchards and open fields hadn't been lost. Although he'd repaid Artemis for the land, the two decided the deed would remain in Arte's name until the times were safe enough to transfer it without raising British ire. As Arte said on the night of Nick's return, the homes, businesses, and lands of traitors had not fared well. In fact, the print shop Primus had owned had been confiscated and recently sold to a loyalist.

The next morning, Nick was out in back of the house chopping wood when he noticed Prince Hall riding up. They hadn't seen each other since the Masons' luncheon.

Prince pulled his mount to a halt and stepped out of his saddle. "Best of mornings, Nicholas."

Nick put down his axe and wiped his face on the sleeve of his hide shirt. "To you as well. Did you come to help me chop wood?"

Prince smiled. "No, but I'd like to speak with you about something if I may?"

Nick surveyed him for a moment, wondering what this might be about. "Let's speak inside."

They went in, and as he warmed himself in front of the parlor's fire, Prince took a seat in one of the upholstered chairs. He glanced around at the furnishings and at the painting over Nick's head. "Your mother was a beautiful woman."

Nick's attention moved up to the stiffly posed woman in blue. In spite of the unsmiling face there was a sparkle in her brown eyes. "That she was. Died giving me birth. I often wondered how it might have been had she lived. Probably a lot less arguing between Primus and myself."

Silence crept into the room and echoed through the house.

Prince said, "It's hard knowing he'll never stand where you are again." He quieted then as if thinking back on his friend, and then grinned. "He told the foulest jokes about the King any of us had ever heard. Left us rolling on the floorboards more times than I can count."

Nick chuckled. "He was one of a kind."

Prince nodded agreement, then sobered. "People will miss him immensely."

Nick found it hard to accept the fact that his father was dead. At the time of their acrimonious parting during the height of the Seven Years' War, it never occurred to him that they wouldn't see each other again, argue again, hunt again. The guilt of not having reconciled with his father continued to plague him. "You wanted to speak with me?"

"Yes, on behalf of the Sons of Liberty."

"Why?"

"The cause needs men with your war experience. We may not be able to beat the British head-on, but if the minutemen can be taught to fight like the Indians, tree to tree, and on the run, we'd stand a chance."

Nick turned back to the flames oscillating in the grate.

"We've already begun to drill and many of the trainers are excellent, but there are not enough of them to go around."

"Are men of color being allowed to drill as well?"

"In some units, yes, in others, no. You'd be helping your race."

"Guilt won't buy me."

"But principle might. This is our fight, too. The hypocrisy inherent in the rebels demanding freedom from the crown while they themselves own slaves is not lost upon any of us. The whole concept is ludicrous, but the Sons of Liberty and the Provincial Congress are being pressured by fair-minded men both here and in England to secure that freedom for everyone."

Nick heartily agreed with him about the hypocrisy.

"And we wish to fight because this is our country, too. We helped build the colonies just as they have, only we've done it with no reward. If Jefferson and his Virginians didn't own slaves they wouldn't have the luxury of riding around the countryside bellowing for freedom. They'd be home behind a plow."

Nick looked his way. "You have been around my father, haven't you?"

Prince's eyes smoldered even as he smiled. "And besides, we've fought in all their other wars. Why should this one be any different? Maybe one day the scales will be balanced and we'll measure up."

Nick nodded in understanding. He'd faced some of that prejudice during the war by both the British and the French, but found the tribes didn't care about a man's skin as long as he fought as fiercely as they. The only color they cared about was the color of *their* freedom. "How many men do you envision?"

"Fifteen, twenty, no more."

"Do they have their own weapons?"

"Most do not."

Nick asked drolly, "Then of what use will they be on the battlefield?"

Prince sighed. "The Provincial Congress has said that each minuteman will be issued a musket, a bayonet, a cartridge box, and thirty-six rounds of ammunition. We've been promised the same."

"Do you believe the promise will be kept?"

"A portion of me does. A portion does not. There's been much debate as to whether men of color, especially the captives, should be allowed to bear arms—slave uprisings and all."

Nick shook his head at the wrongheaded thinking of the colonists. "If I agree, I'll make certain you have the weapons you need."

Prince stared.

Nick didn't say more, instead he asked, "What follows? Where will we drill?"

Prince was still studying him as if wanting to know more but then replied, "We're secluded enough out here on your land. As long as we're not firing the guns we should be safe from prying British eyes."

Nick weighed that. "Anything else besides drilling?"

"Yes. The Sons would like for you to pick up your father's standard on the intelligence side as well. What is siphoned to you, you would send on to me just as he did."

"Why can't you fill his role?"

"My residence like many others inside the city is watched day and night by the British. It is harder for them to know what is happening out here in the countryside. Being outside the city is one of the reasons Primus was able to be successful for as long as he was. He did most of his contact work here rather than his shop in town." Prince added, "There is also the connection to the Lady Midnight."

Nick turned and faced Prince. "The carrot," he stated.

Prince gave him a half smile. "It can be viewed as such, yes. She contacted one of the Sons directly a few days back about Gage bringing in more soldiers. She's done it before. He has no idea how she accomplishes it, but the information she sends is always very valuable."

"And you don't know who she is?"

"No. I knew of her from your father, but he never shared her true name."

"Is that what you're after?"

He shook his head. "We don't need to know her identity. We just wish for her to continue relaying what she knows."

"How do you know that she will?"

"We don't."

At least he was honest, Nick thought. The idea that the Lady Midnight might be able to give him answers he was seeking about his father's arrest was tempting enough to make him want to say yes to Prince, but this was too serious an endeavor to agree without more thought. "How soon do you need my reply?"

"As quickly as possible."

Nicholas asked, "And how will she know that I've replaced my father?"

"I have the means, but the question remains, will she work with anyone other than Primus?"

He found this turn of the tale interesting, "So someone does knows her true identity, and how to reach her?"

"Yes. Maybe more than one. We, meaning the Sons, just don't know. I assume her circle of contacts to be quite small. For her to be able to give us such pertinent and timely news says she has to be close to the British higher-ups. Guarding her identity is no doubt a necessity."

Lady Midnight. Nick thought about the midnight sojourn of Faith Kingston. She and her father were staunch loyalists, so it made little sense that she'd be a rebel spy. Primus and the Widow Lawson had been friends for many years. Could Blythe be Lady Midnight?

Prince's voice cut into his thoughts. "Later this afternoon, there will be a fund-raiser at the Friends' church if you care to attend."

"For guns?"

He smiled and shook his head. "No, for a man named Octavius Freeman wanting to purchase his wife's freedom. The great Phillis Wheatley is supposed to make an appearance."

"The poetess?"

"Yes. Are you familiar with her writings?"

"Probably not as well as most, but I do know of her."

"Then come along as my guest. A good percentage

of the free population is bound to attend and you can make the acquaintance of some of the minutemen of color."

"I'll think about it. Would you write down the name of the church and the address?"

Prince did, and then stood. He held out his hand. "Thank you for listening."

Nick gave him a firm shake in response and walked with him back outdoors.

Prince mounted. He offered a nod of farewell and rode off in the direction of the road. Nick hefted his axe and went back to work.

Chapter 4

When Faith and her father reached the church for the fund-raiser, they carried in the food Faith had spent most of the morning preparing. Once everything was unloaded, he drove the wagon to the adjacent field to park while she hurried inside.

In the kitchen a small group of women were already at work. Blythe Lawson was quartering her roasted hens, while others saw to breads, vegetables, cakes, and trifles.

"Afternoon, everyone," Faith called out. Heads rose. Most greeted her with smiles, but there were also a few sniffs. Eva Potts was one who sniffed. In some Black loyalist households, Faith was a pariah. Not only was she unmarried, she was well-read and handled her father's ledgers. In a time and place where a woman was supposed to be seen and not heard, some considered Faith loud as cannon fire.

Charity Trotter was working beside Blythe. Faith made her way over to where they were. "Where's the baby?"

"My mother has him."

"Is all well?"

Charity nodded and smiled. "All's well."

It was their way of communicating about the letter Faith had put in her care. Charity's affirmative response meant the letter had reached its target. Pleased, Faith jumped in to help with the work. Her contribution to the buffet was a large kettle of baked beans, fresh biscuits, and a large apple charlotte.

When the women were done, they left the food warming and went to join the affair.

Many of the area's free Black population were milling around the room greeting and talking to each other, and Faith was pleased by the turnout. Although women were not allowed to speak from the podium to *promiscuous* audiences, as mixed-gender gatherings like these were termed, the free women of Boston and its surrounding towns had shown up in great numbers. They were laundresses, maids, seamstresses, and cooks, and like Faith they'd come to support Mr. Freeman's quest to free his wife, Letty, from bondage.

A small percentage of the community had been free for generations, but a majority of the people in the room had at some point in their lives been slaves, or as it was more politely termed in the northeastern colonies, *servants for life*. Some had been allowed to purchase their freedom, while others had been legally freed by Quaker owners at the age of eighteen, per the custom of many of the Friends. A few men and women had been freed for meritorious service or given their freedom upon the death of their owners, but many had come to freedom by wit and guile as runaways.

Although everyone in attendance knew the value of freedom, the community was divided over the future direction of the colonies. Her father and his Tory friends supported the King, while many of the younger men, led by Prince Hall, were rebels and minutemen. She just hoped both sides remained civil, and placed Mr. Freeman and poor Letty's plight above politics. The last thing needed would be a heated argument or fisticuffs.

She saw her father approaching with Will Case, and she very much wanted to melt into the floor and disappear. To Faith, Will with his tall, sticklike frame resembled a praying mantis. Because of his successful soap-making business, many mothers in the area were constantly throwing their daughters in the middle-aged bachelor's path, but he kept stepping over them in a quest to secure Faith's hand. However, he was as boring as he was pompous, and she wanted nothing to do with him.

"Ah, here you are," her father said brightly. He'd worn his best coat and breeches for the occasion and she thought the cravat around his throat made him appear very distinguished. She, however, was wearing the same mended gown she always wore for special occasions. "Is everything ready for the repast?" he asked.

"Yes, Father." She turned to his companion. "Good afternoon, Will."

"Faith," he intoned, bowing at the waist. "How are you." His nasally voice always made him sound like he'd smelled sour milk.

"I am well, and you, sir?"

"As well as a loyalist can be in these trying times."

She smiled woodenly. "It is a struggle." Almost as much as her struggle to show an interest in his welfare, she thought.

He continued, "I was just telling your father that I've recently signed a contract with some prominent customers in London. That's quite a feather in my cap, wouldn't you say?"

"I would indeed."

"The British Army is showing an interest as well. Should the negotiations prove successful, I stand to become one of the wealthiest men in Boston, Black or White."

"Then I'm sure you will share some of your blessings with Mr. Freeman this afternoon. His need is very dire, wouldn't you say?"

By the startled look on his light brown face she could tell that he'd had no intentions what-so-ever, but she'd known that from the beginning. She'd had enough. Giving him a curtsy and a smile that she hoped didn't appear too forced, she said, "I should go and see if Blythe needs my help with anything. It's been a pleasure hearing about your successes."

Faith didn't have to look back to know that her father was displeased by her hasty exit, but she had no intention of spending her time listening to Will go on and on about himself. She found Blythe talking with Ingram and Charity. "Rescue me, please."

"From what?" Charity asked with a laugh.

"William Case."

Ingram smiled. "Still trying to win you, is he?"

"I've explained to both him and Father that the race is lost, but they seem to be deaf."

Blythe said, "You could do worse, I suppose. He owns his own business and is quite successful."

"I'm aware of his accomplishments because that's all he talks about."

Ingram nodded. "I have to agree, he is quite self-centered. But you should be married, Faith."

"You sound like Father."

He turned to his wife. "Charity, don't you think it's high time she married?"

"It'll be high time when she says it is."

"Thank you," Faith said of her friend's support.

Blythe added, "He feigned an interest in me some years back, but only as a ruse to get his hands on my property. I told him plainly that were I to marry him, I'd sign all I owned over to the church and shoot myself within a week. He stopped coming around."

They laughed at the dry remark. Faith looked around the gathering. Some of the race's White supporters were in the room now, too. Many of Boston's radical thinkers not only supported events like this one, but often gave as generously as they could. "So do you believe Phillis

Wheatley will really be here?" she asked her friends.

Blythe replied, "I hear she's under the weather again. She's always been sickly, even when she was a child. We'll have to wait and see."

As a way to boost attendance, the sponsors of this event had let it be known that the great poetess might attend and read from a few of her works. Although Faith preferred the ribald plays and poems of the Bard, she enjoyed Miss Wheatley's poetry. As everyone across the colonies knew, Phillis had been only seven years of age when she was captured in western Africa and brought to Boston and sold to the wealthy tailor John Wheatley and his wife, Susannah. In the years since, she'd written many lines of poetry and held the honor of being one of the first women of the race to have her words published. She'd recently returned to Boston from a trip to London, where according to the newspapers she'd received many accolades while being squired around by one of her biggest sponsors, Selina Shirley, Countess of Huntingdon. Rumor had it that the Wheatleys had given her her freedom but Faith had no idea if the rumors were based on fact.

Blythe said, "Ah. Prince Hall has arrived, along with Nicholas."

Faith turned and saw Hall at the entrance shaking hands and greeting those nearby. However, Nicholas Grey's eyes were directed her way. Having that intense gaze burn her from across the room made her heart race. After offering her an almost imperceptible nod, he turned his attention to the man Hall was introducing him to. Shaken, she glanced her father's way, hoping he'd been too occupied by his conversation to notice the silent exchange, but his terse eyes told all.

"Who is he?" Charity asked.

Ingram must have seen the contact, too, because he met Faith's eyes with a frown reminiscent of her father's.

Blythe explained.

Charity, who'd grown up in Lexington, responded with surprise in her voice. "That's Primus's son?" Her eye still on him, she asked her husband, "Did you and Faith know him when you were younger?"

Ingram was studying him, too. "No, he was nearly a decade older than we were so I didn't know him well. Did you, Faith?"

She shook her head negatively. "No."

Ingram added, "He supposedly he went over to the French during the war."

Faith wondered how Primus had felt about his son fighting for the supposed enemy.

Charity's voice cut into her thoughts. "Was it my imagination or was he looking directly at you, Faith?"

Before Faith could form an answer, the commanding sound of Prince Hall's voice rang out. "My friends! Let us begin."

Standing beside him was Octavius Freeman, a brown-skinned man of average height.

Prince introduced him to the crowd. The applause

that followed seemed to embarrass Freeman. He nodded shyly as he acknowledged their support.

Prince intoned, "Through ingenuity and hard work, Mr. Freeman has already amassed twenty of the eighty pounds his wife's owners have set as the price. We know that many of you have given to his cause before, but if you have even an extra coin to spare, please place it in the basket circulating the room."

When Nicholas Grey walked out to where the men stood, the crowd quieted. Faith caught the raised eyebrow Charity shot her way. A quick glance over at her father showed his tightly set lips. She wondered if he knew what Primus's son was about to do or say.

With all eyes on him, he began, "Please excuse my interruption, but I'd like to offer Mr. Freeman the sixty pounds that he needs."

While Prince and Freeman stared at him with shock, Grey reached into his coat and withdrew a small drawstring pouch. He handed it to Freeman, who took it with wide eyes.

Grey then said quietly, "May you and your wife have a long life."

Wild applause erupted. Prince was shaking Grey's hand as if he might break it off at the wrist. Her father appeared to be stunned, and beside him, Will Case looked both skeptical and irritated. Faith didn't know what to think but found the gesture outstanding. Sixty pounds was an incredible amount of money to simply hand to a stranger. She wanted to believe that Primus was somewhere up above smiling down in response to the extraordinary gift.

Prince shouted for the crowd's attention. Freeman seemed unable to look away from the pouch in his hand. By the distance in Grey's manner it was hard to determine if he was pleased with the results of his charitable gesture or not.

As the crowd quieted, Prince said to them, "I've been told that due to poor health, Miss Wheatley wouldn't be able to join us this afternoon, but I had no idea that in her stead we'd witness something equally as moving. Ladies and gentlemen, this generous man is Nicholas Grey, son of the late Primus Grey."

Surprised gasps came just before yet another round of applause. Grey bowed gallantly and Faith heard some of the women nearby sigh aloud in response. She wondered if he was aware of how many eligible young ladies the community had. His splendid features and obvious wealth were sure to have their mothers eyeing him speculatively.

Prince then announced, "Well, I suppose, there's no need for any speechmaking this afternoon, is there?"

Everyone laughingly agreed.

"Then let's ask the ladies to set out the food and we'll celebrate Mr. Freeman's good fortune instead."

As the crowd descended upon the men to offer their congratulations, Charity whispered to Faith, "Nicholas Grey is very nice to look at, isn't he?"

Faith shook her head in amusement and wondered

what Ingram might say if he knew his wife was eyeing Primus's son like a lollipop. "We're needed in the kitchen."

As the buffet line formed and began to move, Blythe, who always headed up the women workers at such events, handed Faith a tray that held three plates piled high with offerings from the buffet. "Take this over to Prince, Nicholas, and Mr. Freeman. The way they're being mobbed, the food will be gone by the time they manage to get over here to the table."

Faith could see a large group of people waiting their turn to speak to the men and she agreed. Making her way through the crowd, she finally reached them and politely interrupted. "Mr. Hall, Blythe sent you food."

Prince excused himself from the man he was talking with and took the tray. "Thank you, Miss Kingston, and thank the Widow Lawson for her foresight."

Behind her, Faith could feel Grey's presence as well as she could her own breathing. Grabbing hold of herself, she turned to face him.

"Miss Kingston. How are you?"

"I'm well, Mr. Grey."

"Thank you for the food," he said.

Looking into his eyes was like looking into flames. "You're welcome." She read a muted sort of amusement in his manner but she had no idea what it might stem from. "That was a very generous gift."

"My father was a warrior for justice. I did it in his honor."

She saw Prince hand a plate to Mr. Freeman, who turned to Faith and bowed.

In response, she said, "You're welcome, sir."

Grey hadn't moved, however. He was still looking down at her and assessing her; for what, she had no idea.

Charity was right; he was nice to look at, especially up close. "I need to get back."

He gave her a simple nod but continued to hold her eyes.

She heard someone behind him say, "Mr. Grey, I knew your father well . . ."

He turned away, and Faith and her wildly beating heart slipped back into the crowd. When she looked over at her father, he was frowning.

The event ended an hour so later. Mr. Freeman left to see to the freedom of his wife, and the crowd began to exit in twos and threes. Charity and Ingram left as well in order to retrieve their son. Faith and the remaining women were in the kitchen attending to the cleanup when her father walked in.

"Faith, some of the Tories would like to meet while we're all in town. Would you mind riding back with Widow Lawson?"

"Not as long as she doesn't mind."

Blythe looked up from the dishes she was washing in a big iron tub. "I'd enjoy the company."

Her father bowed. "Thank you, widow. Faith, I will see you this evening."

"Be careful on the roads."

He nodded and left them to their work.

The kitchen was set to rights a short time later and the women began to leave for their homes. While Blythe made room in the back of her wagon bed, Faith carried out the items that were going inside. The last load was a large, heavy crate holding kettles and the gridirons the meats had cooked upon. Struggling with the weight, she stepped outside and stopped at the sight of Nicholas Grey talking with Blythe beside the wagon. Upon seeing her so loaded down, he came to her aid.

"Let me help you."

Without argument the grateful Faith passed him the crate. "Thank you." He was chivalrous as well as generous. She reminded herself that he also held her father responsible for Primus's arrest.

When they reached the wagon Blythe said, "I'll be back in a few moments. I need to speak with Mrs. Carstairs before she drives off. Faith, make sure we didn't leave anything behind."

"I will."

Blythe hurried away, calling to and waving at Mrs. Carstairs.

"Where would you like this placed?" he asked, bringing her attention back to him.

She indicated an empty spot near the front of the wagon bed and he set it down.

Avoiding his captivating eyes she said, "I'm going to

run back in and do as she asked. Thank you again for your help."

"I'm giving a reception next week so that I may meet more of the community. May I interest you in being my hostess?"

Faith stopped and said, "You know I can't agree to such a proposal."

"Suppose I hire you to provide the meal then?"

"At a price, I'm assuming?" She and her father could use some extra funds.

"Name it."

Faith rattled off a price she hoped would make him choke and rescind his offer, but he met her eyes as blandly as if she'd quoted the temperature. "Fine," he said to her. "I'll stop by the inn tomorrow and we can discuss the menu."

She almost choked. "You'd pay so much?"

Enjoying himself more than he ever thought he would, Nick said, "I'd pay twice that amount for your services, Miss Kingston."

"You make it sound as if I'm offering something illicit."

"Are you?"

In response to his tone and his eyes, a shimmering warmth flooded Faith that she'd never experienced before. She managed to say, "Of course not."

"Pity," he replied softly.

He was so dazzling, she felt dizzy for a moment.

Fighting to regain her equilibrium, she told him, "Go away," but the demand lacked strength. He was entirely too handsome and volatile for such an inexperienced woman as herself.

"I'll go, but only because if I don't, I'll be asking you rude questions like: Have you ever been kissed, Faith Kingston?"

Faith had to close her eyes or fall over.

"Good-bye, Miss Kingston."

When she opened her eyes he was walking away. She fell back against the wagon with relief.

"Are you all right, dear?" Blythe asked, walking up.

Faith hastily straightened. "Yes. Are you ready to leave?"

Blyth turned to watch Nicholas ride away before turning back. She eyed Faith for a quiet moment before saying, "I'm ready when you are."

Chapter 5

Did you know my father was passing secrets to the rebels?" Nicholas asked Blythe. During their short conversation outside the church, they'd arranged to meet here at her home after the fund-raisor so he could speak with her about his father's arrest. They were seated in her well-furnished parlor.

"May I ask why you'd think I would?"

"Because of what you were to each other."

She smiled softly, "And that was?"

"Friends. Confidants. Lovers."

Her sigh of response barely rippled the silence. "I miss him so."

Seated in a nearby chair, Nicholas waited.

"He was all of that to me and more. Much more. When I heard he'd been arrested I paid bribes, called in favors. I tried to move heaven and earth to get him released."

"But you couldn't."

"No. One of the soldiers said they wanted to make an

example of him to the rest of the race as to how dangerous it is to support the rebels. They're hoping we won't get involved in the fight, but we already are, or at least some of us are. Men like Kingston and his Tories are the exception."

"I've heard rumors that Kingston might have been involved with the arrest."

"The only thing I know for certain is that he hated Primus."

"Do you know why?"

"No. Primus never talked about why, only that they were best friends growing up, which surprised me, but after they settled here something changed."

Yet another mystery, Nicholas thought. "Tell me about his daughter. I'm surprised such a beauty isn't married."

"There's a strong mind beneath that lovely face and some men are put off by that. Faith's no meek miss waiting to do a husband's biding."

That jibed with what Faith had revealed, but he'd wanted to hear Blythe's take, too. "Does she follow her father's thinking?"

"You'll have to ask her."

"That's a cryptic answer."

"These are cryptic times, no?"

He allowed her that, so he turned his thoughts away from Mistress Kingston and back to his father's arrest. "Did Primus ever mention a Lady Midnight? I asked

Prince about her, but he was purposefully vague, I'm thinking."

"As I said, these are cryptic times. Some things are not to be shared."

"Not even with the man stepping into my father's shoes?"

She paused and gauged him closely. "Really?"

"Prince asked me this morning if I would consider it, and I gave him my reply at the church."

"And you said yes."

He nodded.

"Your father would approve."

Her response gave him the answer to the question he'd sought at the beginning of their conversation. "So you did know about his secret work with the rebels?"

"Your father and I were links in a long and circuitous chain. Why are you curious about the Lady Midnight?"

"According to Artemis Clegg, she visited Primus just before the arrest, so I am anxious to speak with her. I'm hoping she can reveal the identity of whoever betrayed him."

Blythe went silent for a few moments, and he wondered what she might be holding back. "Your thoughts?" he asked.

"I would like to know who betrayed him as well. I have made some discreet inquiries, but so far nothing tangible has come to light."

"Has anyone else been arrested in the interim?"

"Yes, but no one with ties to the free Black community. Although we do wonder who else may be on Gage's list."

"Prince said that his flat is under constant watch."

"As are many others."

"And you?"

"I've seen nothing that indicates such, but it is more difficult for the British to keep watch out here in the countryside. They are too busy with all that is going on in the city."

"Prince also said that only a few people know how to contact Lady Midnight. I assume my father was one and that possibly you are another?"

Again she studied him but finally admitted, "Yes, I am, but know this, Nicholas. I will betray you before I bring the British down on her head. Should she be exposed, she will hang, and I would not like to see that happen."

He met her eyes and saw the quiet determination they held. "All right. I will not press you further on the matter of her identity, but will she continue to work through me?"

"There is no guarantee. She trusted your father with her life. She may not feel the same about you."

"One last question. Why weren't you the one to take over my father's contacts?"

"Although we were links in the same chain, our positions on that chain were different. His information went directly into Boston. Mine flows elsewhere."

Nicholas thought about all that he'd learned. This was a deadly game he'd signed on to play and any wrong moves could leave him with a noose around his throat. He'd have to proceed with stealth and caution. "You will let the Lady Midnight know about the new arrangement?"

"I will, and we will see how she responds."

"Thank you for allowing me to monopolize your evening, and for being so forthright with your replies to my many questions."

"Your father would have expected no less. So what have you been doing with your life since the war?"

He told her about the years he spent trapping and guiding and living with the Iroquois, but left out being shanghaied and his subsequent life as a smuggler. "Made a veritable fortune, but had no idea Primus would leave this life without me having a chance to wish him Godspeed."

"I'm sure he felt the same."

Nick's laugh was harsh. "No need to lie to me, Blythe."

"It's true. You've no idea how pleased he was to receive your letters."

Nick found that surprising. "But he never acknowledged them with a reply."

"He could be stubborn, but he cherished your words and he worried when they stopped coming for a while. He'd given you up for dead until your letters started to arrive again."

Nick had stopped writing because of the hell he'd found himself in after being impressed.

"You haven't married?" Blythe asked.

"No. No desire to put down the roots a wife and family require."

"And now?"

He shrugged, and Faith's face flashed across his mind's eye. "I could be ready with the right woman. It's good for a man to have sons."

"And daughters," she reminded him sagely.

Amusement lit his tone. "And daughters. I'd like to give a reception next Saturday in order to reintroduce myself to the community. I'd be honored if you would be my hostess."

"I'd love to. Would you like for me to prepare the guest list?"

"That would be helpful. Miss Kingston has offered to help with the food."

"Really? And her father's allowing it?"

"I've no idea what he will say, but if he's the man I believe him to be, the price I'm offering for her services should appease him."

She eyed him for a long moment before saying, "I'll not have you trifling with her feelings, Nicholas."

"I don't trifle, Blythe. She's a wonderful cook."

"She is, but—"

Their eyes met.

"Never mind," Blythe said. "I trust you will be a gentleman."

Nick inclined his head. "Thank you."

"I'll include some of the area's eligible young ladies on the guest list just in case you decide you do want a wife. Would you like to have the reception here? It may be more convenient than attempting to get your own home ready for such an event."

Nick liked the sound of that. "That makes sense, so yes, if it isn't an inconvenience."

"I'd enjoy it."

"As to the young women on the guest list. No insipid ones, please. My ideal candidate will be someone able to hold a decent conversation without having her eyes glaze over."

She replied with a soft peal of laughter. "I will keep that in mind."

Nicholas got to his feet and she followed.

As she walked with him to the front door, she said, "It's been lovely chatting with you."

"For me as well." He paused for a moment, then pledged, "I'll not stop looking for the person who betrayed my father."

"I know you won't because neither will I."

He nodded. "Good night, Blythe."

"Be well."

The following morning Faith was up before dawn tossing wood on the fire in the kitchen's big stone grate to begin the day. The room was cold as it always was at that time. Shivering, she pulled her gray shawl closer and used the poker on the logs to prod the flames higher. It would take a while for the wood to be consumed enough to cook on, so she got out her wooden dough bowl to start the biscuits. As she worked, the kitchen gradually warmed and the fire reduced some of the fat logs to the charcoal-like ash necessary to cook on. Wiping her dough-covered hands clean, she hiked up her skirts and petticoats and tucked the hems into the waistband of her skirt, leaving her stocking-covered legs exposed. Many women died from fires started by sparks on their long skirts, and Faith had no desire to be among their number. It was indecent, yes, but a commonly accepted safety precaution practiced by every cook.

She checked the bacon frying in the skillets sitting on top of the raised gridirons near the front of the fire, then stirred the breakfast stew of meat and vegetables cooking nicely in the big iron pot hanging on the rod fixed into the back of the grate. Each portion of the big fireplace was a different temperature, and it took skill to have everything done in the same time span. Once she placed the biscuits in the Dutch oven, she put the lid on and placed it near the front of the fire. She then used a long-handled fire shovel to pile some of the charcoal on top of the lid. Now that she had everything cooking, she paused to take a breath. She heard voices coming from the main room. Curious as to who it might be at such an early hour, she stepped out to find her father conversing with a British soldier. When the conversation ended, the soldier departed.

"What did he want so early?"

"He's a scout sent ahead by General Gage and his officers. They'll be here in under an hour to eat. Make sure everything's ready."

Nodding, she went back into the kitchen.

The general and his men arrived forty minutes later and immediately headed down to the cellar room. When she had everything ready, she placed the food onto a tray and carried it down the earth-carved steps to the cellar. As she approached, she heard Gage snarl, "I've had enough. We will put an end to this rebel nonsense as soon as and as quickly as we can. By mid April it will be over."

Surprised etched her face and she stopped. The ramifications of his words were enormous. Composing herself, she entered the room. All conversation ceased.

Once done with the serving, she left them as silently as she'd come. Hoping Gage might continue the conversation, she quickly went into the wood bin and was just getting herself into position when she heard behind her, "What are you doing?"

Startled, she turned and came face to face with one of the aides. "I'm getting more wood for the grates, sir," she managed to say without stammering. Her heart was thumping against her chest.

He eyed her suspiciously. "Then get about it."

"Yes, sir."

Under his watchful stance, Faith hastily filled her arms with some of the rough-cut wood, and after giving him a nod, moved past him and headed up the stairs. She could feel his eyes on her back, so she didn't turn around.

Once alone in the kitchen, she waited until her galloping heart slowed and then thanked providence that he'd shown up when he had. Had it been a few moments later, she would have had a harder time explaining why she was in the room and not already gone. In the future she might have to find another way to eavesdrop, but for the present, she pondered what she'd heard. If Gage was indeed planning an imminent move against the rebels, word needed to be spread so that preparations could be made to meet the assault. She supposed she could send word to the Sons of Liberty by Charity again, although she preferred another way. Should Ingram ever find out her role, their marriage might be destroyed and Charity cast out. Although Charity had undoubtedly weighed the risks when she began her tradecraft, Faith preferred not to use her too often. She supposed she could pass on what she'd heard to Blythe and let her handle it from there. As far as Faith knew, no one had been appointed to replace Primus. She assumed the role would be filled eventually, but she had no way of knowing if it would be someone she could trust. If all else failed she could take a chance on leaving a message at the home of John Hancock. It would mean sneaking out of the house again, but Gage's plans were important enough to take the risk.

While trying to decide on the best course of action, she added the wood in her arms to the stack by the grate. She was checking the biscuits still cooking in the Dutch oven when her father entered.

"Are they served?" he asked.

"Yes. You'd think they would offer some words of thanks for it." She continued to be offended by their lack of manners.

"Don't be disrespectful, child. The general shows his appreciation in other ways. Add these coins to the safe." He placed a small leather pouch on the table and walked out.

Faith opened the bag. The pile of sovereigns inside widened her eyes. Grabbing it up, she went after him. "What is this for?"

"Bills."

"I mean why would he pay you such a large sum?"

"For the good service, of course."

She swore he looked evasive. "Are you certain?"

"What other reason would there be? Now go put it in the safe like I asked."

So she did, but not without wondering why he'd looked the way he had in response to her question. Many of the homes and inns in the area had been forced to house British troops with no compensation to the owners. To the people of Boston the foisting had come to be known as one of the Intolerable Acts. The general and his aides had been taking meals at the inn for months now, but Faith never remembered them paying her father so much as a farthing, so why now? Closing the safe, she supposed her suspicions were simply a product of the times.

The sun had just risen when Nicholas breached the surface of the ice-cold creek and shook the water from his face and head. Shivering, he strode naked up the bank and quickly wrapped himself in the warmth of the thick pelt blanket before pushing his bare feet into the worn deer-hide moccasins. Looking like an Iroquois in winter, he made his way through the forest and silently covered the short distance across his fields to the house. Inside, he stood by the fire and warmed himself. Although the creek had been running with the first melting of spring, the frigid temperature was invigorating; not only did it erase the sluggish remnants of sleep, it left his thinking sharp and clear. The early morning ritual was one of the many ways he'd been changed by living inside the Iroquois Confederation. At first, their way of life had seemed strange to a young man whose entire world had consisted of his father's farm and the surrounding environs, but the longer he lived with them, the more he saw the world through their eyes, and the more he came to appreciate their ways and beliefs.

Living the smuggler's life had changed him as well; hardening him, making him more cynical and more apt not to care about the consequences of his actions. He'd enjoyed the danger, the meetings in back rooms, the working of a deal. He'd made friends and enemies, and enjoyed women in port cities all over the world, and now? Coming back to live in polite society had him thinking about what he wanted to do with the remainder of his life. The money he had stashed away in banks in Philadelphia, London, and Montreal made working for a living unnecessary, yet he was not the type to sit idly by until the time came to be buried next to his parents. He needed purpose; always had. It was something he'd put his mind to once the quest to avenge his father was laid to rest, but not until then.

Warmer now, Nicholas dressed and sat down to a simple meal of bark tea, strips of dried pemmican, and a skillet of eggs. He thought about the reception he and Blythe had planned. Her offer to compile a list of potential wives wasn't something he'd dismissed out of hand, but he doubted anything would come of it. He supposed he owed it to his father to do what he could to ensure the Grey name survived, so he spent a few moments imagining himself spending the rest of his life as a farmer and married to a boring woman, and he frowned. If he did decide to marry he'd be more inclined to marry someone like Faith Kingston, whose wit and fire would at least keep him awake. With that in mind, he wondered if her father would forbid her to help with the reception. He hoped not because the more he was around her, the more she intrigued him, in spite of the fact that she wasn't the woman for him. He was supposed to meet her today to go over the food selections. Seeing her again was something he was looking forward to. A knock at his door caught his attention.

When he opened it, he found Prince Hall standing on the threshold. "Morning, Nicholas. Did you forget that we are drilling today?"

He lied, "No, but where are the others?"

"They'll be arriving shortly."

Nick invited him in. His meeting with the beguiling Faith Kingston would have to wait.

Just as he was about to close the door, a young man driving a wagon pulled up and called out to Nicholas. "You Nick Grey?"

"Yes."

"Got a letter for you."

A curious Nick walked out and took the letter. He give the driver a few coins for his trouble and as the man departed, Nick opened the black ribbon holding the missive closed. What he read inside made him smile.

After informing her father that she was going to visit Blythe, but would be back in time to prepare the late afternoon meal, Faith hurried outside to their small stable to hook their old mare, Susie, to the front of the flatbed wagon. Once everything was in order, she drove away.

The sun was shining brightly out of a blue sky as she traveled down the slushy Concord Road. Although the temperature was still cold enough to need her heavy cape, the breeze held the warm promise of spring. The month of April was only two weeks away, and once spring arrived in earnest everyone could shake off the isolation forced on them since mid November. There would be outdoor gatherings at the church again. The benevolent societies could be more active in their efforts to keep the race rising through their work with children, the poor, and the elderly. There would be parades—if the British allowed them—lobster bakes, and fishing, one of her favorite pastimes. In fact, if there was time and the fates were kind, she hoped to catch a few fish for dinner later that day. After months of dried, salted, or smoked meat, something fresh caught would be a godsend.

Since she had to pass the Trotter house, she decided to stop in and pay them a visit, but no one was home, so Faith drove Susie to the next side road that led to Blythe's. It was muddy going. Susie didn't like the slop but Faith urged her to keep moving so that the wagon wouldn't get stuck.

Knocks at Blythe's door went unanswered as well. Sighing with frustration, she supposed she'd have to hold on to Gage's words until she reached her, but she prayed the general didn't implement his plans early. Faith reached into the pocket of her cloak and withdrew the white quartz stone she always used a signal when she needed to speak with Blythe. Placing it at the base of the front door, she climbed back up into the wagon and drove away.

Her next destination was the creek that flowed through Primus's property. When he was alive he hadn't minded her fishing there. She doubted Nicholas would mind, either, but in a way, she was hoping he wasn't at home. She had no idea how to handle a man like him, not that she had experience handling any man, but something about him made her very aware of how much she didn't know about the games men and women played. The few suitors she'd had in her life had run screaming for the door once they took her measure, and as she told Nicholas the night on the road, many men didn't appreciate a woman of intelligence. They wanted to do her thinking for her and very few acknowledged that a woman had a mind at all. It was one of the reasons she couldn't abide Will Case. He was pompous enough to believe himself capable of thinking circles around anyone, especially a woman, and had grumbled on numerous occasions that her father had wasted his money by educating her. But Faith knew he was wrong. She didn't have much fun or happiness or variety in her life, but without her precious books, she would just be existing. At least the Bard offered her stories of lives filled with adventure, pathos, and comedy; stories she could lose herself in and forget about having to work each day from dawn to dark in the service of her father and his needs. Many mothers of eligible daughters thought Will Case quite the catch. Faith would rather catch fish.

Chapter 6

When she reached Primus's land, she turned on to the property. Straight ahead, the big, white, two-story house with its welcoming porch sat like a queen in the sunlight. The drive was a muddy quagmire of melted snow, dirt, and gravel. Although there were a number of other wheel marks and hoof prints in the drive she didn't see any other vehicles or horses tied up at the post near the house. She knew Nicholas had just moved back so maybe the tracks were from recent visitors or deliveries.

Her bad luck held. No one answered her knock. Slogging through the mud with her hems held above the muck, she went around to the back and saw nothing but the barns, the open fields, and the thick stand of trees that encircled the open land. As a matter of courtesy she'd wanted to make certain he had no objections to her being on his land, but seeing as he wasn't at home, she shrugged. Walking back to the wagon, she climbed up and guided Susie over to the tether post. After retrieving the bucket that held her fishing gear, she got down again, secured the horse's reins, and began the long trek to the creek.

A large stand of pines flanked the open fields, and the creek lay behind them. Once inside the cover of the trees, she could hear birds alerting their neighbors to her presence and she had to watch her step to keep from tripping over the roots and boulders hidden beneath the snow. The sound of voices made her stop and look around. For a moment she thought she might have imagined it, but then it came again, a lone voice, shouting. Confused and concerned, she stealthily made her way in that direction, carefully placing her steps so as to not give away her presence. What she saw was surprising. Prince Hall and a small group of men were drilling back and forth and Nicholas Grey appeared to be in command. This certainly wasn't what she'd expected to see, but more importantly, when had he become involved with the rebels? She also saw his neighbor Mr. Clegg among the men. Were they to be seen by a passing British patrol, they'd all be arrested and questioned, which was why most of the rebel drilling and preparations were done in secret. It came to her then that she needed to leave before they spotted her. She was member of a Tory family, and with Tories spying on rebels, she doubted they'd believe she'd just come to fish.

Nicholas looked out at Prince's untrained minutemen and had to agree; they were untrained. They didn't know how to march in formation, had little experience with firearms, and a few were in such bad physical condition that after an hour of marching and drilling they were on the ground wheezing. What impressed him, though, was that they were aware of their shortcomings, eager to improve, and to a man filled with the spirit of freedom. When he talked to them earlier about their reasons for wanting to fight, they gave him much the same reasons Prince had. It was their hope that the freedom the Sons of Liberty were espousing would be applied to all citizens equally, and the men of African descent, both slave and free, were willing to give their lives to add their weight to the scales.

But in order for them to be even moderately successful on a battlefield they had a lot to learn. In addition to the fifty commands they needed to be familiar with in order to fight together as a unit, they had to be taught to fire in three ranks; one line of kneeling men and two rows of standing men behind them, reloading and firing as swiftly as they could. Nicholas was just about to make them practice the lines again when a movement in the trees caught his attention. He called Prince over and while keeping an eye on the spot in the trees, he said. "Have the men rest for a moment. I believe we have a visitor."

Prince froze.

"Don't worry. I'll take care of it." He could see the worry on Prince's face. The last thing any of them needed was for their activities to be reported to the British authorities.

When Faith saw Nicholas Grey heading straight for her position she knew she'd been seen, and her first instinct was to flee like a child in trouble, but running away would only add to the appearance of guilt, so she stepped out of the trees, fully exposing herself.

The move seemed to catch him by surprise. He stopped, looked at her, and she looked back. Her chin rose defiantly because she had nothing to hide.

To say that Nicholas was surprised to see Faith Kingston was an understatement. He had no idea what the raven-eyed beauty with her gorgeous mouth was doing out here. Spying on them perhaps. She did have the pedigree for it. And why was she carrying a bucket?

Nicholas left her fearless glance for a moment to look around the trees for anyone that might have accompanied her, but saw no one else. Only then did he begin to close the distance between them, giving himself ample time as he walked to view the band of shining hair above the flat, dun brown hat on her head, the gray cloak shrouding her small frame, and then the face. She was beautiful enough to have stepped out of an African legend. The aforementioned dark eyes and well-shaped mouth accented the flawless skin. Were he in another time and place he would have already swept her up and stolen her away. Reminding himself that these were not the thoughts of a supposedly civilized man, he stopped before her, took in the coolness in her gaze, and asked, "Are you paying me back for lurking in your trees?"

"I came to fish." She held up the bucket so he could see the net and fishing lines inside.

He scanned the bucket, then slid his gaze back to hers. "Why here?"

"Because it's where I always come. Your father never minded."

"Then I shan't, either." Yes, he thought, steal her away, but there were other more pressing matters at stake. No one was supposed to know what he and Hall's men were doing. "How much have you seen?"

"Enough," she told him plainly.

"And you'll tell your father?"

"Nothing. What you do on your land is none of my business, Mr. Grey."

"Interesting answer."

"Why?"

"Your father is a loyalist. I'd think he'd want to know about rebel activity so close to his home."

"So he can tell General Gage?"

"That does come to mind."

"You still believe my father played a role in your father's arrest."

"I do."

"What do I have to do to convince you how misguided that is?"

"Find Lady Midnight so that I might speak with her."

Faith went cold inside but hid it well. "Who is Lady Midnight?"

"Supposedly the woman who brought Primus the warning about his arrest."

"I know no one of that name." She met his eyes and hoped her gaze was as bland as she thought. "I'll fish another time."

"I appreciate that. I'll stop in later to go over the food selections."

"That will be fine." She turned and walked determinedly back towards the house.

As Nick watched her leave he pondered this latest encounter. First he'd seen her climbing out windows in the middle of the night, and now today she'd shown up lurking in his trees claiming to want to fish, of all things. The male in him enjoyed sparring with her even as he wondered if the visit by Faith Kingston had been just an innocent coincidence, or something more.

Driving home, Faith realized she was shaking. She applauded herself for not fainting when he mentioned Lady Midnight, but she had to wonder if he was on to her. As far as she knew, she was the last person to see Primus, but how had Nicholas come to know that? Surely he didn't think she was responsible for the arrest. The way he'd asked about her alter ego made her believe he was very interested in locating her, but for what purpose? She had enough to worry about, and now this. She'd planned to leave a message for John Hancock tonight about Gage's intentions but now she wasn't sure if she should risk it. What if Nicholas learned she was the woman he was after, and what might he do with the information?

Blythe stopped at the inn late that evening. Faith was in the kitchen gathering the ingredients and the Dutch ovens she'd need for the week's baking she'd planned on doing the next day. Blythe removed her cloak and said quietly, "I saw your rock, so I came as quickly as I could."

Faith took the rock from Blythe's hand and slipped it back into the pocket of her skirt. Keeping her voice down so that her father and the two guests in the main room wouldn't hear, she said, "Gage is talking of moving against the rebels."

"When?"

Faith told her what she'd heard, adding, "Too bad he wasn't more specific about the date, but mid April is precise enough for our purposes."

"I agree. This will mean war."

Faith nodded solemnly. "The Sons in Boston need to be alerted. Has someone taken Primus's place?"

"Yes. His son, Nicholas."

Faith went still. That was not what she wanted to hear.

"What's wrong? He can be trusted."

"We had an encounter today. He's looking for Lady Midnight."

"I know."

Faith stared.

Blythe told her about her conversation with Nicholas and his desire to find Lady Midnight.

Faith replied, "But I don't know who the betrayer is, or how Gage found out. Father said Primus was going to be arrested and I went to him as soon as I could."

"How'd your father know?"

"I assumed Gage mentioned it in passing."

Blythe then looked into Faith's eyes and said earnestly, "Faith, you need to know that your father's name has come up quite a bit in all the speculation swirling around the arrest."

"You're jesting."

"No, and I don't want you to be caught off guard if you hear the talk."

"But he wasn't involved. We both know that."

Blythe responded quietly, "The only certainty I know is that sometimes certainty is not what we think."

"Blythe, you can't believe he would do something so dastardly."

"It doesn't matter what I believe. What matters most to me is that you be very careful."

"I will but—" Faith was all but speechless. Her father wasn't the nicest or politest person to her or anyone else, but she believed him to be an ethical man. Until she heard it from the general's own lips, she'd never believe he had anything to do with Primus's arrest. "I still say my father was not involved."

Blythe didn't respond.

Piqued, Faith asked, "What do we really know about Nicholas? He shows up here virtually out of nowhere, tossing coin around and ingratiating himself into the community. Suppose he's a British spy. Are the Sons convinced he can be trusted?"

"I spoke with Prince Hall this afternoon, and he is as certain as anyone can be, considering the times, that Nicholas can be."

"Hall doesn't know I'm Lady Midnight does he?"

Blythe showed a soft smile. "No dear. Only you and I know her true identity. I made my pledge to you and to Primus to keep the secret and I will."

"But how will I manage to get news to Nicholas? Primus and I had a prearranged signal that let him know when I needed to speak with him."

"That's something you will have to work out with Nicholas, I suppose. Maybe you should disguise yourself as you did the first few times you worked with his father."

Faith mulled that over. Maybe a disguise would be the answer. Presently she couldn't think of any other method that didn't involve her revealing her true identity to him, so she let the dilemma go for now, in hopes of having an epiphany sometime soon.

Blythe said, "While you chew on that, Nicholas says he's contracted with you for his reception. Have you told your father?"

"Not yet."

"If it will help, the reception will be at my house and not his. Maybe your father won't object if he knows that."

"That will certainly be in my favor."

"Nicholas wants me to invite some of the eligible

ladies and their families. He may be in the market for a wife."

Faith wondered why that bothered her. "Does that mean he'll be settling here permanently?"

"I'm not certain, but he asked that I not include any insipid women though. His words."

"That should narrow the field," Faith replied sarcastically.

Blythe chuckled. "True, but either way, he doesn't have much to choose from. I thought I'd ask Hazel Carstairs, Winnie Potts, and Elizabeth Sutter."

The names were familiar to Faith, as were the personalities. She thought it might be nice to be a fly on the wall and watch the play unfold. "What time should I arrive?"

Blythe gave her the time, then said, "The Sons leadership should be told of Gage's plans as soon as possible."

"I'd planned on getting a message to John Hancock tonight."

"What about Nicholas?"

Faith didn't know. "I figure if I let Hancock know, everyone else with a need to know will be informed, including Nicholas and his contacts."

"But there is no guarantee the men of color will be included."

Faith knew she was right. With all the controversy swirling about whether Blacks would really be allowed to fight, who knew what Prince and the others might or might not be told. "Nicholas will have to be told."

"Yes, he will. Do you want me to pass this news along to him?"

"I would."

"All right, but remember, come next week I'll be visiting my daughter in New York, and will be away until after she has her baby. If anything important arises, you will have to go to Nicholas on your own."

Faith blew out a breath. "I'll try and devise a suitable solution while you're gone."

"That's my girl. Now, I'm going home. I'll see you Saturday if not before."

They shared a hug, and Blythe left Faith alone to deal with her problems.

Later, Faith pored over the inn's ledgers. According to the numbers, she and her father were very close to being in the black. Due to the tensions between the British and the colonists, people weren't traveling as much and the Kingston Inn hadn't had a steady number of guests seeking a room in weeks. Most of the coin flowing into the coffers came from the occasional diner stopping by.

As she added up the numbers from the small pile of receipts, her father came in. She was surprised to see him all dressed up.

"How do I look?" he asked.

"Very prosperous. May I ask the occasion?"

"I'm courting."

Faith stared. "Courting."

"Decided I need sons."

Confused but wearing a false smile she asked, "And do I know the lucky woman?"

"Yes, but for now I'm keeping her name to myself. Her parents and I haven't finalized a satisfactory contract as of yet."

"I see." That meant the woman was young enough to still be in her parents' home. A widow or a spinster living on her own wouldn't need parental involvement. Faith knew her opinion wouldn't matter but she wasn't sure how she felt about this new surprising news. "Why sons?"

"So that I can pass the inn on to them, of course."

"Ah," she replied, hiding her disappointment. She'd hoped to be the one to inherit. After all, the inn had belonged to her mother originally. It had passed to him after her death, but she supposed he'd conveniently forgotten that fact. He did look nice in his new clothes, however, even though she was wearing drawers with patched bottoms.

"I'll be back in a few hours."

"Have a good time."

"I plan to."

Once he was gone, Faith wondered who the woman might be. He'd been out in the evenings quite often lately, always professing to be visiting friends, but now she could only assume he'd been out courting, but who? He'd said the woman was someone known to Faith, but she couldn't for the life of her think of who it might be.

She also assumed the new wife would be living at the inn, so did he expect Faith to remain the worker bee while he and the new queen lapped up all the honey? Faith looked down at her hands. They were red and raw from the lye soap she used to keep everything clean, from the linens on the beds to the wood floors. Would the new wife help with the cleaning, make the trips to the creamery, take the grain to the miller in the summer, and draw water every morning at dawn? If she was young enough to still need a parental contract, she probably had a mother to do all the things that Faith did every day. Faith had a bad feeling about this, but knew that there was nothing she could do about it. Her father would do what he felt best for him, and Faith would have to go along with the ride.

Shaking her head, she went back to her ledgers.

The front door opened and she looked up expecting to see her father returning for something he'd forgotten, but instead Nicholas Grey stood there. She slowly rose to her feet. "Good evening." Looking over at him filled her with the oddest sensation. She knew she shouldn't be affected by his handsomeness, but it was difficult not to be. His dark eyes were so intense she wanted to look elsewhere, but forced herself to hold his gaze.

"Good evening, Faith. I came to talk about the reception and to offer you something in compensation for your cancelled fishing expedition earlier today."

"That isn't necessary. I left because I assumed you thought I might be spying, especially knowing how you feel about my father, as misguided as it might be."

He let her see a brief smile. "Regardless, if you would wait for me to return while I go out to the wagon."

She nodded. Once he was gone she exhaled, unaware that she'd been holding her breath. She knew they had an appointment this evening but she wondered if he was also intent upon discerning whether she'd shared what she'd seen in his woods today with her father. The night she found him spying on her from the trees, she'd made a vow to find out more about him, but other than Blythe there was no one in her sphere who would know the truth. He hadn't lived in Boston in over a decade. She'd been assured by Blythe that he could be trusted, but how could anyone really know?

He returned carrying a small copper's barrel that he set on a table. Curious, she walked over and looked inside. Fish. They were gutted, scaled, and packed in snow. She looked up at him with muted delight. "Thank you."

"You're welcome. Is this ample compensation?"

The timbre of his voice and the look in his eyes made her pause for a moment before replying, "Yes."

"Good. I don't wish to be at odds with you."

Another pause, and she seemed to feel the heat of him on the front of her body beneath her blouse and skirt. She felt compelled to say, "My father played no role in the arrest."

"If you're correct, I'll bring you more fish."

She couldn't hold back her smile. "This is more serious than fish."

"Men bring you fish often then?"

"No." No man had ever brought her fish or anything before, but she had no intention of revealing that fact.

He very boldly reached out and turned her chin so she faced him again. His finger slid slowly down her cheek. Shaking from his warm touch and the heat in his gaze, Faith took a small step back. "You're very bold, sir."

"I don't bring fish to just any woman."

She had trouble breathing, and so said softly, "I believe it's time for us to discuss your menu."

"Is your father here, so that we may get his approval?"

"No, he's out courting," she replied.

"Courting?" he echoed with a small chuckle. "Is she someone you know?"

"He says yes, but is keeping her name a secret until the contract is worked out."

"Which means she is a young woman with parents."

"I believe so." Faith gestured for him to take a seat.

He obliged. "How do you feel about having a stepmother?"

"I'm sure it doesn't matter."

"Why not?"

She shrugged. "My father's life is his own."

Faith closed the ledger that lay open between them. Next thing she knew he had a gentle hold on her hand and she froze.

"Lye?" he asked with concern.

Embarrassed, she pulled her red, roughened hand free. "Yes."

"Your father doesn't have a hired washerwoman?"

"No."

"Most inns do."

"I know, but he has me to do the wash, so why waste the coin."

The displeasure on his face was plain. "So, do you do all the chores?"

"Yes, and have done so since my mother died."

"How long has that been?"

"Since I was eight."

Nick knew that her answer was common. Many children were worked from dawn to dusk, but that didn't make it right or something he wanted to hear. "He should hire some help."

She shook her head. "We really can't afford it, and even if we could, I doubt he'd want to waste the coin when he has me."

"And how do you feel about that?"

She shrugged. "It's my life, Mr. Grey. There's no changing it. There are many women in far worse situations."

Nick agreed, but finding out she was being worked half to death didn't sit well.

"What would you like to serve at your reception?"

He didn't want to talk about the reception; he wanted to talk about easing her burdens. "I've been looking for a housekeeper. Would you consider working for me?"

"My father would never allow it. Besides, word is you're looking for a wife."

"Would you consider that?"

Amused, Faith shook her head. "The menu, Mr. Grey."

They shared smiles and got down to work. As they talked about his choices and the logistics involving purchase and transport of the food to Blythe's home, Nicholas found himself discreetly observing things like the tattered thin band of lace on the top of her high-necked blouse, her red and blistered hands, the weariness in her shoulders and eyes. Her faded overblouse was patched beneath the arms and the cuffs were frayed. She was too beautiful to be wearing rags. Although her garments were clean, they should have been banished to a dustbin long ago. The tiredness he saw in her face troubled him most, however. Were she under his charge he'd make certain she never worked another day in her life.

Her voice cut into his thoughts. "Mr. Grey, are you listening?"

He shook himself back to the moment. "My apologies. What did you say?"

"I asked how long you intend the reception to last. Blythe told me the time to arrive, but not how long I might have to stay."

They discussed that and decided on two hours at the most.

"That's fine," she responded. "Is there anything else I need to know?"

Nick settled his eyes on the beautiful woman that he knew was not for him and replied, "No, Miss Kingston. I believe we have covered everything of importance."

"Excellent. Remember, I must still obtain my father's approval, so you may wish to place another iron in the fire, just in case."

"I have faith in your powers of persuasion and in the power of the coin I've promised you for your help."

"You think so little of him that you believe he'd be moved by your money."

"I believe we will deal better if we don't discuss your father."

Faith eyed him. He was right of course. "Then I shall refrain."

"Thank you."

There was a hint of tension in the air, so Faith decided now might be the time to wish him good night. "If we are done, I'll let you get on with your evening."

Nick didn't want to go, but knew she was correct. He stood. "Thank you for the conversation and the help. I'm looking forward to Saturday."

"Good evening, Mr. Grey."

He bowed and departed.

Faith took the fish outside so they would stay frozen. She could still feel his touch against her cheek and no matter how much she tried to banish it, the memory remained. Walking back into the kitchen, she checked on the two loaves of bread she had baking on the fire and then returned to the ledgers.

Her father returned an hour later looking pleased. Faith wanted to know more about this courtship, but knew better than to ask. He'd tell her in his own time and not a second before.

"Did you enjoy yourself?"

"I did. Make sure you get that floor in the cellar room mopped first thing in the morning. If the general comes, I want it clean."

"Yes, Father."

"Good night, Faith."

"Good night."

And he made his exit. She supposed they'd have to talk about Nicholas's reception some other time. Looking over at the clock, she closed the ledgers and checked on the bread. In two hours he'd be sound asleep and Lady Midnight could make her way into Boston. Hopefully by then she'd be able to forget Nicholas's warm touch and the heat in his eyes because she couldn't afford to be distracted.

Chapter 7

Astride Hades and filled with memories of Faith Kingston, Nicholas rode towards Boston. He hadn't intended to touch her, but now that he had he wanted to further explore the satiny skin of her cheek and the texture of her shapely lips. He also hadn't expected to be moved by the challenges in her life, but he had and she was proving to be quite the distraction. He was supposed to be focusing on what he was on to next, not imagining what she'd feel like in his arms or how she'd looked perfumed and nude in his bed. She was the daughter of his father's nemesis and he had no business being attracted to her but damned if he wasn't. He'd always preferred his women tall and bearing curves that filled his hands. Faith didn't fit the model, but her spirit would do an Iroquois clan mother proud and he supposed that was what drew him. Docile, meek women didn't appeal to him. He preferred those who challenged him and then denied him even if it wasn't for long. He sensed all those attributes in Stuart Kingston's daughter, and a growing part of him wanted to know more. However, he noted again that he wasn't supposed to be thinking of her even as he mused upon how he might relieve her of some of the work she was carrying on her slender shoulders.

It was dark and the wind was blowing briskly when Nicholas tied up his horse and entered the shadowy confines of the noisy Boston tavern. Apparently those inside had left their politics at the door because there were uniformed soldiers seated around the tables raising tankards of ale, while commonly dressed locals occupied others. Once the ale flowed, anything might happen, though, so he planned to conduct his business and depart.

As he made his way through the noise and fiddle music, a few of the barmaids gave him smiles, but he didn't tarry. He found the two men he was seeking seated at a back table near one of the few windows.

Seeing him, both men smiled, and Nick smiled in response as he greeted them. "Dom. Gaspar. How are you two?"

Dominic LeVeq grinned. "Nicholas. It's good to see you, old friend."

Gaspar nodded. "Nick."

Nicholas sat down. He'd met sea captain Dominic LeVeq and his blood brother Gaspar the night of the mutiny that freed Nick from his impressment with the Royal Navy. They'd rescued him and the stallion now named Hades, along with a few other men who were in the water as the burning British ship sank. Nick was fairly sure at the time that Dom and his crew were more intent upon saving the admiral's prized stallion than anything else, but he owed them his life.

Dominic asked, "I assume you got my letter?"

"Yes, this morning. How long will you be in Boston?"

"Long enough to conduct some business, but we wanted to see how you fared. Are you and your father reconciled?"

"No." They knew his story, just as he knew that Dom was the bastard son of a French duke.

One of the barmaids walked up carrying a tray holding three tankards of ale. She set one vessel down in front of each of them. Gaspar paid her, but before leaving them, she said slyly, "We offer more than ale here, gentlemen, so if you are in need of a more personal service, my name is Ginny."

They acknowledged her with nods, but no one took her up on the offer.

Once they were alone again, Nick told them the story of his father and all the intrigue swirling around his arrest and death.

"My condolences," Gaspar said solemnly.

Dom offered the same. "So you are looking for this Lady Midnight?"

Nick nodded. "She's the only key I have."

Dom cracked, "You could threaten to slit Kingston's throat if he doesn't offer up the truth."

Nick chuckled. "Don't think I haven't considered

it, but I'm sure his daughter wouldn't care for that approach."

Gaspar shook his head. "Why is there always a woman involved with the two of you?"

Dom drawled, "Possibly because Nick and I are always involved with women."

Nick grinned and saluted his former captain with his ale. "However, this one is a good woman."

Dom shook his head. "Good women are nothing but trouble, my friend. It's best to avoid them, always."

"True, but in this case easier said than done."

Gaspar and Dom searched his face, and Dom asked, "How serious are you about the daughter?"

"That's none of your business."

Dom and Gaspar shared an amused look before Dom declared, "You're doomed, Nick."

Nick didn't dispute the fact. "Maybe you'll be doomed sometime in the future, too, Dominic."

Dom shook his head. "I'm too wily for that."

They shared the smiles of men who'd come to know each other well, then began a discussion of the business Nick hoped they could help him with. "I need muskets."

"How many?"

"As many as you can provide."

"When?"

"Soon."

Dom replied, "There're rumors that once the war starts the colonial government will be issuing letters of marque, and I'd love to be able to legally poke the British in the eyes as often as possible. As for the muskets, I'm certain it won't take long to get you what you need."

Nick was pleased with that answer. He happened to look towards the window. A woman passed by. The brisk wind blew her hood back from her face. She quickly raised it back over her head again but not quick enough to keep her familiar face from widening his eyes. He immediately jumped to his feet. "I have to go. Right now."

Dominic and Gaspar looked confused.

He hastily put on his coat. "Get me those guns."

While Dom and Gaspar stared, Nick all but ran from the tavern.

Once outside, he sprinted down the alley that led to the street that the tavern window had looked out on and glanced wildly back and forth, but he didn't see her. Had he imagined her? he asked himself. He began walking quickly in the direction he'd seen her heading in hopes of catching another sight but saw no woman in a gray cape. Suddenly, a few feet up ahead, he spotted her crossing the street. He grinned and followed, but kept a safe distance. *What are you up to tonight, Faith Kingston? Fetching eggs again, no doubt.*

Faith kept her steps quick and measured. At that time of night the streets of Boston could prove dangerous for a woman alone, from both soldiers and brigands, and she wanted no dealings with either. Her destination was the home of rebel leader John Hancock. She knew where he lived, as did every other citizen in the area. It was her hope that British spies would not be watching his home at this hour but there was no guarantee. She kept casting discreet glances behind her to make sure she wasn't being followed but even though she saw no one, there was no guarantee she wasn't. With her hood up, she doubted she'd draw attention, and if she did, passersby would see nothing more than a woman hurrying home. As she turned the corner onto the street where Hancock lived she casually looked around for soldiers. Seeing none she kept up her pace. However, as she approached his home, she saw three uniformed men posted out in front of the entrance. Gathering her nerve, she approached them. "I'm here to deliver bread to Mr. Hancock. May I do so?"

She reached into the sack and withdrew one of the two loaves inside to show them. It was still warm and the fresh-baked scent drifted fragrantly in the wind.

"A bit late for deliveries, miss."

"True, but the regular delivery woman took ill and won't be able to come in the morning. I told my employer I'd make sure Hancock got these on my way home."

"He's not in," one of them pointed out.

Another soldier cracked. "He's over in Concord getting his neck measured for a noose."

They laughed. Hancock not being home was to her advantage but by the light of the fire they had burning in a barrel to keep warm, she could see them eyeing her with suspicion. She added emotion to her performance.

"Please, I'll have nothing but trouble tomorrow if it isn't left tonight. In fact, you may have one of the loaves if you just let allow me to leave the other."

And with that she was certain she had them. Everyone knew how poorly paid and underfed the soldiers were. In fact, many had taken side jobs at taverns and other businesses just to make ends meet. It was her hope that these three were hungry enough to take the offering and let her go on her way.

One of the soldiers took the offered loaf and motioned her forward. "Go on."

"I was told to leave it around back."

They were already dividing the loaf between them. One nodded his approval, so she drew in a sigh of relief and hastened to the back of the large home. In the darkness she lifted her skirt, pulled the coded message free of her petticoat, and stuck it into the sack beneath the bread. Placing the sack at the foot of the steps, she quickly made her way back to the street. "Thank you. Long live the King."

The soldiers offered farewells around the mouthfuls of bread, and a pleased Faith set off into the darkness to retrieve the mare she'd left tied up outside the church.

Watching her depart from his position in the darkened doorway of a closed shop down the street, Nick didn't know what to make of what he'd just witnessed. Why was she delivering bread at such a late hour? Was it another one of her many chores? He wasn't yet familiar enough with present-day Boston to know who might be living in the home she'd visited but the soldiers posted out front offered two possibilities: either a high-ranking British official or someone needing to be watched, such as a rebel leader. He tried to make out the address so that he could ask Prince about the residence the next time they were together, then left the doorway to follow her.

As he remained careful to keep her in sight, the conundrum surrounding her continued to plague him. On one hand her actions could have been simply what they seemed, nothing more than a delivery; he'd tasted her bread and it was superb. Or was there more to this than met the eye? He now had two choices: either stop her and confront her, or let her go and make himself batty trying to figure it out. He chose the former.

When she passed the tavern where he'd left Hades tied up, he quickly retrieved the stallion and mounted. He had no idea if Dom and Gaspar were still inside but he didn't have the time to enter and see.

He caught up to her and reined the horse to a walk. "Good evening, Miss Kingston."

Faith startled and looked over with surprise to see Nicholas Grey. "Mr. Grey. What are you doing here?" She pulled in a breath to calm herself. His unexpected appearance had been frightening.

"I could ask you the same question. You didn't mention coming into town."

Her wits now in hand, she tossed back, "Neither did you."

"Are you on your way home?"

Faith wondered if he'd seen her leave the inn and had been following her the entire time. She prayed she'd not have to explain herself. "I am. My mare is just up the street."

"Then let me ride you there. It isn't safe for a woman to be out this late."

"That isn't necessary."

"I insist."

Faith could tell by his tone that he wouldn't be taking no for an answer, and the longer she stood here debating the matter with him, the longer it would take her to return home. "Then I will avail myself of your generosity."

He leaned down and before she could blink, his hands were around her waist and she was being lifted into the air. She came to rest in front of him. The warmth of his hands and the heat of his body pressing against her were enough to make her swoon.

"Hold on to me, so that you don't fall."

Faith looked up into his strong face. She'd never ridden with a man this way. It was both intimate and overwhelming. However, she didn't want to fall, so she complied but attempted to keep their bodies separated.

"You'll have to lean back a bit so that I can see ahead."

She got the sense that he was amused by her plight, but she had no choice but to comply and hoped he would be a gentleman. When his arm circled her and eased her closer to make certain she was secure, she was startled by it, but before she could react further, he urged the horse forward and set it on a slow pace.

"What are you doing out so late?"

"I had bread to deliver. And you?" she added quickly to keep him from quizzing her further.

"I was at a tavern with friends when I saw you walk past the window."

Faith would have preferred the horse move faster so that this unsettling encounter might end sooner, but Grey seemed intent upon this slow pace. "I really need to get to my mare and home, Mr. Grey."

"I think we've known each other long enough for you to refrain from calling me Mr. Grey, don't you?"

Faith had no response for that. She was too befuddled by the close positioning of their bodies, the gentle strength in the arm encircling her, and how she felt being held against the soft wool of his coat.

He peered down at her face in the darkness. "No?"

"I—I don't know." It was hard to think. She'd already acknowledged how much he affected her. Addressing him by his given name would remove one of the barriers she needed to keep herself aloof when he was near, not that any barriers seemed to have worked thus far.

"How about this? In public you may be formal, but when it is just you and I, I'd like you to call me Nick."

She couldn't think of a reason to deny the request so she agreed. "I suppose that would be all right."

"Thank you."

Faith was glad for the late hour. More than likely anyone who knew her wouldn't be out and about and report the sighting of her and Nicholas to her father. Had she happened on to an acquaintance while on the way to Hancock, the bread delivery would have offered a sufficient explanation. However, no explanation would be sufficient enough to cover her present situation.

She was been ridden through the dark streets of Boston by a man so totally out of her sphere, she was shaking with nervous reaction because she couldn't turn her mind or her senses away from how close she was being held against him. Every inch of her body could feel every inch of his and the pleasure it gave her wasn't anything a good woman should admit, even as she imagined what it might be like if he were her intended. Were that the case, she could savor their closeness and the faint spicy scent of his cologne and melt against his hard but comforting chest and not be expected to maintain her distance as she was unsuccessfully attempting to do now. What would his kisses be like? she wondered. The breezy, starry night seemed perfect for a lovers' tryst. Appalled by the direction her thoughts had taken, she dragged her mind back to saner realms, and again hoped they'd reach her horse soon.

They finally came upon the church, and as he brought the horse to a halt, she tried to straighten up but his arm kept her in place.

"I'll ride beside you to make certain you arrive home safe."

"But—"

He reached down and tenderly raised her chin. "No buts."

And then he kissed her.

Faith felt the sweetness pour into her with so much force that she would have melted down the horse's flanks had his arm not been holding her secure. The kiss was so wonderful and so unlike anything she'd ever experienced that all she could do was surrender to the tantalizing lure of his masterful lips against her untutored own. Her virgin mouth answered him hesitantly at first; enjoying the tastes and textures, letting herself be swept away by the swell of pleasure until her shyness took flight and was replaced by an age-old knowing of the woman awakening inside. His lips brushed against her cheek and she shimmered in response as they traveled up her jaw before settling possessively against her mouth once more. She couldn't breathe or think. The sensations sparked by this interlude were creating a storm.

"Nick," she rasped in a strangled voice. "We must stop," but she didn't want him to. He was gifting her with short, heated presses of his lips, punctuating them with lazy strokes of his flame-tipped tongue against her mouth's parted corners and she had to stop this or die.

"Please," she pleaded, and drew away. She was breathless. Trying to find herself in the haze around her, she looked up into his handsome face and saw the glitter of his eyes in the moonlight.

Nick was totally enthralled. Back at the tavern, Dominic had termed him doomed and Nick thought maybe his old friend was right. He wanted to hold her against him this way until the oceans went dry. He didn't care about the feud between their fathers, their difference in class, or what she'd really been doing tonight, all he wanted to do was to ride away with her and never let her go, but because reality dictated otherwise, the fulfillment of his fantasies would have to be set aside, for now. He slowly traced her trembling mouth one last time, kissed her passionately, and set her back down on the ground. The slight wobble she showed as she walked over to her old mare made him smile. Apparently he wasn't the only one enthralled, and the male in him was pleased at that. He'd tasted passion in the mysterious Miss Kingston, and he planned to taste much more.

On the ride out of Boston, Faith did her best to act as if his kisses hadn't sent her over the moon but it was difficult. Each and every time she glanced at him riding beside her, the memories returned and her senses sent him a silent call that begged response. Her mind pointed out how disastrous being attracted to him could be. After all, he was set upon discovering Lady Midnight, and who knew what his plans for her might be. On the other hand, revealing herself might offer the closure he was after, but at what price to her? Again, she didn't really know anything about him. As she mused earlier, even though he appeared to be supporting the rebels, there was the distinct possibility that he could be a British double agent, and she had no desire to be so befuddled by his kisses that she wound up with a noose around her neck. Lady Midnight was relieved that he hadn't attempted to kiss her again, while Faith wished he would. Both of her personas were facing a double-edged sword with blades capable of inflicting a life-altering cut.

Nicholas glanced over at the plodding sorry excuse for a horse she was riding and was pleased she didn't have a horse of Hades' caliber, otherwise the journey would have ended sooner than he wanted. Although she'd yet to utter a word, he was enjoying her company just the same. The sweetness of her continued to resonate within, and as he noted earlier, he craved more. "Do you often make late night deliveries?"

"Only when necessary."

"Does your father know you're out?"

"No, because he wouldn't approve of me trying to accumulate a bit of extra income." And that was the truth, even if it was told within the context of a lie.

"It isn't safe."

She didn't respond.

"The next time you need to do this, will you let me know so that I may accompany you?"

"I'm not in need of a keeper, Mr.— I mean, Nicholas."

"I believe you are."

"Not every woman needs a man about in order to conduct her business."

"True, however I am not talking about every woman. It's you I'm concerned with."

"I appreciate that, but I can assure you I will not be asking for your escort when none is necessary."

"You're a very stubborn woman."

"On that we can agree."

Nick took a chance. "So, what else was in that sack?"

"Sack?"

"The one you had the bread in."

She halted the horse and spun on him accusingly. "You followed me?"

"And watched you with the soldiers."

"Your spying is becoming quite tiresome."

"No more tiresome than chasing around after you in the dark."

"You are no gentleman."

"Agreed."

She kicked her mount into motion again and he and Hades matched the pace.

After a few moments of silence, she stated, "If you must know, there was nothing in the sack but loaves of bread, and I'd appreciate you staying out of my business."

"But you liked my kisses."

"We are not talking about that."

"Did you?"

"Are you truly that conceited? In truth, I've had better."

"Faith Kingston, you are such a liar," he countered, laughing.

"You don't know anything about my life."

"I know it hasn't included much kissing, if any at all."

"Now you are an authority on me?"

He smiled. "You're being awfully defensive."

"Your questioning is offensive."

"My apology." Nick wasn't put off by her show of claws. Her temper just made him want to drag her back onto his lap and kiss her until she melted again. "Who lives in that house?"

"What house?"

"Where you delivered the bread."

"Why are you being so nosey?"

He met her eyes. "I'm a nosey man."

"On that we agree."

"All right. I'll cease my questions."

"Thank the heavens."

He grinned.

Faith drew in a mental sigh of relief and hoped he was being truthful. She was floored knowing he had followed her and seen her interacting with the soldiers. She also felt as if he were toying with her. Did he already know she was Lady Midnight? She couldn't wait for her home to come into view so she could escape his questioning and her body's desire for more of his kisses.

Susie was old and slow, however, so it took some time.

Arriving at the inn filled her with great relief.

He asked, "I suppose you plan to enter via the window?"

"Yes."

They were astride their mounts and hidden by the stand of trees that ran alongside the inn.

"Good night, Nicholas."

Nick decided he liked having her address him by his full name. "Good night, Faith. No more running around in the dark."

"I will see you Saturday."

He smiled at her formal and distant tone. The way he'd been questioning her, he supposed he deserved no less. She would probably box his ears if he attempted to kiss her again, so he dampened the urge. "I assume you don't need me to help stable the mare."

"No, I don't, but thank you for the offer."

He nodded. "Saturday it is then, but let me know if your father proves difficult."

"I will."

That said, she turned the mare and headed off to the barn in the back of the inn. She could feel Nicholas's amused gaze follow her departure, but she forced herself not to look back at him.

Chapter 8

In the days that followed, tensions increased in Boston and the surrounding countryside. Rumors were rife. The number of daily skirmishes and rock-throwing confrontations between the troops and the citizens escalated. In the taverns and pubs favored by rebel supporters, word was that arms were being amassed and stored under direction of the Committees of Correspondence, the official governing body of the colonies in revolt, and that if the British wanted a fight, they'd get one. The air was fraught with anticipation, and everywhere one went there were whispers.

The rising tension showed itself in the increased British patrols. They were on the road day and night. Faith watched them from the front porch on the inn whenever she was outside. As always, they were looking for weapons caches. According to her father and his Tory friends, the soldiers did find a few, but for every one discovered another three or four went undetected, hidden in the lofts of barns, the bell towers of churches, and underground in cellars and holes dug in the middle of mud-filled fields. From Boston to Concord, to Lexington, Cambridge and back, the Massachusetts Bay Colony prepared for war.

During Friday's supper, Faith looked over at her father and asked, "Do you think there will be war?"

"Rebels are making it hard for the crown not to do something with all this civil disobedience and storing weapons. When Gage acts, there'll be many dead colonists simply because men like Hancock, Jefferson, and that hothead Patrick Henry refuse to accept the policies of the King. I'm thinking of moving us to New York. The crown is strong there."

It was the first time she'd heard mention of this and it took her as much by surprise as had his courting claim. "And what will become of the inn? I thought you planned to pass it on to your sons?"

"Will Case has expressed an interest if I decide to go."

Case's name made her snarl inwardly.

"All this upheaval has hurt business," he said.

"It's true business has been slow for months, but we are still above water."

"Barely," he noted. "Just barely."

Faith had never lived anywhere else. She'd been born here; taken her first breath in her parents' bedroom upstairs. It had never occurred to her that she might have to spend the rest of her days somewhere new. She wasn't sure how she felt about such a possibility.

Her father looked up from his plate. "Enough about war and such for now. What do you know about this reception Widow Lawson is giving tomorrow?"

"It's a gathering for Nicholas Grey. She asked if I would assist her with the food and he is going to pay me for my service."

"How much?"

When she told him, his eyes grew large. "Where's all this money of his come from?"

"I've no idea."

"Well, since he's paying you, I'll give you my approval. Just make sure you serve the food and nothing else. Man like him, who knows what else he may expect for such a grand sum. And make sure you bring the money right home and place it in the safe."

"Yes, Father. Are you planning to attend?"

"No, but Will Case said he may."

"Why? I didn't know he was a friend of the Grey family."

"He isn't. He's hoping to interest Grey in a business proposition."

"I see." Nicholas Grey didn't impress her as being partial to blowhards. "The widow asked if I could arrive as early as possible, so I'll leave here at sunrise."

"Keep to the main road where the patrols are."

"I will."

He met her eyes for a long moment as if he had something else he wanted to say, so she asked, "Yes?"

"You need a husband, Faith."

"Father, must we keep beating this horse? I'm way past the age of being desirable or submissive."

"You have to secure your future."

"My future is here, at this inn."

"Not if I sell."

"It can be, if you sell it to me."

He sighed and shook his head. "No."

"There are women business owners."

"True, but you can't match or top what Case has offered."

She went still. "You've already discussed price with him?"

He nodded.

"I understand that you didn't have to consult me, but you might have."

"To what end? You have no money or collateral."

"I have Mother's funds."

He looked away.

Holding on to her rising alarm she asked, "The funds are still in the bank in London, aren't they?"

He shook his head and said quietly, "No. It's what we've been living on for the past year."

"But what about the money you've had me putting in the safe each month?"

"That's where it comes from. I had the full amount transferred here to Boston and have been doling it out a bit at a time."

"Why didn't you tell me?"

"Because there was no need."

Faith wanted to scream at him about the unfairness of his actions. That was how she'd planned to secure her future once he passed on. "And how much is left? If it's not being disrespectful to ask."

"It is," he replied pointedly. "However, so that you'll know, only a small portion remains, but thanks to the general's recent generosity, we've enough to get by until late spring."

Faith was stunned. Late spring would be here soon. "And this is why you want to sell to Case?"

"Need to sell to Case. It will also help my marriage suit."

Faith didn't know what to say. She was both angry and hurt that he hadn't revealed the true nature of their finances and that he didn't seem to care that she'd be left penniless when he married this mysterious new wife. Had she known, she could have taken in wash or sold bread to help make ends meet. Now it appeared to be too late. "I wish you had told me."

"And that's why I want you to secure your future by getting married."

"I'll not marry Will Case."

"And if your choice is the almshouse?"

Almshouses held the poor and indigent. "I'll take in wash, sell fresh bread. I'll do whatever need be to make my way, but I will not sell myself and especially not to him."

"You're a stubborn woman."

"I come from stubborn stock."

He placed his hand atop hers and squeezed it until she winced. "Either find yourself a husband, or I'll have to include your hand in the contract I have with Will. He's anxious to marry you. You should be grateful that he wants a woman of your age." Getting to his feet, he left her sitting at the table and walked away.

She crossed her arms and sighed furiously.

Her fury turned to alarm as she saw a group of British soldiers enter. They were not accompanied by General Gage and she worried who they were and why they'd come. To her surprise one was Black. She knew there were many men of color serving the crown but she'd not seen any since the occupation began. She saw him glance over at her and then smoothly away as her father moved to greet them.

"Welcome to the Kingston Inn, gentlemen. I'm Stuart Kingston. What may I do for you?"

The Black man, who appeared to outrank the others, replied, "We hear your fare is honest and good."

"Yes it is. This way, please."

Faith was relieved that they were only after food.

Her father steered them to one of the three tables set up in the otherwise unoccupied room and Faith got to her feet and walked over. He introduced her. "This is my daughter, Faith."

"Pleased to meet you," she said.

The soldier bowed gallantly. "Honored to make your acquaintance, Miss Kingston. I'm Lieutenant Henri Giles." And he took a moment to introduce his companions.

"There's steak and ale on the fire in the kitchen. Would you care for some?"

They indicated they would, so she offered a quick curtsy and left the room.

She returned with their plates and added a loaf of bread. She was aware of Giles's interested eyes, but she stayed focused on her task and then left them to their meal.

Her father entered the kitchen a short while later. "He seems like a gentleman."

Faith checked the skillets on the fire. "Who?"

"Henri Giles."

She shrugged her shoulders. "I suppose."

"He's unmarried."

She slowly turned his way. "You've asked him?"

"I did."

"Are you going to troll the Great Road next?"

He didn't appear to appreciate her humor. "You need a husband."

She shook her head with amusement and turned back to the fire. "I know nothing about him."

"To remedy that, I've invited him to supper on Sunday."

Startled, she faced him. From the serious set of his features she knew he was not going to let this go, so she sighed. "That's fine."

"You will be pleasant?"

"I will be pleasant."

Seemingly satisfied, he left her alone.

Although Henri Giles impressed Faith as being a true gentleman, she doubted he'd be interested in the hand of a woman her age, but to satisfy her father she would go through the motions. For reasons unknown, thinking about Giles made the face of Nicholas Grey float across her mind's eye. She hadn't seen him since the night in Boston. He had a way of showing up out of thin air and playing havoc with all she considered herself to be and that included her senses. Her naturally curious nature made her want to know why that was, and what else his potent kisses might make her feel, but well-brought-up women weren't supposed to contemplate such things. Besides, she had no plans to offer herself as a dalliance while she combed the countryside in search of his mythical Judas. Knowing she might have to deal with him as Lady Midnight in the near future was worrisome enough.

Blythe's husband had been an English earl when he arrived in the colonies in the late 1730s. He'd hired her, a free Black woman, to be his housekeeper and they immediately fell in love. When he passed away a decade later, Blythe inherited all he owned, including one of the largest and grandest homes in the colony. Usually the large formal front parlor was kept closed, but for special occasions like Nicholas's gathering, it was opened and the table outfitted with her finest china, crystal, and cutlery.

Faith's job was to oversee the kitchen and the two

women Blythe had hired to help with the serving. They were Irish, a mother and daughter named Patricia and Laine O'Hara. They were neighbors who lived up the road, and their men were rumored to be strong rebel supporters. Faith had known them all her life and liked them because they were kind people and didn't mind a hard day's work.

By the time the guests began arriving late that afternoon, the food was ready and the buffet table set. While Blythe was ushering the guests into the parlor, Faith came out of the kitchen to make sure there was nothing else the buffet needed. When she looked up, Nicholas Grey was standing on the other side of the table. Memories of being in his arms flooded her like water rolling over a dam.

He said to her, "You never told me if you enjoyed the fish?"

"They were very good." Her heart was pounding as it always seemed to do whenever he came near, but this time, the kisses they'd shared added themselves to the pot. She could see the curious looks on the faces of some of the women in the room who were watching him speak with her, but she did her best to ignore them.

"Thank you for the help with the food."

"You're welcome."

"Did your father approve of my price for your services?"

Her chin rose. "Yes, he did."

"Good."

He was the best-dressed man in the room and wore his clothing as if the current fashion had been designed with him in mind. The coat and breeches were of the highest quality and the shirt beneath was showy but tasteful. The neck cloth appeared to be made from silk, and his snow white hose as well. However, he'd eschewed the wigs favored by the men, nor had he powdered his hair.

Faith knew she should return to the kitchen but she couldn't seem to move. He seemed to be having the same problem but didn't appear bothered by it.

They were interrupted by the arrival of Blythe, who had with her shy, twenty-year-old Winnie Potts and her overbearing mother, Eva. Eva was one of the women in the community who couldn't tolerate Faith because of her education and unorthodox ways. Faith didn't like her any better and hoped Grey was prepared for Mrs. Potts's overbearing manner.

Blythe said, "Nicholas. I want to introduce Mrs. Eva Potts and her daughter Winifred."

He inclined his head.

Eva Potts smiled up at him as if he were something good to eat. Noticing Faith standing on the other side of the table, her eyes narrowed. "Don't you have duties in the kitchen, Faith?"

Faith knew it was Eva's way of trying to put her in her place. Eva's husband owned a large tract of land and she never let anyone forget how wealthy and important she considered her family to be. Faith raised an angry eyebrow but before she could respond, Nicholas asked coolly, "Are you always so rude, Mrs. Potts?"

Eva's eyes widened. Winnie looked down at her slippers.

There was really no good reply to such an incriminating question, so with that said, he turned away from the woman's tight face and extended his arm to Blythe. "Is there someone else you wish me to meet?"

Beaming, Blythe placed her hand on his arm. "Yes, I do."

Nicholas bowed in Faith's direction. "Thank you again, Miss Kingston."

"You're welcome, Mr. Grey."

He escorted Blythe away. A satisfied Faith went back to her duties in the kitchen. The fuming Eva was left standing at the table with her teary-eyed daughter.

As Blythe walked with Nick, she said softly, "Let Prince know that Gage will be moving against the rebels come mid April."

He kept his face bland at the surprising words.

She added, "Prince should alert his contacts as soon as he can. You may wish to let Artemis know as well."

Raising her voice and tone as a friend entered, she trilled, "Mrs. Carstairs. Let me introduce you to Nicholas."

For the rest of the afternoon, the parlor filled up with old acquaintances of the Grey family and others unfamiliar to him. A few of the acquaintances were men he'd been seeking in order to ask them about his father's arrest. He quizzed them discreetly while making the rounds of the parlor but none was able to offer him any information that might shed new light on the matter.

Prince Hall arrived at the height of the affair along with some of the minutemen under his command. Nick planned to tell him Blythe's news before he departed.

Blyth had invited a few of the eligible women so that he could make their acquaintance, but truthfully, they left him unmoved. Eighteen-year-old Hazel Carstairs was a giggler who couldn't seem to do anything else. At first he thought she might simply be nervous, but the more he engaged her in conversation, the more she giggled, so he gave up and smoothly excused himself from her and her grandmother. The second potential candidate was a sly-eyed beauty named Elizabeth Sutter. Her mother kept praising the seventeen-year-old Elizabeth's chaste character but the flirty look in the daughter's eyes told him an entirely different story, as did her clothing. Her gown, though fashionable, had a lower cut than those of the other women in attendance, offering any man who cared to see a good view of the tops of her young breasts. Were he in the market for a dalliance she'd be on the list, but after a short conversation, he bowed gracefully and moved on.

Throughout it all, his eyes kept straying back to the buffet table in hopes of catching another glimpse of Faith, but no matter how many times he glanced that way she was never there.

While the guests mingled, ate, and conversed, he did

the same, picking up snippets of conversations here and there about planting, relatives in England, and the anticipated war. Most of the twenty-five guests seemed to favor the rebels, but there were Tory supporters in the room as well. One in particular, a tall, pock-faced man named William Case, was a late arrival, who upon entering the parlor made a beeline for Nick, who was speaking with Hall and minuteman George Middleton, a commander of a group of Black patriots calling themselves the Bucks of America.

"Mr. Grey. My name is William Case. We met at the church."

Nick excused himself from Prince. Truthfully, he didn't remember meeting the thin, dour-looking man, but he played along. "Nice to see you again."

"Have you settled into your father's home?"

"I have."

"I'm a successful businessman and I'm wondering if I could speak with you about an investment opportunity."

Nick studied him. "What sort of investment?"

He looked around as if to make sure they weren't being overheard. "There's a business I'd like to acquire, but I may need additional coin."

Nicholas could see Eva Potts shooting daggers his way but he ignored her. "And this business is?"

"It's the inn owned by Stuart Kingston. Like everyone else, I know he and your father shared a grudge, but he's thinking of selling."

Nick's mind immediately went to Faith. "May I ask why?"

"He's a bit in debt, shall we say," he explained with a satisfied grin. "Needs the money."

At that moment Faith appeared behind the buffet table to replenish one of the dishes. Apparently Case saw her, too. "Lovely girl, isn't she?" he said.

Nick turned back to the man, but before he could respond, Case added, "Stubborn little bitch though. Prideful, too. Never understood why Kingston wasted perfectly good coin educating her but he said it had something to do with his late wife's estate. Who cares what a woman has in her head. It's what's between her legs that matters to a man. Don't you agree?"

It took all Nick had to hang on to his composure. "Never heard it put in such a crude and succinct manner, Mr. Case."

Nick's rebuke seemed to go right over the man's head.

"I've asked for her hand, but her father is allowing her to make her own choice."

"I see." Nick found this one of the most interesting conversations of the afternoon. "And has she agreed?"

"No."

"Ah." Nicholas felt better. "Some women can be quite stubborn."

"Too stubborn, but I'll have her, whether she wants me or not. She's the main reason I wish to buy the inn. I'll take Kingston's debts and his daughter. No right-thinking man would refuse such an offer."

Nick kept his distaste for Case hidden. "You certainly have it all well thought out."

"Indeed. I'm a success for a reason."

Prince Hall walked up. "Nicholas, there's someone I want you to meet."

Nicholas nodded. "It's been a pleasure speaking with you, Mr. Case. I'll think over your proposal."

As he and Prince made their way to the other side of the room, Nick said with genuine feeling, "Thank you."

"He's a Tory toad. You looked like you needed rescuing."

"And I did. He was telling me of his coarse plans for Faith Kingston."

"Really. He and her father are fast friends."

Nick kept his voice down. "Her father's deep in debt. Case wants to buy the inn and expects Kingston to throw her in as a condition of the sale."

Prince shook his head. "It wouldn't be the first time."

"I know. Women, especially daughters, have few rights."

Prince studied Nick's face. "And what are you planning?"

"How do you know that I am?"

"Because your father often had that same look in his eye when he was plotting."

Nick shrugged. "She's a beautiful woman. Hate to have all that wasted on a rube like Case."

And he said no more. "Do you think any of the women here are the Lady Midnight?"

Prince sipped his ale. "You are determined to find her, aren't you?"

"I am, but in the meantime alert the Sons that General Gage plans to move on the rebels mid April."

Prince kept his poise. "I'll let them know. This will mean war."

Nick agreed.

"All right. I hadn't planned on being here long but am glad I stayed long enough for you to pass along this news."

"I am as well."

"Thank you, Nicholas."

"You're welcome. One last thing, I was in town a few nights ago and saw soldiers posted in front of a home." He gave Prince the street and address of the home Faith had visited. "Do you know who lives there?"

"Mr. John Hancock."

"I see. I was simply curious."

"I'll see you later. I'll be riding back to Boston to share your news as soon as I give my regards to our hostess."

"Godspeed."

Prince inclined his head and Nick watched him make his way over to Blythe. A few moments later he'd retrieved his coat and gone out the door.

Chapter 9

As the affair came to an end, Faith sighed wearily. She always worked from sunup to sundown so the exhaustion was familiar, but still her shoulders ached from lifting the heavy pots on and off the rods in hot ash-filled grate. She was perspiring, her clothing spotted with dust from the ash, and the tiny burns on her left hand, caused by an ember that sparked when she was moving a gridiron farther into the heat, were letting her know they were there. She wiped her hand across her damp brow and continued washing Blythe's delicate china. The two hired women were done for the day and were putting on coats and leaving by the back entrance. She called out her thanks and they called back in kind.

And now the kitchen was quiet. The silence let her exhale and relax. She washed up the last of the plates and dried her hands. She wanted to go back out to the parlor and make certain there was nothing left to be washed before dumping the barrel of water outside. She saw that there were still a few people in the parlor, particularly Nicholas and Will Case but she focused on her task. Seeing nothing that needed to be returned to the kitchen, she started back when she heard Case call from behind her, "Miss Kingston, may I speak with you?"

She sighed and walked over to where he and Nicholas were standing. "Yes?"

"The food was very good. I'll be looking forward to your skills when we marry."

She had no time for his arrogance. "Is there anything else? I have duties to finish."

He turned to Nicholas and grumbled, "This is what I mean. Have you ever witnessed such a disrespectful female?"

Nicholas didn't respond.

Faith was in no mood to be dressed down and so walked away, but Case grabbed her wrist and held on painfully. "I didn't dismiss you."

Angry, Faith tried to pull away.

"Let her go."

The menace in Nicholas's tone brought Case up short.

"How dare you intercede in—"

Employing an icy calm voice that only they could hear, he echoed, "Let her go, or I will kill you where you stand."

Case's eyes grew large as pumpkins and he released his hold.

Nicholas added, "Now, I believe it is time for you to

give the widow your regards and leave here."

Case eyed him for a silent moment, then sneered malevolently at both of them before he walked off in a huff. Moments later, he exited the premises.

Nicholas turned his eyes back to Faith. "Now, where were we?"

She could only stare.

"Should I have been firmer?"

She finally found speech and whispered, "You shouldn't joke that way."

"I wasn't joking, by any means."

She blinked.

"If he threatens you ever again you are to tell me."

He was so overwhelming, for a second she thought she might fall. Why did this particular man affect her so?

"Faith? Are you unwell?"

She spun to find Ingram Trotter standing there looking between her and Nicholas with concern. "No. I mean, yes, Ingram. I'm fine. I just—"

Her eyes went back to Nicholas, who was viewing Ingram as if he were trespassing in his domain. "Ingram, this is Nicholas Grey. Nicholas, this is Ingram Trotter. He's a lifelong friend." She viewed Ingram fondly as he and Nicholas exchanged cool nods. "Mr. Grey aided me in a quarrelsome situation with Will Case. I didn't see you come in."

"I just arrived, but only to drop off a letter to the widow that I picked up for her in town. My apologies for missing your reception, Mr. Grey. My son is ill so my wife and I can't take him out into the weather."

"Understandable."

The men continued to assess each other.

Ingram asked her, "Do you need assistance loading the wagon or anything before I go? It looks as if the party's all but done."

Faith opened her mouth to respond, only to hear Nicholas say smoothly, "I've already offered my assistance, Mr. Trotter. I'm sure you'd like to hurry home to your wife and child."

Faith found herself staring at him once again. Not pleased with his actions at all, she told her friend, "I've everything in hand, Ingram. Thank you. Give my love to Charity and the baby. I hope he feels better soon."

"Thank you." After casting Nicholas a final glance, he left them.

In the silence after his departure, Faith told him, "You're very adept at lying."

"Only when I want my way."

She studied him.

"How long have you loved him?" he asked.

Her eyes widened before she could stop them. How he was able to read her with such clarity, she didn't know, but she was left shocked and irritated. "I have tasks needing my attention."

And she stalked off.

If Faith thought she was done with him, she was mistaken. She'd just removed her apron when he entered the kitchen accompanied by Blythe, who said, "Nicholas has offered to help you load the wagon. Do you have anything he needs to carry out for you?"

Faith met his eyes and then spoke to Blythe. "No, most of the large pots we used were yours. I only have a small barrel holding the things I need to take back with me."

"Where is it?" he asked.

"I can carry it."

He waited.

She blew out a frustrated breath. "There," she said, pointing at the barrel she'd placed by the door.

Blythe said, "All right. Let me go and say good-bye to the last of the guests. Be safe driving home, Faith, and thank you so very much again for your service today."

"You're welcome. I'll see you at church tomorrow. When do you leave for New York?"

"Monday morning."

"Ah. Have a good evening."

Blythe smiled, waved, and left the kitchen.

Nicholas stood waiting at the back door.

She told him again, "I can manage the barrel."

"So can I. Lead the way."

Tight-lipped, she complied.

She'd parked her wagon near the stand of birch trees behind the house. He followed her across the muddy field and placed the barrel in the bed of the wagon.

"Thank you," she offered crisply. "And thank you again for your rescue from Mr. Case. I need to get home."

"I never took you for a fleeing woman."

She stopped. "And I'm not."

They were only a few inches apart and Faith swore her heart was going to beat out of her chest. One part of her wanted to be kissed again and other parts were alarmed by the thought. He slowly and boldly reached out and gently raised her gaze to his. "I miss your kisses."

It took all Faith had to keep from fainting dead away. "I think you are toying with me, Nicholas, and don't believe I care for it."

"I'm not toying with you, Faith. Why would I?"

She backed out of his hold so that she could think. "To play games with a country girl, to get back at my father. You choose."

"And if neither applies, then what?"

"You tell me."

Nicholas was enjoying this. "Then it has to be something else, say, attraction?"

"And again, I say that you are toying with me."

"You don't think I'm attracted to you?"

"You and Case, who's sniffing around me as if I'm a bitch in heat, but the question becomes am I attracted in return?"

His eyes were lit with surprise. "There's that tart tongue again."

"Thank you."

He smiled, finding her fascinating all over again. "And the answer to the question?"

She boldly met his challenge. "The answer is undoubtedly yes, I am attracted to you. However, I'm not silly enough to believe you'd do right by me, so that is that."

Nicholas folded his arms over his chest. "Why wouldn't I do right by you?"

"I'm twenty-six years old, and although untouched, hardly what society deems wife material, so that leaves scandal, and I value myself too highly to take on that role."

Nicholas couldn't remember ever meeting a more frank woman.

"Rebuttal?" she asked.

He had to admit he didn't have one. Instead he reached into his coat and withdrew the small pouch holding the money she was owed for her work.

"Thank you," she said, taking it from his hand, and began to make the walk around to the seat on the front of the wagon.

"Faith?"

She stopped and turned his way.

"This only heightens the attraction between us."

"I know."

While he watched, she climbed up onto the seat of the wagon and picked up the reins. He then asked, "How often do you take bread to John Hancock?"

Her face didn't change. "Good day, Nicholas."

She slapped the reins down over Susie's back and drove away.

Nick watched her leave. He'd also wanted to ask her about the man named Trotter, but he was content to let her escape for now. Their mutual attraction would bring them together again soon enough.

Back at the inn, Faith placed the items she'd come home with in their proper places and tried to rid herself of Nicholas Grey. So he'd learned who lived in that house. She didn't let that worry her because he had no proof that she was at Hancock's for any reason other than the one she'd given him. What worried her more was that he'd been correct about their time together adding to the attraction she felt for him. It didn't seem to matter to her inner self that she didn't want to be attracted to him; it was there and rising each time she encountered him. She would just have to be more vigilant, if only because he hadn't been able to dispute her claim that he wouldn't do right by her. He'd probably left a trail of women in his wake and she had no desire to add her name to the undoubtedly extensive list. With her duties now done in the kitchen and everything put away, she left it and found her father seated at one of the tables in the dining room.

"How was the reception?" he asked.

"I spent most of my time in the kitchen but it seemed to go well." She placed the bag of coins Nick had given her on the table. He immediately took it and began to count what was inside.

"Did you see Will?" he asked.

"Yes. It wasn't a particularly nice encounter though. He grabbed me."

His eyes narrowed. "Why?"

"Because I took issue with him chastising me." She told him the rest of the story.

"Can't have him putting his hand on you that way."

"Nicholas Grey took exception to it as well."

He looked suspicious. "Explain?"

So she did and ended by telling him about the threat he'd made to Will. "I told him it wasn't right to make jokes like that."

"And he said?"

"That he wasn't joking."

He sat up. "So, he's as much a menace as his father."

"He was protecting me. The only menace was Will."

She could tell by his face that he didn't agree and it angered her that he didn't place her safety above all else. "I'm going to my room."

"Grey is not for you."

"I heard you the first time, Father."

Faith entered her bedroom still caught by her mood. He was right but again she noted that her inner self insisted on responding in ways she couldn't control. His touch set off a warmth in her blood that was as wondrous as it was disturbing. Having no mother and being a female of her times, she knew next to nothing about her body and how it performed, and according to society, being curious about such things would only place oneself on a fast wagon to hell. However, she knew this was lust, but she didn't know how to make it stop. It was as if he'd touched off a small blaze inside her and each time they met it rose higher. She frowned. And how had he known about her lingering feelings for Ingram? Had it been so obvious? Oddly enough, during all the years she'd considered herself in love with him, she'd never felt this same heat. So what did that mean? Lust wasn't something a good woman was supposed to feel, was it? And if she did, what kind of woman did that make her? Faith ran her hands over her eyes. She was making herself batty again. All that mattered was that she stay away from Nicholas Grey.

Chapter 10

Sunday morning, Faith and her father drove the wagon into Boston for church. They attended services with the Friends. Many members of the sect educated their slaves and freed them upon the age of eighteen. The members were also vocal in denouncing the continuation of the slave trade, they supported equal representation under the law for all, and the free Black community considered them friends indeed. However, that friendship only applied to the world outside Quaker churches. Inside, Blacks were set apart from the main congregation and made to sit in the small cramped balcony in the back of the sanctuary, a practice mirrored by most Christian churches throughout the colonies.

After the service, Faith and her father stood outside and talked with friends. Faith joined Blythe and a small group of ladies. Now that the weather was breaking, more people were able to venture out. Some in the congregation hadn't seen each other since mid December when the snow began to fall in earnest, and were now pleased to be able to lay eyes upon their acquaintances and relatives.

Faith turned to say something to Blythe but froze at the sight of the redcoats marching up the street. They were six abreast, their bayoneted guns prominently displayed. From the length of the line of men trailing behind the officers there looked to be at least three hundred. As they marched, they sang a stanza from the British version of "Yankee Doodle."

Yankee Doodle came to town
For to buy a flintlock.
We will tar and feather him—and so will we John Hancock!

It was an impressive show of force. On the walks in front of the shops, tavern, and homes, colonists stood watching with anger and contempt, while others hissed and booed. Her father, however, was beaming. He and a few other Tories began applauding the display, which only drew the ire of the colonists standing near, but Faith kept her face impassive as the King's hated troops streamed by.

The captain in charge called a halt to the procession and the spectators looked on warily. No one knew why they'd stopped. Were they about to arrest someone? The answer lay in a liberty pole planted in the earth in front of a tavern. The poles were one of the symbolic signs of the rebellion. They varied in size and shape but all flew a standard upon which a variety of messages were written or embroidered. This one read *RESIST!* The officer walked over, snatched it out of the ground, then broke it over his thigh. Hisses and curses from those on the walks greeted the action, but he paid them no mind. After contemptuously tossing the pieces aside he signaled, and the march and singing taunts resumed.

Her father looked happy as a child at Christmas, but Faith knew this would be yet another mark against the King's forces. After all, it was Sunday; not that wars cared, but the people did, and for the captain and his men to be strutting around on the Lord's Day putting the rebels in their place made the British appear to be the godless heathens the opposition claimed them to be.

Once the troops had passed from sight, the congregation bade farewells to their friends and hastened to their vehicles for the journey home.

"Wasn't that something to see?" her father asked excitedly. They were now on the outskirts of the city.

"It was," she said, hoping he didn't hear her lack of enthusiasm.

"Those rebels will rue the day they decided to tweak the King's nose."

And a very large nose it was indeed from what Faith understood. King George was the third Hanoverian king to wear the English crown, but only the first in his royal line to speak English.

Her father glanced over at her. "You do remember the soldier is coming for dinner this evening."

"I do." She wasn't looking forward to it but she did remember.

"And you promised to be pleasant."

"He isn't going to ask for my hand."

"And you promised to be pleasant."

"I did promise and I will honor it."

"Good," he replied, sounding satisfied.

Later that afternoon, as Faith watched over the food cooking in various spots inside the big grate, she wondered if other women meeting a man for the first time had to cook the dinner themselves. One day before she died, she wanted to have a special meal cooked for her that was prepared by someone else's hands. It would probably be her funeral dinner, she noted dryly and put the thoughts aside. She padded her hands with two towels and lifted the Dutch oven out of the ashes. Inside was a loaf of bread. Her special bread, made from meal, flour, and molasses. The recipe had won her much acclaim at the local fairs and it was said that no one made bread as tasty. However, molasses were getting harder and harder to come by due to the ongoing blockade of Boston Harbor by the British Navy. It was one of the first of the Intolerable Acts implemented by General Gage upon his return to the colony last year. Luckily she'd laid in a large stock before the blockade went into effect, so she had plenty on hand.

With the bread cooling and the hens on the spit, done roasting, Faith pulled her skirts free from her waistband, smoothed the wrinkles as best she could, and left the kitchen to be pleasant to Henri Giles.

Dinner went well. Giles played the perfect gentleman and her father refrained from asking the man to marry her before he took his seat at the table. Giles talked about living in Quebec and asked her father about his past.

"I was born in Jamaica to a slave mother and grew up working in the house. Her master liked how industrious I was, and when he left to return to England he took me with him as his manservant. As I aged, he promised to free me upon his death, and when he died, he did."

"How old were you?"

"Twenty or thereabouts. Came to the colonies a few months after the burial and been here since."

Faith noted he'd left out meeting her mother and the marriage that resulted but she supposed her father felt that too personal a detail to reveal.

He added, though, "Lost Faith's mother to the pox outbreak during the fifties, so she hasn't had much female influence in her life."

Giles looked Faith's way. "It doesn't seem to have affected her in a negative manner."

Her father offered a smile. "Made the mistake of letting her learn. Haven't been able to control her since."

Giles asked Faith, "You can read?"

"Yes. A good number of colonial women can, although some people believe it a waste; after all, what use is a learned woman?"

Her father said warningly, "Faith."

Giles was studying her as if he wasn't quite sure what to make of her.

Her father added a bit hastily, "I'm sure she'll make some man a fine wife one day."

But to Faith, Giles appeared as if he wasn't sure he agreed. She sighed inwardly, but determined to remain pleasant, asked, "Can your sisters read and write?"

"No."

"Ah," was all she said.

"Although they have expressed a desire."

"They are to be commended then."

But he didn't appear as if he agreed with that, either.

Inevitably the conversation turned to the chances of war becoming a reality.

Her father said, "We saw a column marching through the streets this morning. Made this old Tory heart beat proudly."

Giles asked, "And you, Miss Kingston?"

"It was quite a sight," she responded smoothly.

Her father said, "I'm hoping that Gage will just get on with it so that some semblance of normality can be restored. The ships holding the harbor have put a strain on everyone."

"There are signs that something will happen soon. Once we arrest Hancock and a few others, the rabble may quiet down."

Faith said, "I'd approve of normalcy. Will these arrests come soon?"

"From all indications, yes."

She kept her face void of reaction. She assumed Hancock and the Sons were on the alert and taking precautions to prevent such a thing from happening, but she decided it was information that needed to be passed along to them. "Well, enough about war. Who's ready for dessert?"

Both men were, so she stood. Giles chivalrously rose to his feet, and she inclined her head in acknowledgment. Her smiling father sat and watched.

While they ate the pudding she'd made for dessert, she had to admit Giles was handsome and looked very dashing in his uniform. His light-colored eyes reminded her of Ingram but he was much taller and more muscular. His build was more similar to Nicholas's. Thinking about Nick opened the floodgates and she found herself comparing the two. Both were handsome, but Giles didn't make her feel the heat that plagued her so when Nick was near. In fact, she wasn't moved by Giles in any way. She wondered if that was because lust was reserved for dalliance and scandal and not for marriage. Having been very young when her mother died, Faith had no memories of how her parents interacted with each other, nor did she have any other married couples in her family. She'd heard of so-called love matches and it was her guess that Charity and Ingram's marriage could be considered that, but she wasn't privy to the private aspects of their life, either. For all her book learning, she was ignorant about how a man and a woman got along day to day, and she wasn't sure if that was a hindrance or not, but considering she had little chance of being a wife, she supposed that ignorance didn't matter. However, Giles was employed, handsome, and polite, and would undoubtedly be a good provider and husband to whomever he chose.

It came time for him to leave, and as he gathered up his overcoat and gun, her father said, "Faith, why don't you send him back with some of the leftover food?"

She nodded and in the kitchen put helpings of everything into a small crock and returned. When she handed it to him he thanked her.

"I promise to return it," he pledged. "In hopes that you will fill it again."

She smiled. "I'm glad you enjoyed my cooking."

"Faith, why don't you walk him out to his mount? We wouldn't want him to get lost in the dark."

She gave her father a look and wondered if he was purposefully trying to put her in a compromising position. A single woman wasn't encouraged to walk in the dark with a man not of her family. It wasn't done.

As if reading her mind, he waved a hand. "Go on ahead. I'm not going to force Giles to marry you."

She wanted to sink into the floorboards at his jest. Instead she said to the amused soldier, "Are you ready?"

"I am."

Outside in the brisk night air, Faith pulled her shawl closer. "My apologies. My father is determined I find a husband, which is why he spent the evening throwing me at you like oysters to a hog."

He chuckled. "None needed." Looking down at her in the moonlight, he was silent for a few moments. "You're a very unconventional woman, Miss Kingston."

"Too unconventional some might say."

"I'd have to agree. No offense, but I want the woman I marry to be traditional."

"I'm not offended."

"But I must admit, having met you has made me re-think some things."

"Then the evening was a success."

"Your father will not think so."

"He's accustomed to being disappointed, believe me."

She saw his smile.

He said genuinely, "I would like to visit you again, if I'm allowed to ask for such a boon."

Faith decided she liked him. "You are, and I'm sure you'll get no argument from Father."

"I had a nice time, and thanks for the food."

"You're welcome."

He mounted his horse. "Good evening, Miss Kingston."

"Good-bye, Lieutenant Giles."

"Will you call me Henri?"

"If you will call me Faith."

He nodded.

She smiled.

He rode away.

When she stepped back inside her father was watching her eagerly, so Faith said, "I'm not for him. He said he wants a more traditional woman."

His face deflated.

"However, he would like to visit us again, and I told him it would be all right."

"Then there is hope," he told her while yawning tiredly. He pulled out his timepiece. "Had no idea it was so late. Think I'll retire. Will you lock up?"

"Yes."

"See you in the morning."

"Pleasant dreams."

As he went upstairs she wondered how the courting was faring but since she knew better than to ask, she set aside the curiosity because she had a more pressing issue to contemplate. The Sons of Liberty needed to be told about what Henri had innocently revealed. John Hancock was one of the wealthiest men in the colony and a leader of the rebellion. His arrest would put quite a feather in General Gage's cap. Hancock in chains would devastate morale, and maybe make the farmers and merchants supporting the movement rethink their allegiances, because if a man as well-to-do and moneyed as Hancock could be tarred with the treason brush, what chance had they?

She locked up, doused the lamps, and went to her room. Entering it, she continued the inner debate. Of course it was possible that the Sons had already ferreted out Gage's plans to arrest Hancock, but what if they hadn't? Either way she had to pass the news on, and therein lay the stumbling block. With Blythe leaving for New York in the morning, and Charity nursing a sick infant, she had to go to Nicholas. She did not want to see him, not as herself and certainly not as Lady Midnight, but to do nothing could enable the British to strike a killing blow that might stamp out the rebels and their cause for some time to come.

Her decision made, she walked to her bed and lifted the thin mattress where the widow's weeds she used in her disguise lay hidden, and began to dress.

It was just past midnight when Faith eased open the shutters and climbed down to the soft earth below. Unfortunately the moon could be seen through the clouds sliding past it, but her hope was that the cold, windy night would become cloudier. Crossing an open field in full moonlight would cast her shadow all the way to Boston.

Taking in a breath to buoy her courage, she set out for the Grey family home. With the increased British patrols, she didn't dare risk taking the road, but it was necessary that she cross it, however, because Nick lived on the opposite side. Accomplishing that quickly, she used the cover of the thick growth of pines to mask her passage. That he lived less than thirty minutes away stood in her favor, and was also one of the reasons she and Primus had been able to communicate so quickly and so well. In order for Primus to get to his shop in Boston he'd had to drive past the inn, so he knew to look for their mutually agreed upon signals that indicated she had information to pass. Sometimes it was the churn she left by the side of the house, others the way she hung the pillow slips and quilts outside on the clothesline to dry on wash day.

Now, however, she was on her way to see his mesmerizing son.

The moon turned out to be a help rather than a hindrance. As she crunched her way through the thin coat of snow, the faint light guided her journey through the forest's maze. In truth, the silence and the moon on the snow would have made for a beautiful night were it not for the cold wind snatching at the hem of her gray cape. She was glad she'd worn it. With the hood up she looked like nothing more than a passing shadow. More importantly, she was warm.

She exited the trees and paused. Ahead lay the cleared farmland owned by the Potts family. Faith wondered if Eva was still steaming over the set-down Nicholas had given her at his reception. She took a quick look up at the house. Seeing no lights, she did another quick survey of the fields, and after seeing nothing to impede her, made a dash for the trees on the other side. Once there, she set off again. She repeated the dash three more times, the final one being onto Grey's land.

Standing in the trees she ran her eyes over the house. There was a small light in one of the rooms upstairs.

Before she could lose her nerve she made her way over to the house and knocked at the back door. After a few moments, she stepped back to keep him from seeing her clearly. Hoping it was far enough away, she lowered the veil over her face, held the edges of her cloak closely, and waited for him to appear.

The door opened and there he stood with a candle boat in his hand. She shrank back from the light and demanded in a harsh whisper that cloaked her true voice, "Douse the light or we'll both hang!"

For a second Nicholas stared frozen, then blew out the flame. *Was this she?* He couldn't make out the facial features, but the person was bent over like a crone. "And you are?"

"Your father knew me as Lady Midnight. Alert Hancock that his arrest is imminent." And she turned to leave.

"Wait!"

She stopped but didn't face him.

"Do you know who betrayed Primus?"

At first he wasn't sure she'd respond, but finally she whispered, "No," and walked away. The wind whipped at him as he stood watching. When she was far enough away to melt back into the night, he closed the door.

He stood there for a long moment thinking. He'd finally gotten a look at the elusive Lady Midnight. In reality it hadn't been much of one, but he was pleased to have finally laid eyes on her. The news about Hancock was disturbing. It meant the British were after the head of the snake. He wasn't sure if the move was out of strength or desperation, but either way, the Sons needed to know. To facilitate that, he drew on his cloak, walked outside and across the road to wake up Arte.

It took only a few knocks to rouse his friend.

Candle in hand, Arte opened the door. "Nicholas?" he asked in sleepy surprise.

"Sorry for the intrusion, but I need to speak with you. This can't wait until morning."

Arte backed up a few steps to let him enter.

Nick kept his voice low. "Hancock's going to be arrested."

Arte eyes widened. "How do you know?"

"My father's Lady paid me a visit a few moments ago."

"Really? Did she say anything else?"

"Other than denying any knowledge of who betrayed Primus, no. After that she left me."

Arte met his eyes. "All right. I'll pass this on. Bekkah's going to tar me for having to ride out now, but as you said, this can't wait until morning."

Nick nodded.

"Thanks again, friend."

Nick left and returned to his bedroom to ponder the appearance of the Lady. Standing before the fire to warm the chill of outside, he noted that it had been impossible to see her face through the shroud of thick lace. Her hunched carriage gave her the impression of advanced age, but would an elderly woman really be skulking about in the middle of the night, considering the weather and all the possible dangers posed by both man and beast? He supposed it depended upon the fervor of the person involved, but if tonight's visit was any indication, his father's spy was very fervent.

However, none of this revealed her identity. He couldn't even be certain that she was a female. In the morning he planned to check the snow for tracks. He might be able to determine which direction she'd taken and maybe more. He had to admit that her appearance had infused him with a measure of excitement because now he felt one step closer to answers. He was supposed to drill with Hall and the men in the morning, so he'd pass along the information about Hancock at that time. A message from Dom a few days ago had informed him that the guns would be arriving soon. He hoped it wasn't too late.

Chapter 11

Faith awakened the following morning before
dawn. She hadn't slept well. In the back of her
mind floated images of dreams that were far too fleeting
to grasp, but were still oddly disturbing. From outside,
the combined sounds of pelting rain and high-pitched
winds rattling the shutters let her know the weather was
foul. This was the time of year when the spring rains
came to battle winter for supremacy, resulting in cold,
raw, wet weather that kept people inside their homes.

She left the bed. The dark room was freezing. Shivering, she stuck the fire iron into the embers in her fireplace to free the few still-burning coals from beneath
the ash, and added more kindling. Tending the small
blaze until it could be left on its own, she crawled back
beneath the quilts to wait for the room to warm.

She wondered if last night's meeting with Nicholas
was the reason she'd had such a fitful night. He hadn't
recognized her, of that she was certain, and she'd ob-
scured her tracks in the snow to keep him from following her steps. It was a trick she'd learned as a child

while playing hide-and-seek in the snowy forest with Ingram and the other children. Who knew she'd grow up and need such a thing, she thought as she watched the fire grow.

While the sleet and rain continued to batter the house and the wind rose and fell, she listened for sounds of her father moving around upstairs. Hearing only silence, she thought back on his disturbing news about their finances, and set her mind to thinking how she might help so he wouldn't have to sell. The inn hadn't been busy in weeks so taking in laundry was an option. The British soldiers were always in need of clean uniforms so there was a ready need. She could ask Henri Giles to help spread the word of her service, which might ensure a steady number of customers, and with spring about to arrive, she'd be able to hang the clothes outside on the lines to dry.

Being a laundress was backbreaking work, not to mention the effects of the lye on the skin. However, if that was what she had to do in order to keep herself in her home, she'd gladly do so. Her other option was to sell bread, and that too came with a ready market among the soldiers. The barracks were full of hungry men. Everyone knew the Kingstons were good Tories so her patronizing the troops wouldn't be out of the question or draw suspicion, but more importantly, both business ideas would offer new avenues for spying on the British.

The only problem was obtaining the funds she'd need to get her enterprise started. If she decided to take in laundry she'd need larger pots and a stock of lye. If she chose to sell bread, there'd be dry ingredients to purchase, and with the British blockading the harbor, necessities like flour had risen in price. She'd also have to purchase many more Dutch ovens in order to make enough loaves to bring in a profit. She knew that no banker would loan her the money without any collateral, so that left her father. It was not a conversation she was looking forward to, but she hoped if she presented the idea logically, he'd see the potential and loan her some of their remaining funds.

The room finally warmed enough for her to move around, so she carefully removed from the fire the basin of water she'd warmed up for washing, and began her morning.

His breakfast done, Nicholas looked out at the foul weather from the window in his bedroom. By now the heavy spring rains had washed away any tracks Lady Midnight might have left behind, so he would have to concede her this round, and he didn't like it. He'd have to wait for her to surface again, but there was no guarantee that she would. There'd be no drilling today either so he'd spend the day gathering the remainder of his father's things so they could be donated to charity.

Faith was in the kitchen getting breakfast ready when her father entered. "Good morning, Father. Did you sleep well?"

"I did, and yourself?"

"Yes," she lied.

"Will Case will be joining us for breakfast."

Faith went still.

"And so that you know, he's made an offer for the inn. Price is fair and reasonable."

"No!" she cried out in protest. "Father, let me try and help us first. If you would loan me a portion of whatever is left of Mother's moneys, I'll sell bread. Everyone says how fine it is, and I think I could sell to a steady clientele of soldiers."

He barked a laugh. "What?"

Feeling desperate, Faith walked over to where he stood, "Father, listen. I'll need to secure more flour and meal, and I'll bake from sunup to sundown to put us above water again if need be, but please, let me try."

He looked at her as if she were someone he'd never seen before. "You want me to make you a loan to sell bread?"

"Yes. Think about it. If I work hard I can do this."

"No."

"But—"

"No. Will's offered me a fair price and the contracts will be signed. And because you'll be in need of a home, I'm giving him your hand in marriage, which as your father is my right."

Her eyes went large. "I will not be his wife!"

"You have no choice!"

"I will not be his wife!" she repeated forcefully.

"Elizabeth does not want you in our new home!"

She froze. "What? Elizabeth who!"

"Elizabeth Sutter."

She couldn't believe her ears.

"We'll be getting married in two weeks' time."

Faith was speechless. There were so many conflicting emotions streaking across her mind, she couldn't have spoken had she desired to. She now knew why he'd kept Elizabeth's name a secret. Faith would have never approved of him courting the vain and questionably chaste seventeen-year-old.

"I want more children, Faith—a woman who'll care for me in my old age, and Elizabeth offers me that."

"Are you in love with her?"

"No, but she's young and beautiful and will grace my table."

"So I am to marry Will so that you may take your new bride?" she asked, outraged.

"You make it sound so harsh."

Faith looked away, her lips pressed. When she thought she could speak calmly, she faced him again and said emotionlessly, "I wish you and Elizabeth every happiness but I will not marry Will Case."

That said, she turned to walk away, but he grabbed her arm and countered angrily, "You will do as I say."

She looked down at his hand and then up at his face. "You would sell me like a barrel of cod so that you can get between Elizabeth's thighs?"

He slapped her and she tumbled to the floor.

"How dare you speak to me that way! You will honor my offer to Will, or you will leave this house immediately, you ungrateful child!"

Faith got to her feet. She had been disrespectful, but she was not going to be sold like a slave or a mindless beast. "I'll get my things."

"You leave here with nothing! The clothes on your back is all I'll allow!"

She stopped at the doorway and looked back. She had never seen him so angry, but she was angrier. She also realized that he didn't believe she'd leave. He appeared certain that his ultimatum would scare her so badly that she'd surrender and stay, and that increased her anger. Without another word, she turned on her heel, exited the kitchen, and headed for the front door. When she snatched it open, the force of the wind and rain almost snatched it back.

Her father came running behind her. "If you leave here, don't return, Faith Kingston! Ever!"

She stepped outside and didn't look back.

The heat of her anger carried for the first ten minutes and then the weather began to take its toll. With no cape, the stinging rain had her thin skirt and blouse plastered to her body in no time. Sleet stung her face and cheeks, and mixed with her tears to form little crystals of ice on her eyelashes, her nose, and the corners of her lips. Her plan had been to walk to Charity and Ingram's. They didn't have room to house her for an extended stay, however, she hoped she could stay until Blythe returned, but as she walked into the howling wind and became colder and wetter, and her steps slowed, and her limbs began to numb and ache, she realized she'd likely succumb to the elements before she reached their home.

Sheer will propelled her forward. As she made her way she prayed she'd see a wagon or someone passing on the road but there was nothing but the elements. A part of her deemed herself a lunatic for making this decision, but no part of her wished to have remained at home to marry Will Case, so she wearily plodded on feet that she could no longer feel.

After what seemed like an eternity of frigid rain and battering winds, she didn't know how long she'd been walking. The only certainty was a deep longing to simply stop, collapse, and let the fates have their way because she couldn't go any farther. She was soaked and frozen . . . The ice in her eyes had rendered her blind and she had no idea where she was, who she was, or where she was going. With the last of her senses she saw a house ahead and knew if she didn't seek help there she would surely die.

Nicholas was inside sorting the items of clothing he'd be donating when he happened to glance out of the window and saw a woman slowly collapse in the road by his front gate. Alarmed, he ran downstairs. Ignoring the stinging rain and wind, he scooped her up and dashed back inside.

Breathing from anxiety and exertion he looked down at the pale, ice-crusted face and his eyes widened with recognition and fear. "Faith!" he called, jostling her gently. She was as unmoving as the dead.

"Faith!" Her limp body felt like a block of ice in his arms. Taking the stairs two at a time, he placed her gently on the bed, then dragged some of pelts he slept on as close to the fire as he dared. Kneeling beside her, he gently removed as much of the ice from her eyes and face as he could.

"Faith!" he called anxiously. He placed his ear on her icy wet blouse and prayed her heart was still beating. It was, albeit faintly. He had a hundred questions or more about what she was doing out in the weather with no cape, but he had to set them aside. He needed to get her dry and warmed as quickly as possible.

First he had to get her out of her wet clothing. Everything she had on was frigid and soaked. He could have debated how to go about it in a way that might have preserved her reputation and modesty, but there wasn't time. If he didn't undress her, her body would never warm enough to survive. Tight-lipped with concern, he dragged the sodden garments away from her cold skin and briskly dried her feet and limbs with a heavy blanket from the bed. The firelight danced over her nudity, providing the perfect backdrop for a tryst, but that was the furthest thing from his mind. His only concern was getting her dry and warm. Once done, he fetched a second blanket from the bed, and moving her as if she were made of the King's crystal, gently wrapped her inside. Placing her down again, he covered her with the bed quilt and then the heaviest bear pelt he owned. It was all he knew to do, then he sat on the floor to watch and wait.

Later, as silence filled the room and the weather continued to rage outside, Nicholas allowed himself a moment to wonder over the whys of her appearance. When he first picked her up out on the road she looked like she'd been washed up on the beach by the sea. Why wasn't she dressed for the weather? Had she been set upon by ruffians and her cape stolen from her? He supposed it made no sense to waste his thoughts on speculations because he had no answers. Was her father out searching for her? Nicholas thought he should probably ride over and apprise Kingston of the situation, but he was afraid to leave her alone. Because it was improper for an unmarried woman to consort with a man outside her family, there might be ramifications if Kingston called foul and word got out, but it had been either leave her to die or bring her inside and offer his aid. Surely a loving father would see the rightness in that decision.

However, a nagging feeling Nick couldn't name made him hesitate over the decision to speak with Kingston. Although he had no answers as to how Faith came to be in such dire straits, he thought he'd wait to hear her explanation first.

Three hours later, she began to stir. Nicholas, eating a bowl of rabbit stew, set it aside and walked over to where she lay beside the fire. Eyes still closed, she was moaning and attempting to pull off her blankets but didn't appear to possess the strength.

"Faith," he called softly as he knelt beside her and gently stroked her sweat-dampened brow. She was burning up with fever.

"I won't marry him," she protested weakly. "I won't!"

"Faith," he echoed more urgently. He had to get her fever down. Placing a kiss on her forehead he hurried down to the kitchen.

He spent the rest of the day and night heating water to sponge her down, talking to her softly, and easing her up so he could offer her spoonfuls of bark tea to calm the fever. He repeated the ministrations over and over; urging her to fight and telling her how proud he was of her when she took the tea, even though she didn't appear to hear a thing.

But he kept it up and when he was ready to drop, he crawled onto the pelt, dragged her back against the heat of his body, and slept.

Faith opened her eyes and peered around. *Where am I?* She moved to rise but was laid low by a surprising lack of strength. Lying there and breathing harshly, she pondered that for a moment and glanced around the unfamiliar room. Nicholas sound asleep in a chair startled her and widened her eyes. Filled with alarm she frantically surveyed the dark room again. *Where am I?* She was still so weary, her eyes began closing. *Maybe it's just a dream.* How long she drifted off she didn't know, but when her eyes opened again, he was still in the chair; however, this time he was awake and watching her. Seated in the firelight, he looked like a king at rest and his expression was impossible to decipher. His long-sleeved shirt was partially undone, revealing a small vee of bare throat and chest. His face was unshaven.

"Good afternoon, Miss Kingston."

Not a dream. "What am I doing here?" she asked. "Where are we?"

"You've been ill and we're in my bedroom."

Her eyes widened. He didn't say anything else so she asked, "Did you bring me here?"

"Yes. I found you outside in the storm."

With those words everything rushed back to her. The fight with her father, her flight from the inn, the storm. Her whole world had suddenly tilted and she forced herself not to acknowledge the ache in her heart. "How long have I been here?"

"This is the evening of the fourth day."

The span of time was shocking. That she'd become so ill after what she'd endured wasn't. Had her father looked for her, or simply said good riddance? That thought brought pain, too, along with the renewed memories of her flight. She saw her herself trying to make her way through the icy rain and how horrible an experience it had been. She was lucky and grateful

to have survived. She was still so tired though. She felt
as if an apple blossom could knock her over. Her eyes
slid closed.

"Are you hungry?"

She never answered. She'd fallen asleep.

Nicholas noted that her breathing sounded more
even than at any time since her arrival, and it made him
believe the crisis had passed. Getting her back on her
feet would now become his focus. After that, he didn't
know, because he had no idea why she'd been out in
the weather. His mind went back to that first afternoon
and her fever-fueled delirium. Whom didn't she wish to
marry? Had Case been bedeviling her again, and was
he somehow tied to her being out in the weather? Once
again, Nicholas had no answers, so he retook his seat
and resumed eating his stew with the hope that she'd
awaken again soon.

It was dark inside the room when Faith reopened
her eyes. This time, the sense of disorientation only
lasted for a moment; she knew where she was. She was
lying by the fire in Nicholas Grey's bedroom and she'd
been ill. The images of the argument with her father
flooded through her mind again and she placed her
hand against her cheek. It still stung where he'd struck
her, but the mental slaps he'd meted out were more hurt-
ful. Elizabeth Sutter. To his credit, during the years he'd
raised her, he'd never dallied with anyone, or at least as
far as she knew. Their lives had centered around each
other and the inn. Now he was feeling like a buck in

rut, proposing to have new children and toss away the old. She brushed away the tears filling her eyes. She refused to cry. She turned her head and found Nicholas watching her from that same chair. He didn't speak and neither did she, but it was yet another situation she'd have to face eventually. She still felt as if she'd been left for dead.

"Thank you for saving me," she said to him. She had no remembrance of telling him that before, but she owed him thanks and more for his help.

"You're welcome. Are you hungry?"

"I am."

"I have stew for you warming downstairs." He got to his feet, adding, "There's a chamber pot behind the screen over there. If you're not strong enough yet, I'll help you when I return."

Faith was embarrassed to her toes. "I believe I can manage to get there myself," she countered, not knowing whether she could or not, but certain she'd faint dead away if he had to assist her with something so personal.

She looked up at him looming above her in the shadows, and for the first time, her vision was clear enough to see the weariness in his eyes. "Have you slept?"

"No."

"Have you been the only person taking care of me?"

"Yes. I didn't want to alert your father until you could tell me why you were out in that storm."

"Then no one knows I'm here?"

"Only my neighbors, Arte and Bekkah Clegg. Bekkah brought over some food."

She met his eyes again. "Thank you," she whispered emotionally.

"I'll get you some stew."

As soon as he departed she forced herself to a sitting position to try and make it over to the screen before he came back. As she sat up straight, the sheets and quilts wrapped around her body slipped down. For the first time she realized that she didn't have a stitch on! Beneath all the covers she was naked as a newborn. All manner of questions screamed at her for an explanation, but it didn't take an advanced education to unravel how this had come about. Nicholas Grey had removed her clothing! She almost did faint then. The implications left her dizzy and appalled. She understood that it had been undoubtedly necessary; she'd probably resembled a shipwreck survivor when he found her, but the ramifications were legion. Realizing time was wasting, she forced herself to stand and on shaking legs rewrapped the blankets around her and made her way to the screen.

Her mission accomplished, she was lying on her back panting from the exertion when he returned. He took one look at her and asked, "I assume you took care of your needs without assistance."

"I did," she whispered.

"Stubborn woman."

"Embarrassed is more applicable."

He showed a small smile and shook his head. "Here's the stew."

"Can I sit in a chair? Maybe that will help me stay awake longer."

He set the bowl down and carried the chair he'd been sitting in over to the fire and set it close. He scooped her up gently, quilts and all, before she could protest. His strong arms and her knowledge that he knew she had no clothes on were both so distracting that it took her a moment to realize that she was not in the chair, but on his lap in the chair. Startled, she tried to get up, but he stayed her gently.

"I'll wield the spoon, you eat."

"I can feed myself," she protested. Although the trip behind the screen had drained the small amount of energy she'd awakened with, this was far too intimate for her to allow. "You must let me up."

Instead, a spoon filled with a delicious-smelling stew floated in front of her face and she looked up into his waiting eyes. Her stomach growled in response to the tempting offering, and she knew she was going to surrender; she was too hungry not to. His intense gaze made her aware of intimacies associated with other kinds of personal surrenders as well, but she chose to concentrate on the food instead.

Nicholas fed her slowly. As she chewed and swallowed he saw the small signs of rebellion in her eyes, but the show of temper proved she was on the mend and that pleased him.

"More?" he asked.

"No," she replied with a shake of her head. "I believe I've had enough for now."

He set the bowl on the floor. She'd eaten far more than he'd expected and that pleased him, too.

As the fire filled the room with flickering light, he gazed down at her and ran his finger gently over the angry bruise on her cheek. It had bloomed to life the first evening and he'd been waiting to ask her about it. "Who struck you?"

She ducked away, eyes downcast.

His touch light, he raised her chin so he could study her face. "Was it Case again?"

For a moment she didn't respond. He could see her mental struggle so he waited calmly. With her hair matted and the signs of sickness showing itself in her tired eyes, she looked awful, but he still found her absolutely mesmerizing.

" 'Twas my father."

He stiffened and searched her eyes with wonder. "Why?"

So she told him the story.

He listened without comment and when she finished Nick was furious. He tenderly gathered her closer, and she let herself be held without a fight.

Faith had never been held this way before. His embrace seemed to offer her both the strength and the solace she'd always sought. For her entire life, she'd taken care of her own emotional needs; eschewing her tears, sadness, and fears because there'd been no one to share them with, not even for a little while. However, his arms were like a balm to all the years alone, and for a moment, in the quietness of the room, she let go of being strong and dutiful, and allowed someone else to help her with her burdens.

Next she knew, she was crying. Where the tears came from she didn't know, but they were rolling silently down her cheeks. Her father had finally broken her heart, and with her world turned upside down the future loomed dark.

"You are the bravest woman I've ever known, Faith Kingston," he whispered above her head, and she felt his lips press reverently against her brow.

He raised her chin and looked down at her face as she slowly wiped at her tears. He kissed each wet eye with equal reverence before asking, "Do you think you will be all right here alone if I leave you for a short while?"

She dragged her palms over her cheeks. "Where are you going?"

"To your father's to retrieve your belongings."

She stiffened with alarm.

"Don't worry, I'll leave him alive."

"He isn't going to let you take them."

"It doesn't matter what he wants. You need your things."

He was right, of course, but she didn't see her father letting him take them without a confrontation, providing he hadn't already disposed of them. She also didn't see Nicholas taking no for an answer. Added to those worries were the spy inks and stationery hidden in her bedroom desk drawer. Had they been discovered? They had to be retrieved as well. Her widow's weeds were kept beneath her mattress but she didn't want to have to explain why they were hidden away. She stopped herself before the worry list grew longer. She was too tired for all this thinking.

"What's the matter?" he asked.

"Tired."

"I'll lay you back down."

Faith was surprised at how comfortable she'd become and in reality would have chosen to stay where she was, but he was neither her husband nor her intended so she had no business even thinking along that vein. If word got around about where she'd been for the past few days it wouldn't matter that he'd saved her life, she'd be shunned at church, and the subject of scandal-fed gossip, maybe for the rest of her life.

"You're certain I can leave you alone? I'm sure Bekkah wouldn't mind sitting with you until I return."

"I will be fine. The less people who know where I am, the better for us, I believe."

He gave her an agreeing nod. "I'm glad you're on the mend."

"So am I. Thank you again for coming to my aid."

"Again, you're welcome. I'm simply glad I was at home."

And she was as well. He laid her back down on the

pelts as carefully as he'd picked her up earlier. Tracing his finger down her unbruised cheek, he said, "I'll be back as quickly as I can."

"Would you bring the contents of my writing desk, too, please?"

"Yes."

Faith watched him depart and then slid back into sleep.

Chapter 12

Nicholas knew he could have easily waited until morning to see Kingston, but his anger was too high. Not only had the man's selfish ultimatum nearly cost Faith her life, he'd struck her hard enough to leave her bruised. That alone made him a candidate for gutting. The vivid memory of how cold and still she'd been when he found her added to the fury. Had the man no heart at all? He didn't care about Kingston wanting to marry the little tart he'd been introduced to at the reception, but he took great exception to the plan to sell Faith to Case as if he she held no more value than a milk cow. The most difficult challenge would be keeping himself from strangling the Tory toad with his bare hands.

Arriving at the inn he saw a wagon parked out front. He had no idea whom it belonged to, nor did he care.

Inside, Kingston was seated at a table with the cadaverous-looking Will Case. The urge to horsewhip them both rose within him.

Kingston looked up with surprise. "What brings you here, Grey?"

"I've come for Faith's things."

Kingston visibly froze. "What things? Where is she?"

"From the story she told me, I'm certain you don't care."

Case snapped. "If you know where she is, I demand you take us to her."

"I'll take you to hell first." He turned his attention back to Kingston. "Where's her room?"

Kingston eyed him for a long moment. "Is she at your home?"

"Again, I ask why you care. You demanded she leave here, and she did, almost at the cost of her life. When I found her lying in the road she was near death!" The force of his fury seemed to blow Kingston back. "And let this be a warning to you. Never put your hands on her in anger again. Now, direct me to her room."

Kingston countered smugly, "She deserved what she got for being disobedient and disrespectful."

Nicholas flashed across the room like lightning, hoisted Kingston up by the lapels, and slammed him into the closest wall. "You outweigh her by nearly a hundred pounds! How dare you hurt her!" He slammed him again.

Kingston whimpered.

"Now where's her room!" Nicholas demanded in a cold, wintry voice.

Kingston pointed. "Back of the house."

Nicholas tossed him aside, not caring that he landed on the floor in a heap.

Fury ruling, he entered her room and lit a lamp so that he could see. As he looked around the quiet interior, his anger momentarily ebbed. His eyes touched her bed that was made up so neatly, and the threadbare patchwork quilt on top. He viewed the polished mahogany armoire and the red shutters on the window he'd watched her sneak through the night that now seemed ages ago.

Removing the slips from the two thin pillows on her bed, he filled them with the frayed stockings and mended underwear he found in the armoire drawers. He wrapped the larger items like her few skirts and blouses in the familiar gray cloak she should have been wearing during the storm. The memories of the way she'd looked when he found her so close to death rose again and his emotions did the same. Forcing away the disturbing images, he walked to her writing desk. She had specifically asked that the contents be retrieved, so he made sure the ink pots were closed tightly before placing everything he found inside the desk drawers into one of the pillow slips. As beautiful and unique as she was, the fact that her personal items didn't even fill up two pillow slips tightened his jaw.

Hefting her things into his arms, he doused the light and walked back to the front of the house. He found Kingston eyeing him angrily over a raised musket. Case had an axe.

The ludicrous scene caused Nick to chuckle softly. He slowly placed Faith's items on a table beside him, and when he turned back to the men across the room he had two silver French pistols, one in each hand. He saw Kingston's eyes go wide before they quickly settled on him once more.

Nick said casually, "Muskets are notoriously inaccurate. Even soldiers have difficulties hitting their targets. Did you prime it correctly? Did you pack the load well enough? Will the bore pull to the left or to the right? Will it blow up in your face?"

Kingston's eyes widened again and the gun shook in his nervous hands.

"Pray you don't miss, because these," and he raised the pistols, "are very accurate. The first shot will be for you, and the other for your friend."

Kingston and Case shared a quick look of panic.

"Put the gun down, sir, before I have to kill you both, and while I may be pleased with that outcome, Faith may not."

Kingston grudgingly drew the gun down.

"Very smart," Nick said. "And yes, Faith is at my home. If either of you set foot on my land I will shoot you without a thought."

He picked up Faith's things and made his exit without a backwards glance.

Kingston came running out. "You can't do that! Damn you! Primus took Adeline from me. I'll not let you make Faith your whore, too!"

Nick stopped. "What did you say?"

Kingston charged him, but Nick being younger and the

better fighter had no trouble besting the innkeeper. His rage high, Nick stood over the man on the ground, and the cold air was thick with the streams of their breaths.

"I curse you!" Kingston stormed, wiping blood from his split lip. "May you and that whore of a daughter both rot in hell!"

Case came out and helped Kingston to his feet. Nicholas ignored them as he tied Faith's things to his saddle and mounted.

"This isn't the end, Grey!" Kingston promised, and continued to hurl threats and curses as Nick rode away.

His fury full-blown, Nick thought back on Kingston's surprising revelation. Could his claim be true? Had his mother, Adeline, really been Stuart Kingston's intended at some point in her life? If so, how had she ended up married to Primus? And could this be the reason for their acrimonious feud? He had no answers, so he put the riddle away for the moment and made his way home to Faith.

Wrapped in the thick quilts Faith watched the glow of the fire while the silence of the house echoed around her. The warmth in the room felt good. Physically she still wasn't up to snuff, but her mind was clearer and she felt stronger, probably due to the stew. She wondered how Nicholas was faring with her father. She just hoped they hadn't had a fight because there was no way her father would come out on top. Not that she wanted him to after what he'd done and said, but he was still her father, and her heart ached at his selfishness, so she put thoughts of him away and turned them towards herself. *What am I going to do?* Being penniless and homeless left her very few options. She knew she could count on Blythe to take her in, but Blythe wouldn't be coming home until after the birth of her grandchild, and there was no way of knowing how long that might be. Of course, she could ask Ingram and Charity to take her in, and they would, but she didn't want to impose on them. Their home was small, and like most people in the area they were bringing in just enough income to get by. Having to house and feed another adult would place them under a serious strain and she loved them both too much to add to their burden.

So where did that leave her? She had no other family, so there was no option of seeking shelter with anyone of that nature. She supposed she could make the round of taverns and inns in Boston and the cities nearby to see if someone would hire her. She could wait tables or pour ale; she'd been doing that most of her life. She could also hire herself out to someone's kitchen or do day work as a housekeeper. *Where would I live?* Some of the tavern owners allowed their women employees to lease rooms on the premises, but many of the women offered themselves as prostitutes to supplement their wages, and the owners often took a cut. She didn't see herself doing that, however. She sighed sadly. All because she refused to marry a man she couldn't abide and because her father— She moved her thoughts away from him again.

The clock on the fireplace mantel showed it to be nearly midnight. Because she had no clear recollection of how long Nicholas had been gone, she wasn't sure if she should be worrying over his absence or not. She was still uncertain about what day it actually was. He'd said she'd been ill for four days. Was this the night of the fourth day or the fifth? She decided not to worry about that since she had so many other pressing things to occupy her mind.

She looked around at what she could see of the well-appointed bedroom. She'd never been in Primus's home before. She'd never been in a man's bedroom before, either; ever. Her presence was going to cause a lot of tongue wagging if word got out, but if her father's anger held, she was certain he'd have no trouble painting her as having deserved his banishment for not surrendering to his demands. She strongly believed her bread making would have been profitable, given the chance, and she vowed to make a go of it once she got back on her feet. There were doubts, of course, but she didn't plan to let that scare her off. All she needed was a plan of action and funds, and eventually life would be good again.

A short while later she heard footsteps on the stairs. Nicholas had returned. She took in a deep breath to steady herself. He entered the room quietly, and upon seeing her and the quilts cozied up in the chair by the fire, walked over to her.

"I thought you'd be sleeping."

"I've been awake for a little while."

"I have your things."

"Was he difficult?"

"Of course."

Silence rose for a few moments.

"How are you feeling?" he asked.

"Better. I'm still a bit weak but I'm hoping it will pass quickly. Is he still angry?"

"Yes."

"So am I," she declared with a small blaze in her eyes.

He gave her a smile. "I have your things downstairs. I remembered your desk items, too."

"Thank you." To the layman's eye, the paper and inks looked very ordinary, so she had no worries of him tying them to her spying activities. Another facet of her life that might be changed.

"What are you thinking?" he asked, and took a seat on the arm of the chair.

"How my life is going to be altered. I need to find work."

"Let's get you up on your feet again first."

"I can't stay here with you."

"At the moment you're in no condition to do anything else, but let's suppose in a few days that you are. Where will you go?"

She shrugged. "If I can hire in at one of the taverns, I may be able to work and live there."

When he didn't offer a response she turned back to

the fire. "Or I could do day work, or housekeep, or do laundry in someone's home. Maybe the people I work for would let me lease a room. I don't know. I've never had to contemplate any of this before."

He still didn't respond so she looked up at him. "Have you nothing to say? Suggestions? Anything to offer?"

He showed his amusement. He shrugged his shoulders. "I have a solution. You stay here."

Faith almost laughed. "In what capacity?"

"My housekeeper."

"Your housekeeper," she echoed doubtfully.

"I'm looking for one. Blythe didn't know of anyone and I haven't found anyone in the area on my own, so the job is open."

Faith held his eyes. "I thought you were looking for a wife."

"Truthfully that was more Blythe's idea."

She studied him in an attempt to glean the seriousness of his offer. "Even if I was addled enough to say yes, I'm still in need of a room."

"I've three here that you may choose from."

"You're serious, aren't you?"

"I am. If you think about it, it is the perfect solution."

"I can't live here alone with you."

"Why not?"

"Because it's just not done. Have you any idea of the scandal that would cause?"

"I thought you told me you weren't a fleeing woman."

She quieted. Thoughts of that day returned and she

was again under the birch trees being set on fire by nothing more than the sound of his voice, the look in his eyes, and the gentle touch of his fingers on her chin. She blinked to pull herself back to the present. "I'm not. Some people have thought me scandalous for varying reasons, but never for salacious behavior."

"Who says it has to be that?"

"Because you're involved, Nicholas."

He laughed. "Then I'll promise to keep my attraction under control."

"And you lie. You've already admitted that you do to get your way."

He paused and said nonchalantly, "There is that."

Faith shook her head and turned her eyes back to the fire.

Nicholas was enjoying her and couldn't wait for her to be fully recovered. This last bit of conversation had him all but convinced that he'd miss out on something very special if he let her leave, and no matter the end result of the attraction between them, his offer of employment continued to be the perfect solution.

"Not to mention, my father would undoubtedly come here and shoot you if he knew I was openly living here with you."

"He's already made an attempt."

Surprise flashed into her face. "When?"

"Tonight, when I was retrieving your things."

She stared speechless.

"I assumed you didn't want him dead so I convinced

him to rethink his plan. Case was there, too. I threatened to shoot them both."

"This is getting far more serious by the moment."

He smiled at the wonder in her voice. "Did you know my mother was once your father's sweetheart?"

Once again, she was caught off guard. "No. Where did you hear that?"

"From your father. He was very angry with me for wanting to take your belongings, mainly because I wasn't a bit polite."

"He makes being polite difficult most times."

"This evening he was even more so."

"I'm sorry."

"No apologies needed. I accomplished the task."

Faith decided that if he were less handsome, he might be easier to deal with. "So what did he say?"

"Something to the effect that my father had taken Adeline from him, and he wasn't going to allow me to do the same with you."

She mulled that over for a few moments before asking, "Do you think this is what caused their disagreement?"

"Possibly."

"He's never said anything about this to me. I wonder what happened?"

"So do I."

Their eyes held, and for a moment as she felt a familiar heat rising, she looked away.

"You still haven't replied to my offer."

"I have. I appreciate your concern but my answer remains no."

"So you have someplace to go when you recover?"

"No," she replied, shaking her head.

He reached out and turned her face to his. "Faith, it doesn't matter what people think of you. It only matters what you think of yourself. Do you honestly want to work in a tavern filled with drunk soldiers?"

"No." She backed out of his hold. "If I could have my wish, my living would be baking bread."

He cocked his head. "Really."

"Yes, I tried to convince my father to give me a loan, but he said no. Our conversation about my making bread so I could help supplement our income is what started the argument that led to his order to leave."

"I thought you said you were arguing about Case?"

"We were, but my proposal was what set everything in motion."

"So explain this idea to me."

She did, and when she was finished, she said to him earnestly, "If you truly wish to help me, then make me a loan so that I may go into business and I will return your funds with interest."

He could see her determination. In truth, he wasn't doing much with his money at the moment besides secretly buying guns for Hall's small regiment of minutemen. He had more than enough to spare, and she was correct about everyone needing bread. It was a staple of life. Soldiers in particular were a ready group because there were never enough rations to satisfy everyone's hunger. "And where do you propose to do the baking?"

"Since I can't do it at the inn, the only other grate I know of large enough is Blythe's, and she's out of town. What size is the one here?"

"A bit larger than hers, I do believe."

"Really? May I see it?"

"You turn down my offer for employment, but you might like to use my grate?"

She smiled at him for the first time. "Possibly."

"Did I tell you the salary?"

"No."

He did, and the amount made her mouth drop.

He asked, "Not enough?"

"Oh goodness, that is more than enough." She searched his face. "And you'll want nothing other than housekeeping?"

"And meals and laundry, and that is the truth, Faith. I wouldn't lie to you about my intentions, nor have I ever forced myself on a woman, so that you'll know."

Faith found his offer astonishing. "With that amount I could easily get myself on my feet and be able to put money away as well."

"Yes, you could."

"But why would you make such a grand offer?"

"Because I want you to take it and because you need it."

He was correct, her needs at the moment were great. "And no strings attached?"

"None. If you're going to be thought scandalous you might as well be compensated for it."

It was the most outrageous offer ever proposed to her; tempting, too. Extremely tempting.

"May I think on it?"

"Of course."

Faith found this hard to believe. He was offering her a way to support herself both now and in the future. No one in her right mind would turn down such a boon. Granted there would be talk, probably a wagon full, but more than likely her father was already telling anyone who'd listen that he'd cast her out for being disrespectful and the talk had already begun. Faith didn't wish to be the subject of gossip, but she didn't wish to remain homeless and penniless forever either. In the end, the decision was an easy one to make. "I'll take the job."

"Good. Welcome to the household."

There'd be no going back now and she felt better than she had since heading out into the ice storm. With hard work, she might be able to make enough to eventually leave Boston and start anew if the gossip became too much to bear. At the moment, however, her world had suddenly brightened and she was grateful. "Thank you."

"My pleasure. I can stop beating the bushes for a housekeeper now."

"I'll start first thing in the morning."

He shook his head. "You'll start when your strength returns. Until then, you get to laze around and do nothing.

I didn't bring you back to life to have you relapse. I'd also like to enjoy a full night's sleep sometime soon."

His weariness was plain and she felt sorry for being the cause of so much strain. "Then go and sleep," she said softly. "I'll be fine now. Is there a tub so I might bathe?"

"There's one down the hall."

"All right. When I get up I'll heat some water and rid myself of the grime. How close is the pump to the house?"

"Why?"

"So I'll know where to look for it. I'll need to pump the water to bathe, you know."

"I'll take care of the water. You're supposed to be recovering, remember?"

"I do, but what time do you rise? I should have strength enough to cook breakfast."

He looked to the heavens as if for strength of his own. "I never knew you were deaf."

"I'm not."

"You must be because you obviously didn't hear me say you are to do nothing for the next few days."

"Oh," she responded. She looked up at him. "This is going to be difficult for me."

"I'm seeing that."

She dropped her head to mask her smile. "I've never been ill before. How will I pass the time?"

"Read? Correspond? Anything that doesn't involve household chores."

"But I'm the housekeeper."

"Not until you are fully well."

She sighed. "All right."

"Good."

"I suppose chopping wood for the fireplaces is out, too?"

He shook his head and smiled. "We'll do well together, I think."

She agreed.

"Do you wish to sleep in the bed?"

She looked over at it and then back to the dark pelts plied high by the fire. "May I ask why you had me sleep on those?"

"So I could place you closer to the fire."

"Are they yours?"

He nodded. "I brought them back with me when I left the Iroquois."

She covered her surprise by asking, "Were they a gift?"

"No, they were my bed."

"During a visit?"

"No. I lived with the Confederation a year or so."

"You're jesting?"

"No."

She'd never known anyone who'd slept on pelts or had lived with a native tribe. She studied him as if there might be a visible sign of his time there. "Were you captured?"

"No, I was there by choice. I'll tell you the story soon

if you are still interested. Now I just wish for you to rest, so that I may do the same."

She preferred to hear his tale, but he was correct, they both needed rest and he especially so. "I'll use the pelts, if I may."

He nodded. "I'll be down the hall in my father's room."

"I'll see you in the morning."

"Good night, Faith."

"Good night."

Later, as Nicholas lay in bed, he thought about the young woman sleeping in his bedroom. He was glad she'd accepted his offer, which in reality had been selfish in nature. With her as his housekeeper, he'd be able to see her, banter with her, and for certain lock horns with her on a daily basis. She would do for female companionship, and because he'd promised to keep his attraction to her under control, he could always engage in a discreet dalliance with someone else should his physical needs become great, but that didn't interest him. She did. He'd never met a *good* woman with her spine and determination, and he certainly had never made a loan to one with a plan to go into business for herself. Her father was an old fool. It was easy to see the potential in her idea, and if she worked as hard as he guessed she might, she'd soon be a force to reckon with. In the meantime, he needed sleep. He could barely keep his eyes open, so he surrendered and let slumber have its way.

Chapter 13

Nick was awakened the following morning by the sounds of pounding. Bleary-eyed, he stared around the dim room. It took him a moment or two to realize where he was and why, but once he conquered that the pounding started again. Someone was knocking on the door, he finally deduced. Not happy, he pulled on a shirt and breeches, picked up his pistol, and padded barefoot to the stairs.

The thundering knocks continued to rattle the door. "I'm coming!" he yelled out in sullen response over the din. He hoped that whoever it was had a damn good reason for pulling him out of his warm bed.

He flung open the door and snarled like a bear whose winter nap had been interrupted, "What do you want!"

"I've come for Faith."

It was Ingram Trotter. Nicholas almost slammed the door in his face, but knew Faith wouldn't approve, so he put the desire aside. "What?"

"I said, I've come for Faith. Her father says she's here. He wants her to return home."

"Oh he does, does he? So he sent you to get shot instead?"

Trotter's eyes widened with surprise. Upon noticing the pistol in Nick's hand they grew even larger and he warily stepped back a pace.

Nick shook his head. "Come in. I'm at my poorest when I've not had enough sleep." Not waiting to see if the man followed him, Nick turned and walked into the parlor and sat. Ingram appeared, and Nick soundlessly gestured him to take a seat.

"Is she here?" Trotter asked.

Nick eyed him balefully. "Yes."

"May I see her?"

"She's sleeping. I'd rather she not be disturbed."

"I demand to see her," he countered.

Nick had seen ground squirrels taller than Trotter. "You demand?"

"Yes."

It was obvious that the short man hadn't any idea what he'd walked into, and Nick felt no obligation to help or to explain. "You don't enter another man's home and demand anything."

"My apologies, but Mr. Kingston's extremely worried, as am I, and I'm not leaving until I see her."

"Then I shall have the pleasure of tossing you out before I go back to bed."

"Nicholas, you will not toss him anywhere," Faith

voiced as she entered the room. Both men got to their feet. Amused, Nicholas held her eyes. She was wearing a gray blouse and skirt, but didn't look any less disheveled than she had last night. She had a few lightning bolts in her eyes that were directed his way. It was easy for him to see that she'd attempted to do something with her thick black hair before joining them, but in reality only succeeded in resembling a woman who'd just stepped out of her lover's bed. By the mildly shocked expression on Trotter's face, he apparently thought the same.

"Good morning, Ingram," she said coolly, looking away from Nick's unrepentant gaze. "What brings you here?"

"Your father sent me to fetch you home."

"See why I wanted to toss him out?" Nicholas explained.

"Behave yourself," Faith chided him, holding on to her smile before replying to Ingram. "I won't be returning."

"May I ask why not?"

"We had an argument; he struck me and asked that I leave, so I did."

Nicholas added coolly, "And out into the teeth of last week's ice storm."

Ingram visibly stilled and confessed, "He didn't tell me that."

Nick replied, "And I'm guessing he didn't tell you

that he planned to sell Faith, along with the inn, to Will Case as if she were part of the furniture."

He stared.

Faith nodded and informed him, "Father is planning to marry Elizabeth Sutter and they would prefer I not be in the way."

Ingram glanced confusedly between the two of them. "But why are you here? Why didn't you come to Charity and me?"

"Because she never made it that far," Nick drawled. "She succumbed to the elements right outside my door. Did I fail to mention that he threw her out without a cloak?"

Ingram's mouth dropped.

Faith asked, "Now do you understand why I can't return, Ingram?"

"Yes, but come home with me," he told her, casting another wary look at Nick. "Our place is small but Charity and I will make room."

Faith shook head. "I appreciate the offer, but I couldn't ask you to take that on. You have enough mouths to feed."

"We wouldn't mind."

"I know, but I would. Everyone is struggling because of the blockade and you two are no exception."

"So you plan to stay here, with him?"

"For the present, yes."

"In what capacity, if I may be so bold to ask."

Faith stilled at the accusatory sound of the question.

Nicholas cracked icily, "You should have let me throw him out."

She shot him a quelling look, but Nick ignored that and said to her, "He's asking you that rude question because your hair looks like you just left your lover's bed."

Embarrassed, her hand quickly went to her hair.

Nicholas wasn't done. With his eyes on Trotter he asked Faith, "Does he always have such salacious thoughts about you, Faith?" Eyes still burning Trotter's way, he asked, "Does your wife even know you're here?"

Faith threw up her hands at Nick's teasing and pinned him with another disapproving glare, but Nick was enjoying his role. He wanted to swat the little man like a fly.

"I'm employed as the housekeeper, Ingram. Nothing more," she explained.

The skepticism on his face was plain.

"Doesn't look like he believes you," Nick pointed out.

"It doesn't matter," Faith said, shooting her disapproval at Ingram this time.

Her glaring must have gotten his attention because he replied hastily, "Faith, I'm terribly sorry. But the way you look—"

"I collapsed in the storm that day, Ingram. I woke up four days later, here. I've been extremely ill, but Nicholas nursed the life back into me. He knows I have no money and nowhere to turn. He's graciously offered me a position in his household. Should I have gone to the almshouse instead, providing I'd lived to do so?"

As Ingram squirmed, Nick remembered her words when he'd accused her father of betraying Primus. *My tongue is tart from having to debate nonsense with men like you . . .* Standing there and listening to her skewer someone else, Nick could almost sympathize with Trotter. Almost. Faith Kingston was not to be toyed with.

"My deepest apologies, Faith. Please forgive me."

"I do, but it would help immensely if you would explain my reasoning to anyone dragging my name through the mud. I'm not counting on my father to be truthful."

"I promise."

He looked to Nicholas. "My apologies to you as well."

Nick nodded tightly.

"Mr. Grey, I'd like your permission for my wife and me to visit Faith occasionally if we may."

"As long as it doesn't interfere with her duties, I see no reason to forbid it."

"Thank you."

Faith turned to Nick, and the warm thanks in her eyes melted his insides like honey in sunshine. He frowned. Nick enjoyed being with a woman who engaged his mind and his senses, but he'd yet to meet one who'd engaged his inner self and feelings. This one apparently had and he wasn't sure what to do with that.

"Is something wrong?" she asked.

He shook his head. "No," he said. "Woolgathering, that's all."

She studied him for a moment longer, then turned her attention back to Trotter.

While she and Ingram chatted about the health of his wife, Charity, and the baby, Nicholas silently watched them. She seemed at ease with Ingram, and although Nicholas knew the two had grown up together, he found himself envying the man's knowledge of her. Trotter knew her in ways Nicholas could never duplicate. He knew what Faith had looked like as an adolescent and if she had been as strong-minded then as she was now. What had they done for fun? Nick wondered. She apparently enjoyed fishing, so had they sat on the creek banks with their lines and their bare feet in the water, while basking in their friendship? The two of them shared memories they'd take to the grave, and Nicholas wondered what that felt like, and if he'd ever find it in his life.

The sound of Faith's voice pulled him back.

"Please give my love to Charity and let her know I am well."

"I will," Trotter told her.

He walked over and extended his hand to Nick, who grasped it in solid response.

"Thank you for aiding her, and again, my apologies for my rudeness. I was simply concerned about Faith."

"I understand."

"Good day."

After giving Nick a respectful bow and tossing Faith a smile, he made his departure.

In the silence that followed, she looked Nick's way. "Would you have really thrown him out?"

"Yes. He woke me up, and was pounding on the door like a redcoat. I almost slammed the door in his face, but I assumed you wouldn't care for that."

"You assumed correctly."

"See, I'm learning what pleases you."

His declaration was as potent as his eyes and voice, Faith decided. She knew he was going to be a handful, but she had no idea she'd have to grow more hands in order to keep pace. He'd played with Ingram like a cat with a mouse. "Thank you for being so nice to him at the end."

"It was difficult."

She smiled. "If I neglected to say good morning—good morning."

"Good morning. How was your sleep?"

"Well. I feel better. I'm past ready to be clean, however. Will you pump the water, since I am not allowed to do so."

He heard the dig. "I see the tart tongue has recovered."

She gave him a quick curtsy.

He laughed. "Let me get my shoes, your majesty, and I'll pump your water."

"Most appreciated, sir."

"But humor me and have a seat in that chair, so that you don't keel over from having done too much already this morning."

Faith knew she wasn't as strong as she wanted, but she'd been determined to ignore the weakness and press on through the day. "Must I?"

He nodded.

She offered a mock snarl and sat. "Happy?" she asked softly.

"Extremely. Now be in the chair when I return and I will be ecstatic."

"I am here to serve."

He chuckled and left to put on his shoes.

While Faith waited for him to return with her bathwater, she thought back on the direction her life had taken since her banishment from the inn. At least now she'd found housing and employment. She had no idea how it would work out but it beat by a large margin having to go to an almshouse. Her father was going to have apoplexy when he learned she'd moved in, and would not be kind in his words about her when talking to his friends, but she didn't care. Nicholas was right, life boiled down to how you felt about yourself. She'd never heard it expressed in such a succinct manner before though. Beneath his gruff and incorrigible nature lay a razor-sharp mind and even sharper wit. She couldn't believe her ears when he asked Ingram if Charity knew his whereabouts. Trotter had looked so stunned, she'd felt sorry for him. Faith had never had anyone champion her before, but now it seemed that she did and she found it rather nice. He was also going to invest in her idea to make herself self-sufficient and that was rather nice, too.

This was her first true look around at the parlor. The furniture was of fine, highly polished woods and the lamps were of good quality as well. She eyed the large painting of a woman hanging above the fireplace mantel. She was dressed in a blue gown and was stiffly posed as was common for the times. Faith wondered if this was Adeline, Primus's wife and the mother of Nicholas. She certainly had been beautiful. Even in the unsmiling pose Faith could see the light in her young eyes and Nicholas's resemblance to her. Had she really been the cause of the rift between their fathers? Nicholas's recounting of her father's angry words about Adeline made Faith even more curious about the unsolved mystery. One day maybe the questions would be answered, but right now the only person with those answers had cut himself out of Faith's life. She sighed.

She heard Nicholas's footsteps as he reentered the house. She moved to get up but remembered she'd been asked to stay seated, so she waited for him to appear. After a short while, he did. "Ecstatic to see me still seated?" she asked.

Nicholas gave her a grin. "Very much so." He could still see the tiredness in her eyes, however, and planned to keep a tight rein on her activities for the rest of the day. "The water is heating and as soon as it is ready, I'll pour it into the tub for you."

"Thank you."

"It's a proper bathing tub, so it may take a bit longer to warm all the water needed to fill it."

"That's fine. I've never bathed in one before. Only hip tubs."

"I believe you will enjoy it."

She turned her eyes to the window and saw the sunshine. "Is it cold outdoors?"

"Not overly so for this time of year. Why? Would you like to go out and get some air?"

"I would maybe later."

Nicholas wasn't sure if that was a sensible idea or not, after all she'd only been up and around less than a day. "We'll see what your strength is like this afternoon."

She nodded.

While they waited for the water to heat, he went into the kitchen and sliced her off some meat, added bread and a cup of coffee, placed everything on a tray, and took it into the parlor. "Here's breakfast."

"Thank you," she said, eyeing the offerings with interest. "I am hungry. Is this coffee?" she asked, looking up from the dark-colored beverage in her cup.

Nicholas took his plate from the tray and took a seat on the floor before the blazing fireplace. "This is a rebel household," he reminded her.

Coffee was the beverage of choice for rebellion

supporters. They began consuming it in response to the boycott of British tea that culminated in the now infamous Boston Tea Party. She took a hesitant sip and frowned. "The taste may take some getting used to. Do you have any honey or molasses?"

He went in the kitchen and returned with a tub of honey. He watched her spoon some into her cup and watched as she took another sip. "Does it help?"

She grimaced. "Only marginally. Are you certain there is no tea?"

"Yes, I am."

"I understand the political choice but this . . ."

"I won't be buying tea."

"I understand."

He scanned her silently. "Is my treasonous household going to ruffle your Tory sensibilities?"

She scanned him in return. "No. Truthfully, I've secretly supported the rebellion for years."

He froze.

"A group of soldiers made sport of Charity and me a few years back and we've both hated the redcoats since."

"What happened?"

"We were walking home from the Negro Election Day festivities and they stopped us, questioned us about why we were out alone, and then took us into the trees." She met his eyes. "They formed themselves into a circle and we were shoved into the center. They pushed us from man to man, laughing and touching us where they could, trying to lift our skirts. We were screaming and crying. I'd never been so terrified."

Anger tightened his jaw.

"They finally tired of us, or maybe they had to be back at their barracks, I don't know, but they released us with the warning that if they ever saw us alone again, it wouldn't be a game the next time."

"Did you tell your father?"

"I was afraid to. He'd forbidden me to go to the celebration. Charity's, too. So she and I made a pact to—" Faith almost said *spy on the British*, but caught herself and finished with "secretly support the rebels, even if our parents didn't."

"What of Charity's husband?"

"Ingram is a staunch loyalist. He shouldn't see anything you don't wish to get back to the patrols."

Nicholas studied her. "Once again, you've surprised me, Faith Kingston."

"I'm glad."

He chuckled softly. "Any other secrets behind those eyes?"

She thought about Lady Midnight. Now that she no longer lived at the inn, her life as Lady Midnight had probably come to an end, but she had no intention of revealing that side of herself ever. Her disclosure might make him ask her to leave if she couldn't give him the answers he was seeking about his father's arrest. "If I tell you, they won't be secrets anymore, will they?"

Hoping to change the subject, she looked up at the portrait above his head. "Is that your mother?"

"Yes."

"You favor her."

He looked up at it. "Wish I had known her."

"I lost my mother, too. Something you and I have in common."

He gazed at her face a few moments longer. "I wonder if we'll ever learn the truth about the root of the trouble?"

"It would be nice to finally put the riddle to rest, wouldn't it?"

"Yes, it would."

By the time they finished the light meal, the water was ready. Returning to the parlor after having gone upstairs to check on it, he asked, "Can you make your way back up the stairs on your own?"

"Yes."

"Will you need help getting into the tub?"

"I should be able to manage that, too. Is there soap?"

"Yes. It isn't scented though."

She stood. "That's all right. I've never used any. My father said the extra money charged for it was a waste."

Nicholas made a mental note to purchase her a few bars as soon as he was able. He was getting the impression that while living under Stuart Kingston's roof, she'd enjoyed very few of the feminine niceties many women took for granted. He'd found no perfumes, salts, or any other scented toiletries in her room when he gathered up her belongings. "When you're done bathing, just pull out the stopper and it will drain the water. The bathing room is down the hall and to the left of my room. I set you out some towels."

"Thank you, and I will remember your instructions for the stopper."

"Are you sure you don't need help?"

"I am, but if that proves wrong, I will call."

"That's all I ask. Enjoy your bath."

She departed and he was left alone.

He waited for her call but when none came, he gave her a few more minutes then went up to his room to gather the things he needed for his daily morning plunge into the creek.

Chapter 14

Faith eyed the bathing tub while she removed her clothing. It was odd contemplating sitting in a tub of water that reached one's waist as opposed to standing up in a short little tub filled with water that was just above ankle high. She wondered how she was supposed to keep her shift dry. No God-fearing woman would lounge in the tub fully unclothed, would she? She'd have to ask Charity about it the next time they were together. Charity was one of the few people Faith knew who'd had such a tub in her home while growing up.

For now, though, she decided to keep the thin shift on and put on her clean one when she finished bathing. She owned only two. She realized Nicholas had probably seen how mended and torn her unmentionables were and that the two pairs of drawers he'd placed inside the pillow slips were old and frayed as well. The knowledge was embarrassing but there was nothing to be done about it. Maybe once she had a bit of extra coin she could ask Charity's seamstress mother to sew her up new ones. Until then she would make do as she'd always done.

She knew of only a few homes that had a room dedicated for bathing, but apparently Primus had been a creature of comfort. The fireplace with its wide mouth held a roaring blaze, and inside sat a large kettle holding more water in case it was needed. The towels Nicholas had mentioned were folded on a three-legged stool at the foot of the tub. She ran her hand over the surface of the one on the top of the pile and noted how soft they felt and that they looked to be thicker than the quilts on her bed back at the inn. Knowing the water wouldn't stay warm forever, she dipped her hand in to see if it needed heating up, but it didn't. She stepped in and the novelty of all the available space when one was accustomed to a hip tub made her smile with wondrous delight.

Once she was in and seated, she decided that this form of bathing had to be a sin because it felt so glorious. She scooped handfuls of the warm water over her shoulders and neck and let it slowly cascade down her shift and back to its source. From that moment forward, a hip bath would run a poor second when she needed to bathe in the future. She could have lounged in the liquid decadence for hours. However, the need to wash away the grime and remnants of her sickness took priority, so she picked up the soap and began.

When she finished, she pulled out the wooden stopper and the water began to slowly drain away. Where it went she had no idea but would ask Nicholas when she had the chance. She'd enjoyed her first experience with a bathing tub very much and she stepped out feeling fresh, clean, and a bit tuckered out. She wrapped one of the towels around her body and the other around her wet hair. With no oils or dressings available, she fashioned it into one long braid. She would worry about dressing it at some point, but it was clean again and she'd settle for that.

There was a window on the room's back wall, and once she was dried and dressed in a clean brown blouse and skirt she'd taken from her pillow slip, she walked over to the window and looked out at the drab day and the muddy open fields and outbuildings behind the house. And then she saw Nicholas walking towards the house. He was wrapped in what appeared to be an Indian blanket of some sort. Confusion lined her face as she wondered where he'd been and why the blanket. He was holding the edges closed against the wind, but his hold slipped for a moment and Faith got her first look at a man's nakedness before he snatched the blanket closed again. She spun away from the window so quickly she almost fell down. With her hand pressed against her gaping mouth and the heat of embarrassment filling her face, she fought to catch her breath. What kind of man walked outside without any clothes? He'd mentioned living with a native tribe. Was this something he'd taken to doing while there, or— She was so speechless she couldn't complete the thought. *Oh my word!* First the pelts and now this? It came to her that she didn't know very much about him at all. Heart still racing, she took in a deep breath and forced herself to calm down. She couldn't fathom having to face him after what she'd seen. Granted, it had been only a flash, but it had been revealing enough to leave her with vivid memory of his lean, dark, muscular legs, and a portion of his male anatomy no unmarried woman was supposed to see. She wondered if she was in the first stages of apoplexy, because she was still finding it hard to breathe. Gathering her belongings, she left the bathing room and hoped she'd recover before she had to face him again.

She didn't, but she masked it well enough so that when he made his appearance a short while later, he didn't ask if something was wrong. She was in his bedroom seated in the rocker before the fire.

"Did you enjoy your bath?"

"I did."

"It's starting to snow so we'll have to cancel your outing. I don't want to risk you slipping back into sickness."

"Neither do I." But she was disappointed.

"Maybe in a few days."

"We'll see."

"So is there anything I might do to help you pass the time? Would you care for a tour of your new realm? I don't think that will be very taxing."

That sounded like a great idea to Faith. "I think I'd like that. You said there were three bedrooms available.

May I see them so I can decide which one might be mine?"

"Of course. There's this room."

"Which is yours so I'll not take this one."

"You may if you like."

She wondered how a man's eyes could be so potently inviting. "No, that wouldn't be right, so let me see the others."

He led the way.

The first room was a smaller room at the back of the house. There was a window and a bed. It was larger than the one she had at home and thus very suitable. "This one will do."

"You should look at the others before making a final decision."

"This is more than sufficient."

"We may have to put you back in bed. I think your hearing's been affected again."

She dropped her head to hide her smile. Looking up into his innocently set face, she gestured to the door and she followed him out.

"Did Primus build this house?" she asked as they walked back down the hall.

"No, he purchased it from a Quaker farmer who wanted to sell so he and his large family could relocate to Pennsylvania. Here's the other room."

The first things she noticed upon entering were the two large windows that looked out over the road. She could see almost to the horizon, and for a moment she stood there and marveled at the magnificent view. Behind her was a large, polished stone fireplace, and near it an enormous, four-poster canopy-topped bed made of gleaming dark wood. A beautiful armoire made from the same wood drew her eye, as did a matching chest with filigree handled drawers and curved claw feet. The bed sat atop a beautiful indigo- and cream-colored rug that she sensed would feel like heaven beneath her feet on a cold winter morning. It was a sumptuous room, larger than many parlors she'd been in, and Faith knew that claiming it for herself wouldn't be proper for the housekeeper. "This is very lovely, but I'll take the other."

"May I ask why?"

"These aren't quarters for a servant. They're far too grand. This should be your room."

"I'm happy where I am."

Faith looked around the interior again almost wistfully. She turned back and found him watching her. "Whose room was this?"

"My mother's."

She stilled.

"My father kept it swept and dusted, and the furniture polished, the entire time I was growing up. When I returned a few weeks ago, the room was shrouded with tarps, so I pulled them back, wondering if everything was the same, and it was."

She viewed the space in a new light.

"I don't think my mother would mind, nor would my father."

In his eyes she saw something she couldn't name; something that reached inside and touched her inner feelings. "No, Nicholas. I can't take this one. This isn't where a housekeeper is supposed to sleep."

"Why not?"

She shrugged. "Because."

"Very succinct reply."

"Stop mocking me," she said, amused.

"Then you will have to come up with a better rebuttal."

She took in his lean, tempting presence standing in the doorway, and wondered how many other women had had this same difficulty telling him no. Probably legions.

Faith scanned the beautifully appointed room again. Her eyes touched the low-slung vanity table with its scrolled, wood-framed mirror and padded bench, then traveled over the elegantly carved writing desk and its companion chair by the windows.

He asked quietly, "Well?"

Claiming the room for herself went against everything Faith had ever been taught about a person's proper station in society, but in the end, she surrendered to him and to yet another of his grand proposals. "All right, I will take this room, but only temporarily. If you marry, it rightfully belongs to your wife."

"That won't be for some time to come, so thank you for pleasing me."

His softly pitched tone sent ripples across her senses and she found herself unable to look away. An inner heat flared up inside, reminding her that he was responsible for its birth, and that if she wasn't vigilant it could consume her as his kisses had done that night on the darkened streets of Boston. "Thank you for yet another boon."

"My pleasure."

Faith wondered why it seemed as if time were slowing and that they were the only two people in the world. With his unshaven face and ever watching eyes, he exuded power like the dominant wolf of a clan and she was scenting him like a bitch in heat.

Nicholas didn't know how much longer he'd be able to hold back the urge to take her into his arms and treat her to the passion he wanted her to taste again. His promise to keep reins on his attraction was wearing on him, and the parts that remembered the sweet taste of her mouth wished he hadn't made such a limiting vow. "Let me show you the rest of the house."

Neither of them wanted to move, but knew they were heading down a road that led to each other and that it would only be a matter of time before they succumbed.

"May I see the kitchen?"

"This way."

He stepped back to let her precede him. When she

passed, her fresh scent wafted across his nostrils and his manhood hardened in response.

In the kitchen, Faith saw that the fireplace was large enough to handle meals of all sizes and that it offered more than enough space for the loaves of bread and biscuits she planned to bake and sell.

"Will this do?" he asked.

"Oh yes. This is more than sufficient."

She glanced around at the wealth of Dutch ovens, kettles, and other cooking vessels and utensils stacked neatly on the shelves attached to the far wall. There was also a large table that could be used for dining or for preparation work. The room was well stocked and she couldn't wait to begin. Granted it might take her a short while to learn to adjust the fire to the temperatures that worked best for cooking the different dishes, meats, and breads, but it was that way with any new kitchen.

"There is also a grate outside for summer cooking."

She marveled at that. That would a godsend on the hot sticky days of July and August. "May I see it?"

"Might be prudent to wait for better weather."

He was right of course. She was so excited she'd forgotten about the snow falling outdoors.

"There's also a large cellar, a smokehouse, and an icehouse."

"I'd like to start my duties in the morning."

"Are you sure you're well enough?"

"It's the only way to know, and I'm anxious to begin. I will make you a promise that if I tire, I will rest. And I won't be lifting the furniture or attempting to have all the floors mopped by noon."

"That's a relief."

Their smiles met and lingered.

A thick silence rose between them, making them even more aware of each other, and Faith wondered if a woman could melt under the heat of a man's eyes. "So shall we talk about my duties? I'd like to know what you expect. You indicated meals, laundry, and cleaning, but is there a certain schedule you'd like for me to adhere to for, say, wash day. Is Monday better than Tuesday? That type of direction would be helpful."

"I have no preference. You can set up a routine that works best for you and I'll follow. If there's anything the household lacks, let me know. I'll be going into Boston in the morning to pick up some items. If you're up to it, you're welcome to ride along, providing the snow has stopped."

She thought about being seen with him and how much gossip might be already in the wind about them, but she told herself she would do her best to face it head on.

"And if you are worried about people whispering behind your back, don't," he said as if having read her thoughts. "Anyone who utters anything other than 'Good day, Faith, how are you' will answer to me."

She nodded and smiled. "I've never had a champion before."

"You do now, and I take my charge very seriously."

"I've noticed." She thought back on poor Ingram.

"When we go into town, I also want you to purchase any personal things you need, like scented soaps, bath salts."

"I don't need scented soaps or bath salts. I'd rather you spend the money on dough bowls or beeswax for the furniture."

"You'll find the house has plenty of both. Next objection, Miss Kingston." He folded his arms with an amused air.

"I don't need frivolities."

"When was the last time you indulged yourself?"

"I'm not sure I understand what you mean."

"You've worked for your father your entire life, correct?"

"Yes."

"Have you ever visited a hairdresser, or purchased a hand lotion that you were fond of, or had a length of silk sewn up for a new shift?"

"No. We never had money for such extravagances."

"Now you do."

She searched his face for the jest but saw only a seriousness in his eyes that made her go still.

"We're going to be lovers, Faith, and we both know it. It's been inevitable since the day we met."

Faith's breath caught in her throat.

"So," he continued quietly, "allow me show you what it means to be desired, so that I can give you the desires of your heart."

The sheer force of him swept over her like a great wave and she was trembling with such reaction, she thought she might fall down.

"I will never take you against your will, but don't let what you've been led to believe about who you are, and what you can't have, deny what you can have."

She closed her eyes, hoping it might slow her racing heart. She'd never had such words directed her way, nor did she know how to respond. "I know nothing of this," she whispered.

"I'm aware of that, so we'll move as slowly as you need."

He was speaking as if it was a foregone conclusion, and in the face of what she was feeling, she supposed he was correct, but: "And the future?"

He shrugged his shoulders. "To be honest, truly honest, I'm near the point of asking for your hand."

She gasped and felt her equilibrium go awry.

"But you may find my half-wild ways not to your liking and want to leave after you've made your fortune selling your bread."

In spite of her shock, her smile peeked through.

"So I'll leave the future to you. However, it's safe to say I've never met a woman who fascinates me the way you do, Faith. And as you have pointed out, I will lie to get what I want, but I can also be truthful."

Faith wondered if he'd had too much ale or had a mind fever or was suffering from some other ailment that would account for this latest grand offer. "But you know nothing about me."

"What I do know makes me hungry for more."

The wave crashed over her again.

Nicholas had no idea any of this was going come out of his mouth, and now that it had, parts of him wondered if he had lost his mind, but the part that was touched by the smile she'd given him this morning during Trotter's visit supported him wholeheartedly. His plan to marry her also had its advantages. By becoming his wife, she'd be spared any future machinations by her father and deny any gossipers further fuel. He wasn't sure how he'd gone from proposing they be lovers to proposing marriage all in the space of a few minutes' time, but it was a testament to just how off balance being around her rendered him. "So, your thoughts?"

She couldn't find words, let alone express them. "You truly wish to marry me?"

"I do. I've no other prospects and apparently neither do you. Why shouldn't we? The attraction is there, which puts us ahead of many couples embarking on a life together."

Faith felt as if she were standing in a windstorm. "But this doesn't make sense."

"Maybe, maybe not, but I believe it will be fun. Think of it as an adventure."

She studied his face. The offer was more than tempting. As he'd stated, they did share an attraction; it wasn't love but Faith didn't need that. "And you will be true?"

"Yes."

She brought her hands to her mouth and tried to make sense of this. They did get along, and granted she knew as little of him as he did of her, but as he'd said, what they did know put them head and shoulders above other intended couples. And it wasn't as if she had suitors beating down the door; more than likely his would be the only desirable proposal for marriage she'd receive in this lifetime, so did she really want to dismiss it out of hand? She knew she did not. Becoming his wife would without a doubt leave her father frothing at the mouth, but that wasn't her concern. As far as she could determine, the issues he'd had with Primus had nothing to do with her and Nicholas. She met his eyes. She'd always liked adventure, and the prospect of being his wife held its own unique draw. "All right. If I say yes, what happens next?"

"We find a preacher to say the words and we cast off."

"You make it sound so simple."

"Would you rather something more complex?"

She shook her head. "No. It's just . . . ." She eyed him, and wondered where this would lead. This man who slept on animal pelts, walked unclothed in the snow, and declared a hunger for her that still made her shake, was offering her the opportunity to turn her drab brown existence into one brighter than the sun. What other choice did she have but to say, "Yes. I will be your wife."

"Even though I am half tamed."

"Maybe because you are half tamed."

He raised his eyebrow. "You do like adventure?"

"Yes, I do." Now that she'd given him her answer, she sensed a bold new facet of herself emerging, one that enjoyed this subtle wooing.

"Then I can unleash my attraction."

"Slowly, remember."

He grinned. "I do."

He walked towards her and Faith's shaking returned in full force. He stood before her for a long moment drinking her in with his eyes, telling her soundlessly, what, she didn't know, but it was powerful. He stroked his finger slowly down her cheek, then leaned over and gently pressed his lips against the tingling spot. Tiny shooting stars burst across Faith's inner sky and her eyes closed.

He straightened and, no longer masking his desire, fed on her visually before bending again to gift her with a fleeting brush of his lips across hers. He repeated the gesture, letting her become reaccustomed to his touch, his nearness, and his desire. He accented the caress with tiny whispery licks from the tip of his tongue, and her mouth parted in trembling response. He raised his head, and as she shimmered under his blazing eyes, he slowly traced the curves of her lips.

"Such a gorgeous mouth . . ." he noted quietly. And to prove it, he kissed her deeply. When he finally backed away, she couldn't even remember her name.

"And this is how it will be with us, Faith. Passion, desire, fun." He offered her a muted smile. He traced her lips again as if they possessed an invisible lure he couldn't resist.

Faith felt as though she were basking in warm, beguiling sunlight. Her nipples were taut, her breath uneven, and there was a sensual thickness between her thighs that had to be a sin. Nothing in her puritan upbringing had prepared her for any of this.

He slanted his mouth across her again and pulled her flush against him. His arm across her spine, the pressure of his kiss, and the solid strength of his thighs against her set off more fires. He ran a heat-filled hand lazily up and down her blouse-covered back and then moved it boldly down to circle her skirt-covered hips.

His dazzling lips traveled over her jaw, the skin beneath her ear, and the skin of her throat above the worn lace collar of her blouse. His hands roaming her waist burned through to her skin, as did everywhere his hard body pressed against hers. Faith had no idea kissing could lead to such mindless hunger. All her life, she'd been warned against the sins of the flesh, and now she knew why. Every press of his mouth made her want more.

For Nicholas she was sweet as a honeycomb and he wanted to taste every tantalizing inch of her. This would only be the opening movement of the sensual song he would create with her; he'd save the crescendo for their wedding night. In the meantime, he contented himself with the softness of her lips, the arousing sound of her breathless sighs, and the feel of her taut nipple against his circling palm.

His hands on her breasts stole what little breath Faith had remaining. Once again, she was caught unawares by just how powerful passion could be. The hunger in her blood increased the throbbing thickness between her thighs. When he placed his mouth over the crest of her nipple and bit her gently the fever made her cry out in a shock-filled moan. This was too much; she backed away.

Breathing hard with desire, her eyes lidded and her lips parted and swollen from his kisses, she fought for calm. "I thought we agreed to go slow."

"This is slow, sweet Faith. You're still dressed."

Her eyes widened and he chuckled.

"All right," he said. "We'll stop. For now."

The implication sent a rush through her blood. While her nipples continued to reel from their brief encounter with his pleasuring, she wondered why women weren't told their bodies could respond to a man this way.

"Are you ready to see the rest of the house?"

She found it hard to think let alone move from where she was standing, but she nodded and let him lead her out.

They stopped next at the den with its book-lined

walls and large desk, and although she was still filled with the echoes of his kisses, her spirits soared at the sight of the many books on the shelves of the bookcases. There was a complete set of the Bard's comedies and dramas. She saw works by Chaucer, and poets like Pope and Spenser. She never realized Primus had such an extensive library.

"May I read when there is time?"

"You may read even when there's not."

She gave him a shy smile. When her father cast her out, one of her biggest losses had been leaving behind her small but precious trove of books, but now she had at her fingertips a collection that would do any public reading room proud. "Thank you," she said sincerely.

"Again, my pleasure.

The word *pleasure* immediately transported her back to being in his arms. She looked up at him and was again filled with wonder that such a remarkable man wanted them to share their lives. "Are you certain you wish for us to marry?"

He answered by easing her into his arms and after a long, silent look down into her eyes, kissed her so thoroughly she swore her knees melted into her shoes. When he released her and she gazed up at him through the haze of desire, she had no more questions.

Chapter 15

With the house tour ended and Faith tired from all she'd done, she chose to go and lie down for a bit in an effort to stay on the path to recovery. Nicholas watched her depart, and he sat at the desk in the den and reviewed their morning. That he'd asked her to be his wife seemed right. As he'd noted earlier that had not been his initial intent, but he didn't regret the offer, nor did he want to back out because even though they knew very little about each other, he continued to believe they would do well. He'd been a loner all his life. Growing up as an only child in a society where, due to the high incidence of infant mortality, parents often waited until their offspring reached adolescence before forming a bond, he'd suffered even more being motherless. Having no extended family that might have supplied him with cousins or other youngsters his age, except for his friendship with Arte, he'd led a very isolated existence in his father's home. As he survived into adolescence, he and his father became closer and shared experiences as they hunted and fished, did the farming, and worked in his print shop, but Nicholas felt as if something was missing from his life. Once he left home to go to war and began to face the world on his own, there'd been no time or opportunities to forge lasting relationships. His times with the Iroquois had been the closest he'd come to having clan members, but having not been born into the Confederation meant he was still somewhat of an outsider in their eyes, and in his own.

So, why Faith? Because from the moment he saw her that first time at the inn, he felt drawn to her, and then when he learned that she had wit and sass and an intelligence many of her sex lacked, the desire to learn more about her increased. But he'd no desire to marry her. He'd resigned himself to finding a compatible woman and leaving it at that. Most marriages were arranged and usually contracted by parents with an eye towards improving social status, acquiring property, or gaining wealth. The average farmer or merchant with little status looked for a mate who was healthy and able to provide the children needed to help keep the business or the farm afloat. Few marriages were love matches or grand passions, so he'd had no illusions about what kind of marriage he would have, and would have been content to just find a woman he could abide, but now it appeared as if he'd stumbled upon one who excited not only his senses, but his mind as well. This unlikely adventure he and Faith were embarking upon could hardly be termed a love match; neither of them was that naïve, but there was passion; grand passion if his feelings for her were any indication.

He thought back on something he'd been told by an old fortune teller he'd encountered in Bombay years ago while sailing as an impressed seaman with the hated British Navy. She'd predicted that he'd find peace with the spawn of an enemy. At the time, he hadn't given her words much credence; the only peace he'd been seeking was escape from the King's navy, but had she truly known that Faith would enter his life? For most of his existence, personal peace had been as fleeting as trying to cage the wind. He'd fought wars, seen the world, and gotten a bellyful of death and man's inhumanity to man. He'd returned to Boston hoping to be greeted by his father, only to find his headstone instead. There'd been very little peace in the world of Nicholas Grey, and now that world included a feisty, raven-eyed innocent who was indeed the spawn of an enemy.

So yes, he would marry her, clothe her, feed her, and do everything in his power to help her achieve all that her heart desired, and maybe, just maybe, she'd turn out to be the instrument of the peace he'd been seeking.

By mid afternoon the snow stopped falling, leaving the outdoors looking as if it lay under a fluffy white blanket. It was the first week of April and Faith hoped this would be one of the last snowfalls because she was sorely tired of winter. As Nicholas entered the dining room carrying plates holding their suppers, Faith turned from the window. He placed one in front of her and his at a spot on the table nearby.

She was still a bit overwhelmed by the morning's events, but under the circumstances she supposed it was natural, seeing as how she'd gone from being his spinster housekeeper to his intended in the blink of an eye.

"Something amiss?"

She tasted the mixture of root vegetables and smoked pheasant and found it quite tasty. "Just wondering when the wedding will take place and where."

"As soon as we can manage, I suppose, and we may as well have it here. Is there anyone in particular you wish to invite?"

"Only Charity and Ingram. How about you?"

"My list is short, too. Arte and Bekkah."

"I don't wish to embarrass you in front of your friends, Nicholas, but I don't own anything suitable to be married in."

"I'm not marrying you for what you have, Faith, and my friends won't think less of you because of how you're dressed. They aren't that way."

That made her feel better.

"Do you know a reputable seamstress?"

"Yes. Charity Trotter's mother is highly sought after. She has a shop in town."

"Do you think you'd like to visit her?"

She eyed him down the table. "I would."

"Then how about we stop in and see her tomorrow?"

For a woman with her pride, it was hard for Faith to admit she needed new clothing. "That would be agreeable." She turned the conversation back to the wedding. "Who will the pastor be?"

"Arte's uncle Absalom. He has a church in Boston. I'll talk to Arte about his availability later."

She studied him and for the hundredth time that day, wondered where this would lead.

"Second thoughts?" he asked.

"No. Not in the least, I'm just wondering where this adventure, as you call it, will take us."

"Hopefully into our old age, with our hair and teeth intact."

The silliness made her chuckle. "That would be helpful, but on a more serious note, I'm simply curious, I suppose."

"I say we let it unfold as it will and enjoy what comes."

That made sense, but Faith wasn't sure it was enough to keep her from wanting to take a peek at their future together.

"It isn't as if we can control what comes and make it dance to our tune, you know."

"True," she admitted, meeting his eyes.

He shrugged.

A knock at the door made them both look up and Nicholas said crossly, "If it's that ground squirrel again—"

The confused Faith echoed, "Ground squirrel?"

He left the table but didn't respond.

It then occurred to her what he might be referencing, and her eyes widened. "Nicholas, you are not talking about Ingram, are you?"

He gave her a grin.

"That's terrible of you!"

But he didn't slow and left the room without a word, causing her to yell, "Be nice!" as he disappeared.

Nicholas opened the door. It wasn't the ground squirrel. It was the ground squirrel's wife.

She said to him, sounding nervous, "Mr. Grey, I know my husband's already visited Faith today, and he said you weren't pleased by it, but I must see her to make certain she is well."

Assessing her, Nicholas remembered Faith's parting shot, but the decision to comply or not was moot as she walked up behind him.

Giving him an amused yet quelling look, she said, "Good evening, Charity. Please come in."

Nicholas smiled and stepped back so Mrs. Trotter could enter, but his eyes were on his soon-to-be housekeeper wife. "I'm wounded that you didn't trust me."

"I'm wounded that you'd think I would."

He threw back his head and laughed.

Charity looked between the two of them.

Faith turned away from his too handsome face and said to her friend, "Pay him no mind. Lack of sleep has made him grouchy all day."

"And whose fault is it that I've had no sleep?"

Charity's eyes grew wide.

Faith wanted to sock him. "As I said, pay him no mind."

He said to her in a soft voice, "I believe this round is mine, sweet Faith."

Charity couldn't seem to hide a grin.

"Go away, Nicholas." It was all Faith had. He was so uncontrollable. "Charity, let's go to the parlor."

Sailing past the grinning Nicholas, Faith escorted Charity to the parlor and wondered where she could buy a barrel of extra hands.

Faith closed the double door and they both sat on the large love seat.

"Well," Charity exclaimed.

Faith ran her hands over her eyes. "He's incorrigible."

"I noticed."

Faith looked her way. "He's asked me to marry him."

"What?"

"Yes."

Charity stared, shocked. "Ingram said you were to be the housekeeper."

"I was, but after he left this morning, things changed."

"Oh my goodness. What did you say?"

"I said yes," she said plainly. "I'd be a fool not to." Faith let her friend digest that for a moment before asking, "Did Ingram tell you what happened between my father and me?"

"He did. I'm so sorry you had to suffer that but it is so good to see that you are well."

"Only because of Nicholas. Implications to the

contrary, his lack of sleep is due to the nursing he gave me. He tended me for four days."

"Very commendable. When I'm ill, Ingram goes and fetches my mother. He doesn't do well around sickness."

Faith wasn't aware of that. She knew it wasn't right to compare the two men, but after being with Nicholas she was certain that her feelings for Ingram were those of a young innocent girl and not a woman full grown.

Charity asked, "So he just up and asked you to marry him?"

"Yes. He's termed it an adventure."

"Sounds wonderful."

"You think so?"

"Have you taken a good look at the man? If I didn't love Ingram with all my heart, I would have already pushed you into the harbor."

Faith grinned and her friend did as well.

Charity asked, "But what is this about your father and Elizabeth Sutter?"

So they spent a few moments discussing that topic, and when they were done Charity looked as disgusted as Faith had been at the news. "That's appalling. Do you think he's the father of her babe?"

Faith straightened. "What babe?"

"Elizabeth is carrying."

"Oh my goodness. How do you know?"

"Mrs. Bentley."

Mrs. Bentley was the local midwife.

"You know that woman can't keep a secret."

Faith was stunned. Could the babe be his? She supposed it had to be because surely Elizabeth wouldn't go into the marriage carrying another man's child. "Has it become common knowledge?"

"Not so far. The people that do know are being discreet, but the cat is out."

Faith shook her head and sighed aloud. "Poor Father."

"You're very Christian to say that in the face of how he treated you. Had my parents tried to give my hand to Will Case I would have run out into an ice storm, too."

Faith thought back on that awful day. Had it not been for Nick, Charity would be helping to plan Faith's funeral. "So, catch me up on what's been going on in Boston. Nick has had me so wrapped in cotton I've no idea if war's started or if Gage has been tarred and feathered and tossed into the bay."

"The city should be so lucky. His soldiers are marching all day every day. People are afraid. Everyone says we are getting closer and closer to war."

Faith thought about General Gage's plan for mid April and hoped things might be settled before then, but the time was looming.

"Does Nicholas know about Lady Midnight?"

Faith shook her head. "No, and I've decided to let her die. The risk is too great, especially since he thinks she may know something about his father's arrest. He may not believe I don't."

"So you won't be telling him anything?"

"Other than that I support the rebels. No."

"Sounds sensible."

"I've debated it, but I can't seem to find a way to bring it up, not that I've tried, but I think remaining silent is best."

Charity nodded her agreement. "He's quite a catch. You're going to make a great number of women green with envy. Are you ready for your wedding night?"

"Honestly, I'm not sure." She thought back on his powerful kisses.

"Understandable. Mine wasn't what I expected at all."

Faith's confusion must have shown on her face.

"Let's just say I expected more."

Faith still didn't understand.

"It was over so quickly, I wasn't sure anything had happened at all." She took a look at Faith's puzzled face and added, "Maybe I should explain."

"Please."

"When I lived with my parents, I slept in the room right below theirs, and on some nights, I'd hear them having relations."

Faith's eyes widened.

"The bed would be knocking around, my papa would be yelling, Mama would be making all kinds of high-pitched shrieks, and frankly it sounded like they were having a good time."

"So are you saying you and Ingram aren't?"

"Aren't. Ever. Never. Pick any word you'd like. He

taps me on the shoulder, does his business, and rolls away. Five minutes later, he's asleep."

Faith didn't know what to say.

"I love him so much, and it's maddening because I know there could be much more. However, I play the dutiful wife and don't complain."

Faith had a good idea of what Nicholas would be wanting, but it never occurred to her that she might have wants, as well.

Charity said sagely, "I don't think you are going to have that problem with your Nicholas, though."

"No?" Faith asked, unable to mask her amusement.

Charity shook her head. "No."

Both women smiled.

A few moments later, Charity asked, "Do you have something to be married in?"

"Nothing that doesn't make me look like the church mouse that I am."

"I probably have something that will fit in my armoire. I'll bring it with me when I come to do your hair."

Faith opened her mouth to protest being fussed over but closed it; she knew better than to argue with Charity. "That's fine."

"Thank goodness you did this without notice, otherwise my mother would want to make a special dress and drive you batty for weeks on end like she did me when I married."

Faith remembered. "We're going into town in the morning. He wants us to stop by her shop and ask if she would sew me up a few new shifts."

"She'd love to, I'm sure." Charity studied her intently. "Are you certain you want to marry him?"

"I do. It isn't like I've suitors lining the walk, and for now, he and I seem to be getting along."

"As long as you are content."

"I am."

"Have you decided when and where you'll marry?"

"No planned date as of yet, but we agreed it should be here in the parlor."

Charity glanced around. "It's a lovely room. Who's the woman in the painting?"

"Primus's wife and Nicholas's mother, Adeline. She died giving him birth."

"That's too bad."

"Yes it is."

"He favors her."

"I think so as well." Faith wondered what kind of person she'd been inside. Had her marriage to Primus been an adventure?

"Should I bring food for the dinner?" Charity asked, bringing Faith back to the wedding plans. "How many others are you inviting?"

"Just two. His neighbors, the Cleggs."

"Then I will bring food and the wedding cake, so you must let me know the date in plenty of time."

"I will."

* * *

While Faith and Charity were sequestered in the parlor, Nicholas made a quick trip over to the Cleggs.

Arte answered the door.

As Nick entered, the red-haired Bekkah appeared and asked, "How is Faith?"

"She's well but Arte, I need your uncle Absalom to marry us."

"Marry whom?" he asked, sounding confused.

"I've asked Faith to marry me and she said yes, so we need a pastor."

Arte held up his hand. "Hold on a moment. How did she go from being deathly ill to your intended?"

"By agreeing to be my housekeeper."

"Have you been drinking?" the puzzled Arte asked.

"Not that I remember."

Bekkah chuckled and said to her husband, "Arte dear, you know how Nick is. He'll have you chasing your own tail until Easter. He loves to tease. You've known that all your life."

Arte dropped his head and grinned. "So you were just jesting?"

"No. I'm quite serious."

Both Cleggs stared, thunderstruck.

Arte asked with alarm, "She's not carrying, is she? Nick, you didn't—"

Nick raised an eyebrow.

"My apologies. None of my business."

"True, but to answer your question, no. So, will you

be seeing your uncle soon, or should I drop by the church while I'm in town tomorrow?"

"I'll see him in the morning when we drill. I'll give you his answer when I return home. Where will the wedding be?"

"My house."

"And the day?"

Nick shrugged. "Friday. Saturday. Whatever day or time is convenient for him."

"All right, I'll ask him."

"Thank you. I'd also be honored if you'd stand up with me."

Arte smiled. "You know I will." After a short pause, he asked Nick, "Do you really wish to marry?"

"To her, yes."

Bekkah said, "You'll need a wedding dinner, so consider that my gift."

"Thank you, Bekkah."

Arte was studying Nick with such a serious face, Nick sought to reassure him. "Everything will be fine, I promise.

"I'm writing that down," he teased.

Nick grinned. "I have to get back. Thank you for your friendship. We'll speak again tomorrow." He departed, leaving the outdone Cleggs to stare at each other in wonder.

Chapter 16

Nick came in the door just as the women were leaving the parlor. Faith blessed him with a beaming smile that melted him inside just as it had before.

"Charity's going home," she said to him.

"It's been a pleasure, Mrs. Trotter."

"For me as well. Congratulations on the upcoming wedding. I know that you will treasure her as much as Ingram and I do."

"That is my intention," he pledged, and saw the satisfaction his words put in Faith's eyes.

"I'm going to be making the wedding cake and bringing food."

"My neighbor Bekkah has volunteered to feed us as well. Faith and I should know the date by late tomorrow."

Faith asked Charity, "You'll be my matron of honor?"

"I'd fight anyone else you asked." She gave Faith an emotional hug, after which she said to Nicholas, "Thank you so much for saving her."

Nicholas noted the sincerity in her eyes. "You're welcome."

After her departure, he and Faith stood together in the silence. "I like Mrs. Ground Squirrel."

Faith dropped her head and chuckled.

"Are you enjoying our adventure so far?" he asked her.

"I am. And you?"

"Yes."

Nicholas used the silence that followed to admire the shape of her mouth, the sheen of her blemish-free skin, and the raven black eyes and matching midnight hair. She was passionate and witty, and he'd chosen her to be his wife. He'd made a good choice. The urge to stroke her soft cheek slid like smoke from beneath the hold he'd placed on himself and next he knew he was doing so. In response, her lids lowered. Leaning down, he kissed her gently and followed it with one filled with his growing ardor. When her parted mouth opened on a breathless sigh, his manhood rose in concert.

He eased her into his arms; kissing, savoring, dying to have her nude so that he could feast his way down her body without restraint and brand her as his alone. Her warm skin was enchanting; her mouth, hot and sweet. Before he knew it, his fingers were conquering the buttons of her blouse and he was tasting each patch of newly bared skin while she trembled. The thin ivory shift covering her body gave his adoring hand access to the soft breasts unbound by stays. He teased the nipples until they ripened and her sighs and moans increased.

Drawn as if by a siren's call, he kissed his way back to
her mouth while his hands on her breasts continued
their play.

Faith was being buffeted by spiraling sensations that
obliterated every lecture she'd ever received about the
conduct of a proper woman. Her lips were parted, her
nipples pleading, and in answer to their soundless cry,
he pulled down the shift and took a bud into his mouth.
It was too much. Her body exploded into a hundred brilliant
pieces and she cried out, shuddering, eyes closed.
Staggered, she backed away from him, her hand over
her pulsing breast, her breathing harsh.

"Welcome to the world of pleasure, sweet Faith."

Faith had never felt such an explosion before.

He smiled into her passion-lidded eyes. "It's your
body's natural response."

The echoes continued to drum inside and remnants
of the silken bliss closed her eyes again.

"Did you enjoy it?"

"I did," she confessed, and wondered if that made her
a fallen woman in the eyes of polite society. In truth, her
body didn't care. Her still pulsing nipples concurred.

Nick knew she was unaware of what an alluring picture
she made with her blouse opened and her shift in
erotic disarray around her bared breasts. It took all he
had to maintain his position and not back her gently
against the door and pleasure her nipples again. She
was indeed sweet, and he wanted to taste her until the
roses bloomed in June.

But he planned to wait until the wedding night. That was important to him, and it also felt right. She wasn't a camp follower or a whore purchased to service drunken sailors or a gilded courtesan he'd contracted with for one night. Faith was a stunning, high-spirited beauty who'd graciously agreed to become his wife. "Would you do something for me?"

"What is it?" she asked softly, her body still humming from being pleasured so well.

"Close your blouse. The sight of you is threatening my hold on myself. I want to wait for the wedding night to be with you fully, but it's difficult to keep my distance when you look the way you do."

Faith nodded. Under the scrutiny of his glittering eyes, her fingers slowly did up the buttons. Watching him watch her gave Faith her inkling of the sensual power a woman wielded over a man.

When she was done, he said in a tone that made the echoes return, "Thank you."

She could tell by his manner that his hold on himself was tenuous. A part of herself eagerly anticipated his loss of control, but she thought it best if she distanced herself and let the air between them cool. "I'm going to fetch a book from the den and go up and read awhile before I sleep."

His eyes moved from her mouth to her eyes. "Then I will see you in the morning."

Memories of the ways he'd kissed her threatened to

distract her so she forced them away. "What time would you like breakfast?"

"Early might be best since we're driving into town."

In the face of the day's myriad happenings, she'd all but forgotten about the trip. "I'm accustomed to starting the fire at four, will that be suitable?"

"Perfectly."

His gaze was holding her with an intensity that made a singular craving rise from between her thighs and slide through her blood.

"Good night, Faith."

"Good night, Nicholas," and she retreated.

Later, lying alone in Adeline's large bed, Faith gave up trying to read *Hamlet* and set the bound volume of the Bard's tragedies aside. How could she read with her body so restless? Everywhere her mind turned he was there, pleasuring and kissing her until the passion carried her away. When she told Charity that she didn't know what to expect, she'd no idea how truthful that admission had been. Who could have imagined such a kaleidoscope of sensations or that her body would bloom and burst the way it had? She was glad he'd had a measure of control because she'd had none and there was no telling how it might have ended. He'd pledged to go slow, but the only slow thing about their encounter down in the foyer had been the pace of his seduction and the explorations of his expert hands. It was obvious he was as well versed in passion as he was with a woman's body. Once again she thought it very unfair that a man would know more about her body than she, but the parts of herself that he'd made croon and plead were glad he did. Now she knew what desire and lust were capable of instilling and that she could lose herself in it as a result. He'd not been wrong in terming their marriage an adventure because it was proving to be just that.

The following morning, Faith had the fire started and was cooking breakfast when he entered.

"Good morning, Faith. Smells good in here. I hope you slept well."

She turned from the fire to reply, "I did, and you?"

The questioning look in his eyes was lit with such humor she wondered what he was about. Attempting to figure it out, she looked down at herself and found the reason. Appalled and embarrassed, she snatched her skirt free of the waistband so it would hide the male wool leggings she always wore for warmth during the cold months. "They keep me warm, and I don't want my skirt to catch fire."

"I don't want you to catch fire, either, sweet Faith."

He'd only just entered the room and Faith was already on the threshold of swooning. Unbidden memories of last night rose to mind. By the light in his gaze she sensed him to be on a similar track so she turned back to the fire and picked up the fork to fiddle with the bacon. "Everything's almost ready. I can bring it out to the dining room if you'd like."

"How about we use the table in here. It'll be warmer."

She nodded.

"Is there anything you need me to assist you with? Water? Butter from the cold box?"

"No, I've everything we need. You can sit if you like."

So he did and she could feel him watching her.

He asked quietly, "Is there something the matter?"

She glanced his way. "I'm just new at this adventure. Not sure where I'm walking."

"I see."

Faith used her towel-padded hand to brush the ashes from the top of the Dutch oven and peeked inside at the biscuits. They appeared to be done so she grabbed another towel and brought the small vessel to the table and set in on a trivet in the center.

Going back over to the grate, she placed the bacon, eggs, and potatoes on a platter, and after placing it on the table, she sat opposite him.

"Everything looks so good. It's going to be a pleasure not having to eat my own cooking."

"Your cooking hasn't been bad."

"You lie well."

Amused, she said to him, "Bless the food so we may eat."

He reached for a piece of the bacon. "I don't pray."

She studied him as he spooned a generous portion of the smothered potatoes and onions onto his plate. "May I ask why not?" she quizzed quietly.

He shrugged. "Too much of a sinner, I suppose."

She eyed him for a moment longer, wondering what that meant. "Then I shall pray for us both."

He bowed his head, she said the words, and when she finished, they began the meal.

They ate in silence for a while until he asked, "Does my lack of religion trouble you?"

She shrugged. "My father wasn't a staunch believer so I'm not shocked by your words, just curious as to what made you give me that reply."

"Too much of a sinner?"

"Yes."

"The life I've led, the things I've done. The things I left undone." He met her eyes. "Maybe we'll talk about this one day."

Faith wanted to hear more, but decided she wouldn't press and would wait until he was ready.

He picked up one of the biscuits on his plate and said. "At the moment, I'd much rather discuss how excellent these biscuits are, Faith Kingston."

She grinned.

"If the bread you're planning to sell is anywhere near as good as these, the populace will crown you queen."

He'd already eaten three and he reached for two more.

She raised an eyebrow. Of the original nine only four remained. "Planning to eat them all, are you?" she asked.

"Yes," he replied, and without a hint of shame.

She laughed. "May I have another before you do?"

"Be my guest."

"You're so kind."

As she secured one for herself, he grinned and popped another piece of biscuit into his mouth.

She shook her head.

After another few moments of silence, he said seriously, "I suppose it's natural to feel unsure. This is new for us both."

She realized he was picking up the unfinished conversation they'd had before she joined him at the table. "I just don't know how I'm supposed to conduct myself."

"As a married woman?"

"Yes, but as a woman married to you. There seems to be a difference."

He grinned. "Explain."

"This attraction, as you call it. Why don't I see any of that from other married couples?"

He shrugged. "Maybe they save it for behind closed doors."

She mulled that over. "So in public they are staid and emotionless."

"And at home, away from prying eyes, they may walk around nude and make love on the dining table."

Her eyes went wide as saucers. "We're not going to do that, are we?"

He laughed at her appalled face. "You may enjoy having me strip you nude and have you for breakfast."

Heat spread through her. His suggestive voice matched his dark eyes and she found it nearly impossible to breathe.

He chuckled. "No?"

"No," she echoed, scandalized.

"Remember you said that."

Faith almost fell sideways out of her chair. She couldn't look at him, nor could she look at the table, and so decided maybe the time had come to change the subject. "Let's talk of something else."

Nicholas nodded his agreement but he enjoyed the provocative banter. Beneath her innocence lay a beguiling, sensual woman just waiting to bloom into life, and as her husband it would be his sovereign duty to make certain the ground stayed fertile and wet. "Then let me continue to praise the meal. If this is an example of how well you cook, I'll be needing wider breeches by summer."

"I'm glad you find it pleasing."

"I do." He found her pleasing as well.

They finished the meal, and as the silence rose between them, thickening the air, Faith fought down her body's attraction to him, and asked, "When will you be ready to leave for town?"

"Whenever you are."

"After I clean up in here."

He nodded. "That's fine. I'll go out and get the horse and wagon ready. Join me when you are done."

After his departure, Faith took in a deep breath.

Who'd ever thought a simple breakfast could have such sensual undertones or that people made love on tabletops. That last had to be Nicholas teasing because she couldn't imagine anybody doing such a thing. She turned her mind away from her half-tamed intended and began the cleanup.

After putting the kitchen back to rights she hurried upstairs to fetch her cloak, hat, and gloves. Once she was adequately clothed for the weather she joined him for what would be her first excursion outdoors since the day of the ice storm. Unlike that freezing cold day, the sun was shining and the weather warmer than it had been in months. Spring was on its way, and she couldn't have been more pleased.

For the most part, the ride into Boston was uneventful. The bright sunshine made it a great day for traveling. She could see buds beginning to emerge on the birch trees growing beside the road, and as the snow on the ground continued to recede, patches of winter gold grass dotted the open fields. The Concord Road was ofttimes difficult to navigate during the winter due to the uneven hilly terrain upon which it was built. Their wagon encountered flooding in some of the low spots but the levels weren't deep enough to impede their progress.

It was slow going. At one point during the journey, Nicholas had to steer the horses to the far side of the road in order to make room for the stagecoach that roared up from behind. The coaches began in 1764

allowing travelers to make it from New York to Philadelphia, the largest city in the colonies, in three days.
Now the coaches were much faster and the same trip
took only two days. Colonists called the fast coaches
flying machines.

After the passing of the stage, Nicholas got the wagon
under way again, and as it seesawed back and forth over
the cobbles, he groused, "I'm envious."

"Of what?"

"Their speed," he replied, indicating the coach pulling farther and farther ahead. "I'm accustomed to being
on horseback when I travel. This wagon will us take all
day. Makes me feel like a farmer."

"You are a farmer."

He shot her a look. She grinned and turned her attention back to the passing landscape of trees, taverns,
and family farms. They passed a wagon heading in the
opposite direction being driven by a man of color. He
was dressed in the fashion of the day, including the
popular tricorn hat, but his clothing looked old, and
on his legs were the blue-striped hose farm slaves were
mandated to wear. As he passed, he nodded a greeting
and they replied in kind.

They were soon approaching the section of the road
that led past her father's inn and Faith steeled her heart
to keep her emotions in check.

Nicholas seemed to sense her mood because he sent
a questioning look her way. "Are you all right?"

"Yes. I'm fine." It was her first look at the place since

her banishment. In truth, a part of her hoped to catch a glimpse of her father to see how he might be faring, but sterner parts chastised her for wanting such a thing in the face of his actions towards her. However, he was still her father; her only parent, and deep down inside the love she'd had for him still echoed with pain.

It was mid morning when they arrived in Boston and because the narrow twisting streets were filled with traffic, they were forced to go slow.

The walks lining the streets were filled with people beginning their day, and the stalls belonging to itinerant businessmen were being pushed in place. Faith noted the increasing number of shuttered shops, businesses, and taverns. General Gage's Intolerable Act of closing the harbor to shipping was taking its toll on the goods available for purchase, leaving angry merchants and shopkeepers little choice but to shutter their businesses or contract with smugglers. The hated blockade was devastating what was once the most robust economy in the colonies.

Up ahead loomed the British custom house which during the 1750s came under attack by the local populace incensed by the Sugar and Stamp Acts. The tax agent was hanged in effigy and an angry mob descended on his place of residence. They broke in, stole everything of value, and destroyed everything else; walls, floors, windows. They were in the process of tearing off the roof when the soldiers arrived and finally put an end to the anarchy. Boston citizens were a major thorn in the crown's side and they were proud of it. As a result the four thousand soldiers were a looming presence.

"So many soldiers," she said to Nick quietly.

"Yes, they seem to be everywhere."

Their red coats made them conspicuous and their strength in numbers made them a significant percentage of the city's population. They stood in groups on street corners, marched in the streets, and were stoned, cursed, and scorned. Almost as numerous were the signs of rebellion. Broadsides exhorting people to fight blared their message in large letters nailed to the sides of buildings and on doors of shops and taverns. Liberty poles bearing the drawing of the severed snake first seen in Ben Franklin's paper, the *Pennsylvania Gazette*, continued to be displayed, no matter how many times the soldiers tore them down. The city was under siege and one could feel the tension in the air.

"Where are we going?" she asked. They passed a town crier ringing a cow's bell and announcing that he'd found a lost boy of about six years of age. Faith saw the little teary-eyed child walking at the crier's side. She hoped his parents would return to claim him soon.

"I want to see if Prince Hall is at home, and then do a bit of shopping. Where is Charity's mother's shop?"

She told him where.

"Then we'll stop there after I talk with Hall."

Prince lived in the northern part of the city that had been home to the small free Black community since the 1640s. People were busily moving around in this part of town as day workers headed off to their jobs as cooks, cleaning women, and apprentices, and business owners hurried to their shops.

He parked as close to the Hall residence as the traffic allowed and stepped down onto the street. "I'll only be a moment."

Faith wondered what he was about but didn't ask. Although they were to be married, they both had secrets.

Nick found Hall working in the shed he used as his leather shop.

"Morning, Nicholas."

Nick watched as he rubbed oil into a large square of tanned leather. "What's that to be?"

"Skin for a war drum. Hoping to get it done before Gage marches on us. Have orders from a few other regiments wanting new skins, too." He glanced up. "What brings you around?"

"Wanted to let you know that the guns for your men will be arriving soon."

Prince stilled and studied him for a long moment. "I suppose I shouldn't ask how you managed that."

"No, but I'll let you know when they arrive."

Prince looked away for a moment, then finally shook his head as if amused. "Who are you really, Nick?"

"Primus's son."

Prince smiled at the simple reply. "All right. My thanks in advance for your help."

"You're welcome."

They took a few moments to discuss the ongoing drilling and Nick departed.

While waiting for Nick to return, Faith glanced up and down the street. She knew that Gage had Hall's residence under surveillance just as he did those of other patriots tied to the rebellion, but she saw no one on the walks who appeared to be serving that purpose. Then she noticed a man standing in the shadow of the doorway of a sweet shop a few doors down and directly across the street. His dirty clothing and face had all the appearance of a vagrant but his eyes, so clear and focused, were riveted on Hall's front door. When he met her eyes, he smoothly looked away and then staggered drunkenly away.

Chapter 17

When Nicholas returned and they were again under way, she said, "I saw a man I believe was watching Hall's home."

Nick nodded. "He knows he's being spied upon so he's being very discreet about who he allows to visit."

That was good to know. She didn't want him to suffer Primus's fate. "Have you made any progress finding Primus's betrayer?"

"No. I've talked to his friends, but I know little more than I did upon my return to Boston."

Faith sighed with the injustice of that. She almost asked if he still considered her father a suspect but kept the question unspoken because after her father's perfidy, she could no longer be sure about anything concerning him. Nicholas had also asked that they not discuss his guilt or innocence and she continued to think that best.

They found a place to park and left the wagon to walk across the street to the shop owned by Charity's mother, Babette Locke. Babette grew up in the French Indies as a slave to a mixed-blood seamstress. She and the mistress left the islands to immigrate to the colonies but the seamstress died on the passage and was buried at sea. Babette spent the remainder of the voyage forging a set of free papers that designated her as the half sister of the dead woman. She entered her new life as a free woman of color, married a free Black man, and became highly sought after by the wealthy women of the colony because of her outstanding needle skills.

Upon seeing Faith enter she threw open her arms. "Ah, Faith."

Faith let herself be enfolded in Babette's well-bosomed embrace and basked in the familiar hug she'd been receiving since the Lockes moved to Boston when Charity was fifteen.

"And who might his be?" Babette asked.

Faith looked to Nicholas. "Mrs. Locke, this is Nicholas Grey."

"Primus's son? The one everyone is speculating about?"

Faith grinned. "He is the son of Primus. I'm not certain about the speculating."

Babette curtsied. "*Enchanté*, Mr. Grey."

Nicholas bowed. "My pleasure, Mrs. Locke."

With the introductions done, Faith asked, "What is this speculating concerning?"

"Which young woman he will choose as his wife, of course."

Nicholas smiled but kept silent.

"He's chosen me."

Babette's green eyes widened with happiness. *"Non!"*

"Yes."

"Oh my. I must take your measurements. I will make you the gown of your dreams." She stopped to gauge Faith critically. "Now for color. Maybe indigo, or a forest green?"

Faith held up her hand before Babette could work herself into a tizzy. "There won't be time. We're to be wed in the next few days, we are hoping."

Babette looked between the two of them. "So soon? Does Charity know about this hasty pudding wedding?"

"Yes, ma'am," Nicholas replied, hiding his smile.

"Then if you are not here for a wedding gown, how may I assist?"

"I need some new shifts."

Babette nodded, "Knowing that miser who calls himself your father, you probably need much more."

Faith didn't want to back Nicholas into a corner by making him pay for more garments than he could afford so she didn't respond.

But he apparently didn't mind corners because he asked, "Would it be too much to ask that you provide her with everything? Shifts, nightclothes, and the rest?"

Faith opened her mouth to protest but Babette was already replying, "My work is not cheap; even with the reduced price you will be receiving due to my love of your intended, the price will be substantial."

"Price is not a problem, madam."

"As you wish," she said, beaming, eyeing him in an entirely new light.

Faith was staring up at him in astonishment. "I simply need a few shifts."

Babette, still assessing Nicholas, said to Faith, "Hush, child. Let your man spend his coin as he sees fit. I will get my tapes."

A defeated Faith sighed audibly as Mrs. Locke hurried into the back of her shop to get her tools of the trade.

While she was away, Faith said to him, "This is a waste of perfectly good coin."

"Faith, your underwear has more patches than a quilt."

Her eyes narrowed warningly, but the return of Mrs. Locke kept her from responding. Instead she stood quietly as the measurements were taken while he looked on, amused. To her further dismay, he asked about purchasing a few day dresses.

"I have some readymade samples in the back that may fit," Mrs. Locke said, sizing Faith up. "Come with me, chèrie."

Once they were alone, Faith got out of her clothes, and after standing for a few moments in her dingy white shift, knee-length drawers, stockings, and ankle boots, she took the ensemble handed to her upon Mrs. Locke's return—a soft gray wool skirt and over jacket.

Faith stared in wonder. Included was a fine-gauge white blouse with long sleeves and lace-edged cuffs meant to be worn beneath the jacket. The skirt and jacket were piped in strips of black velvet, and they were beautiful, the most beautiful garments she'd ever held in her hands. "How much will all this cost, Mrs. Locke?" the overwhelmed Faith asked.

Babette shook her head. "Does Charity know how you and the *très magnifique* Mr. Grey came to be together?"

"Yes."

"Then I'll hear the tale when I visit her tonight. In the meantime it's time for you to get dressed. No more questions. Your man is waiting."

Faith looked down at the lovely ensemble lying across her arm and then up at Charity's mother. "But Mrs. Locke—"

Babette held up a silencing, well-manicured finger. "Faith, you are blessed enough to have a man who is willing to provide for you in a way that is rare. Whatever the circumstances surrounding this sudden marriage, he cares about you. It's in his eyes. You are not to throw it back into his face."

Faith dropped her head. "I'm just—"

"I know, just being the very frugal Faith Kingston that Charity and I know and love. That is not a detriment. Being frugal is a strength, one you have had to master your entire life."

"But suppose he's spending himself into the poorhouse showing me he cares."

"And suppose he is not? Suppose he can afford this and more for the rest of your lives? What then?"

Faith went quiet.

Babette hugged her shoulders affectionately. "Let the man be nice to you. And if you do wind up in the alms-house, at least you will be well dressed."

Faith laughed softly and slipped on the blouse.

When they returned to the front of the store, they found Nicholas seated in one of the chairs and leafing through the shop's pattern book. He looked up at their entrance and upon seeing Faith, he stopped, slowly set the book aside, and got to his feet. "You look grand."

Faith gave him an embarrassed smile. "And it's really warm. Much warmer than my cotton dress."

Nicholas found the transformation stunning. The gray jacket and skirt fit perfectly and the cut of the jacket gracefully accented her curves. The snow white blouse peeking out underneath the cuffs and neckline made her look as fashionable as any other woman on the streets of the city.

Mrs. Locke added, "The ensemble has a matching cape and bonnet. Did you want to add those also?"

"Yes," he replied, unable to take his eyes off the lovely picture Faith made. He'd wrap her in diamonds if he could. His inner voice questioned where that shocking thought had originated but he paid it no mind. He was hooked on this woman like a bass on a line. It made little sense, and he had no explanation, but it didn't matter. "How long will it take you to finish the other garments?"

Babette shrugged. "A month."

"If you can make it two weeks, you may add a five percent bonus to my bill."

She smiled. "Then two weeks it will be."

"Agreed."

Babette looked affectionately in Faith's direction. "Take care of her, Mr. Grey. She is very precious. And I expect to be invited to the wedding."

"You are more than welcome to join us," Faith said sincerely. "I'll send word by Charity about the date."

"Excellent. I will see you then, and congratulations to you both."

As they started to the door, Nicholas spotted a display that held a variety of bath salts, small bottles of hand lotions, and scents. Stopping, he picked up a few and brought them to his nose. Faith watched silently, but Mrs. Locke walked over to see if he needed assistance. The two of them spent a few minutes narrowing down his choices, and without consulting Faith he purchased them, and once they were placed in a small sack, he and Faith left the store.

Faith asked, "Are you always this flippant with your coin?"

"Buying you new drawers is not being flippant."

A scandalized Faith looked around to see if he'd been overhead by the people they were passing on the walks. "Mrs. Locke says I'm not to argue with you about this."

"Then she is both beautiful and wise." Nicholas didn't know whether to be upset with her or amused. She obviously felt strongly about his spending, but to be frank, she'd been dressed like waif since the first day they met. The hems of the two skirts she owned were frayed, as was the lace around the necks of her two blouses, and the cuffs of the long sleeves. Her father, on the other hand, had always been well outfitted in handsome breeches and coats. Yet another sin to add to Stuart Kingston's slate, he grumbled inwardly. As they crossed the street he looked over at her in fashionable bonnet and matching cape and declared, "I'm about to spend more unnecessary money on you, Faith, so prepare yourself."

Her smile peeked out. "All right. Where now?"

"Wherever you purchase your Dutch ovens. You said you'd need more for your bread baking."

Faith stopped and studied his eyes. As people passed by them on the crowded walk, she asked quietly, "You're actually going to help me with this?"

"I said I would. Have you changed your mind?"

"No, I—" She was moved and a bit overcome. "Thank you, Nicholas."

"You're welcome. No more lectures?"

"No," she pledged. "No more. Ever."

"Which we both know is a lie," he countered, chuckling.

She dropped her head.

He lifted her chin and stared down into her eyes, and Faith's body heard his silent call. "You'd probably sock me if I kissed you out here in front of God and everybody, so I'll wait until we are alone."

Faith was shaking as if they were alone. "The shop is a few blocks west."

Amusement in his gaze, he ran a caressing finger down her chin before saying, "Lead the way."

On the wagon ride home, Faith couldn't remember ever being so content. She was pleased with her new cape and clothing, the Dutch ovens, the trivets, and everything else he'd laid out coin for, from flour, spices, and new linens for her bed, to big fat candles for her to read by at night. She was content, but her head was spinning as well. No one had ever spent time shopping exclusively for her needs; her father certainly hadn't. Asking for new clothing had at times led to arguments as to whether her needs were dear enough. Now, however, she was wearing the first new clothes she'd had in years and they were made of wool so fine and soft, she felt wealthy and important. Charity's mother was correct, she was blessed to have Nicholas in her life.

The drive took them past her father's inn again. She noticed that there were a number of wagons, horses, and carriages parked out front. As she wondered what might be going on inside, Elizabeth Sutter and her mother stepped out of a carriage, and Faith stilled. Elizabeth was wearing a black velvet cape over what appeared to be a beautiful blue gown. Was the wedding about to take place? She looked over at Nicholas. He viewed the scene for a moment and then said, "I believe your father may be heading for a different type of adventure."

She agreed, especially in the face of the rumors that Elizabeth was carrying a child. "I hope he'll be happy."

"He won't be, but spoken like a true daughter."

She chuckled and settled in for the rest of the ride.

When they drove up to the house there was a small group of mounted British soldiers waiting out front. Faith stiffened and asked, "Do you have anything incriminating on your person?"

"Only a copy of the *Massachusetts Spy*."

The *Spy* was the newspaper published by Isaiah Thomas. His scathing editorials flayed the British mercilessly. Many people, mostly Tories, labeled his writings treasonous, but so far Gage hadn't had him arrested.

Faith's second shock came when she realized that one of the soldiers was Henri Giles.

Nicholas stopped the wagon and set the brake. "Afternoon, Henri."

"Nick."

Faith's third shock.

"Miss Kingston, how are you?"

"I'm well, Lieutenant Giles, and you, sir?"

It was Nicholas's turn to be shocked. "I take it you two have been introduced."

Henri nodded. "Miss Kingston and her father were nice enough to invite me over for supper a few weeks back."

Nicholas looked curiously over at Faith and then back to Giles. "What brings you to my door?"

"A matter that needs discussing." He turned to the members of the patrol. "Mr. Grey is an acquaintance. I'll speak with him and get this matter resolved. Continue the patrol and I'll meet you later."

They nodded and rode away.

After the departure, Nicholas asked, "Well?"

"Mr. Kingston wants you arrested for holding his daughter against her will."

Faith stared.

Nicholas shook his head. "Let me unhitch the wagon and we'll go inside."

A short while later they convened in the parlor.

Nicholas asked, "So he's claiming Faith is being harmed?"

"Yes, and that she was in serious distress."

Faith asked, "Do I appear to be in distress, Henri?"

"No. In truth you look rather well."

"Thank you."

Nicholas glanced between the two and wondered if this was what jealousy felt like.

"Is something wrong?" she asked him, peering at him closely.

"No."

Giles smiled Nick's way as if he knew what Nick had been thinking, and then asked her, "So how did you come to be here?"

"My father became angry and cast me out."

"He cast you out?"

So once again, Faith related the circumstances that led to her being at the Grey home.

At the conclusion of her tale, he shook his head. "My apologies. I had no idea he was lying to me about the situation."

Faith said, "And here I had just wished him happiness in his marriage."

Nicholas added yet another sin to Kingston's slate. "So what will you tell your superiors?"

"The truth. The only reason we were sent was because Kingston appealed to General Gage for assistance."

Nicholas did not like the sound of that. The last thing he needed was to draw Gage's eye, especially in light of his father's fate and the guns he was hoping to take possession of soon.

Faith snapped, "How dare he go to Gage when he is the cause of all this, and I resent his underhanded ways of attempting to make me return simply because Elizabeth can't cook a decent breakfast, or whatever his reason is. He made it plain to me that he and Elizabeth didn't want me in their home. I bowed to his wishes." She looked Giles in the eye and said, "And make certain you tell your superiors that Nicholas and I are to be married, just in case my morals are called into question and Father wants some ridiculous tribunal convened to decide my fate."

"You're marrying? Nick?"

"You sound as if that's troubling, Lieutenant," she stated, eyeing him coolly.

Nicholas smiled and hoped Giles had the sense to stow whatever else he had to say before she filleted him like a trout.

"No, Miss Kingston," he offered up hastily. "Not troubling in the least. In fact, let me offer my congratulations."

Smart man, Nicholas thought.

Giles glanced Nick's way but Nicholas kept his amusement hidden.

"I hope you both will be very happy."

"Thank you. And now"—she paused and stood—"I shall you leave you two to catch up on old times. Nicholas, I'll be upstairs. I had a wonderful day."

Both men rose chivalrously.

Nicholas inclined his head.

She looked to Giles. "Henri. It's been a pleasure seeing you again."

"Pleasure seeing you as well."

She exited and closed the doors so they could converse privately.

After her departure, Henri remarked, "She's quite a fiery woman."

"That she is," Nicholas agreed. "And her father, the village idiot."

"Appears that way. I should apologize to you as well."

Nick waved him off. "I'm accused of abducting women all the time."

Henri nodded and grinned. "Glad to see you made it off the *Stella* alive."

"Looked for you in the madness, but had to go overboard to save myself. Many men died in the fire. Many more when it sank."

The *Stella* had been a British frigate. With over one hundred impressed sailors among the crew, the mutiny that occurred during Nick's tenth month at sea seemed inevitable. It was not a pleasant time in either man's life. "Where'd you go after the fire?" Nick asked.

"Found some smugglers who were sailing east and signed on. Spent a couple of years with them and various others in the trade. Rather liked it. Worked my way back to England and then to Canada and home. What about you?"

"Merchant ship that cast off the following morning. Took at least five of us on and the admiral's stallion. He was a smuggler, too. Guns."

"Always a market for those."

"Always. Especially if your clients are maroon villages in Jamaica and the Indies. He also did some business here in the colonies as well. I never knew there were so many maroon encampments in the southern swamps."

"Not something the slave owners want known.

Escaped slaves armed and living free? Other slaves might escape to join them and then chaos would result."

They shared a look and Nicholas chuckled.

Henri asked, "So how'd you end up in Boston?"

"Was born here. In this very house in fact."

"I didn't know that. When did you return?"

"Last month. Have been in New York for the past few years. It's where I was living when the Royal Marines shanghaied me."

"At least we are alive to tell the story."

"And for that I am grateful. And now you are wearing a British uniform."

"Let's just say there's a profit in it."

"Still smuggling, I take it."

Henri smiled. "Just enough to send money home to my mother and sisters, and to keep me from having to beg employment at the taverns like some of the soldiers are forced to do. King George doesn't pay enough for his men to subsist on, and the food and lodgings are worse. So one has to be inventive to survive."

"I've a few irons in the fire as well." He didn't say more. Henri didn't need to know anything about Nick's business dealings.

"If I can assist, let me know."

"I'll keep it in mind. Are you planning on being here for the duration?"

"I hope not. There's going to be a war. I've no stomach for more death and dying."

"Neither do I."

Henri looked at the small clock on the mantel. "I should rejoin my fellows." He stood and Nicholas did the same. Nicholas walked him to the front door.

"Give Miss Kingston my regards?" Henri said.

"I will."

"You're a lucky man, Nicholas Grey."

"Yes, I am."

"I assume you are supporting the rebels?"

"I'd support hogs over the British," Nick replied fiercely.

"I understand. I've no idea how much longer I'll be in Boston, but if I don't see you again, be well and enjoy your life."

"You do the same." Nicholas watched until he rode away before closing the door.

Chapter 18

Upstairs in her room, Faith finally stopped the angry pacing caused by her father's actions. She realized there was nothing to be done about him for the moment, so she focused on undressing and hanging her cape and the rest of her new ensemble in the armoire. Giving the soft fabric one last appreciative stroke, she drew on one of her old skirts, added a blouse, and did up the buttons. Her mind strayed to Nicholas. She'd made him a promise that she wouldn't question his spending, but she couldn't help but wonder how he'd made the fortune he seemed to have, and of less importance, how and where he and Henri first met.

A knock on the door made her look up. "Yes?"

"May I come in?" It was Nicholas.

"Yes, of course."

She went to the door but he was already entering. It came to her that he was without a doubt the most handsome man she'd ever seen. "Has Henri gone?"

"Yes. He sends his regards."

"Where did you two meet?"

"On a British frigate. I'd been impressed and so had he."

Faith shook her head sadly. "I've heard terrible stories."

"All of them true, no doubt. I was in a tavern on the docks of New York when a group of Royal Marines entered. They announced their intentions, a fight ensued, and I was hit over the head and knocked out. When I woke up, I was on a ship in the middle of the Atlantic."

Faith's heart went out to him. "How long did you serve?"

"Almost a year. Henri and I both managed to escape when the crew mutinied and the ship was set afire."

"I'm sorry you were forced to endure impressments."

"So am I."

Impressed men were sometimes chained and whipped to keep them in line. She hoped he hadn't been subjected to that as well, but the granitelike set of his features told all. To lighten the mood, she said, "Thank you again for my purchases."

"Again, you are welcome, and thank you for changing the subject. Those are times I'd rather not revisit."

"I understand. How about I let you revisit my traitorous father instead, and you can tar and feather him this time for siccing the patrol on us."

"If I thought you meant it, I'd already be on my horse," he replied with amusement in his eyes.

She laughed softly. "Whatever are we going to do about him?"

Nicholas walked to her and draped his arms loosely around her waist, and said, looking down at her, "We aren't going to do anything. At least not this minute. Right now, you are going to let me kiss you the way I wanted to on the street."

She raised an eyebrow and replied with humor-laden skepticism, "And if I say no?"

He traced a slow finger over her lips, bent down, and whispered, "Then you'll be missing this . . ."

It was the first kiss of the day, and the brushes of his lips, coupled with the seductive timbre of his voice, made denying him unthinkable. His fervent mouth made hers catch fire instantaneously, and they pulled each other closer. Roaming hands, breathless sighs, and kisses that traveled over lips, jaws, and the planes of cheeks stoked passion higher. In the timeless moments that followed she lost touch with everything but his caresses and her soaring response. She'd no remembrance of him opening her blouse, but when her shift was pulled aside and his mouth found her breasts, she moaned and tightened with scandalous delight. He lingered, teasing and tonguing until her moans turned to groans. His hand moved up and down her shift-covered torso, then circled low to possessively cup her hips. When he raised himself to capture her lips again, he shoved her skirt gently up her thighs and moved the bunched-up fabric freely over the loose-fitting drawers. The heat of his exploring palm pierced the worn, patched cotton, and Faith knew she was going to dissolve into steam.

"Someone's knocking at the door downstairs," he whispered against her ear. "Let's bring you to pleasure and then I'll go shoot whoever it is."

Faith hadn't heard a thing. Her entire world was filled with sensations, so when he boldly slipped his hands into the long slit of her drawers and stroked the damp vent between her thighs, she shattered like a glass hit by a stone. Her high-pitched yell combined with the now familiar shuddering that accompanied her body's uninhibited release rocked her like the boom of cannon. She was still riding the remnants of the storm when he kissed her softly and departed, leaving her breathless, shuddering, and alone.

Downstairs, Nick snatched the door open. "What?"

It was Arte. "Good afternoon to you, too," he cracked. "Why're you growling at me?"

"What do you want?" Nick asked, holding on to his patience.

"Did I catch you at a bad time?"

"You can say that."

Arte looked chagrined. "My apologies. Just came to let you know that Uncle Ab will be here on Saturday at two, to marry you and Faith, if that's agreeable."

"It is. Thank you."

"Sorry again." He left the porch quickly and Nick closed the door.

Upstairs, she was standing just as he'd left her; clothes in disarray, lips swollen from his kisses.

"Who was at the door?" she asked quietly.

"Arte. We're to be married at two on Saturday."

Her eyes lingered on his mouth, then rose slowly to his face. "That will give Charity time to make the cake."

He walked over to where she stood by the fire and dragged a slow finger over the soft tops of her velvet breasts and down the valley between. Leaning in, he used the tip of his tongue to taste the spot and pressed his lips against the nook of her throat. His manhood was hard as a length of mahogany. He wanted her to touch him, but knew it was too soon to ask that of her; she was still new at this dance, so he concentrated on her pleasuring instead.

The fog rose up again to enclose Faith in a world where only they and desire existed. Sunlight poured through the room's many windows, highlighting something else she didn't know. She thought lovemaking was only done while lying in bed at night, but that was obviously not true. What was true was that he was an expert at this, and when his fingers between her thighs showed how much, she shattered and cried out again.

Nicholas was breathing as if he'd run a race and he forced himself to move away from her or break his vow to wait for her to become his wife. He retreated across the room and took up a position near the windows, hoping the distance might help him regain control.

He saw that she was breathing just as harshly. As she stood there with her nipples hard and her lips parted, the hunger in her passion-lidded eyes made him turn away or be lost. "I need you to right your clothing again, Faith."

Because he had his back turned he missed the slow smile that crossed her lips as she complied. After a few moments of silence, he heard her say, "I'm done, Nicholas."

He turned and saw that although she was dressed, it would be a while before the way she tasted and felt faded from his body's memory. In truth, he'd want her for a lifetime, but for the moment, he just needed his desire to retreat long enough for his breathing to normalize and his manhood to stop its virile pulsing. "You're very tempting, Miss Kingston."

"As are you, Mr. Grey."

"Are you enjoying this part of our adventure?"

"Very much."

Nick wondered what their children might look like. Would there be raven-eyed daughters who were miniatures of their mother, or tall, lean boys with features reminiscent of him and their late grandfather. He'd settle for either just as long as he could continue to visually feast on her loveliness.

Later, they shared dinner at the small table in the kitchen. The warmth and light emanating from the fire made the atmosphere in the room very cozy.

Nicholas watched her moving around the kitchen

putting up the last of the dishes and utensils they'd used for the meal, and he admitted that he knew next to nothing about her other than how much he craved her kisses, but he wanted to know more about Faith, the woman. "Have you and your father done much traveling?"

She shook her head as she retook her seat at the table. All the chores were done for the day. "Other than to Lexington and Concord for church events, no."

"Never been to Philadelphia or New York?"

"Or down South, or to Rhode Island, or anywhere else but here. How did you come to live with the Iroquois?"

He didn't respond for a few moments due to the flow of his memories. "It was during the Seven Years' War. My father and I were with a British unit in New York. We were split into two patrols; he was in one, I was in the other. One morning, my unit came across an Iroquois village made of four longhouses."

"What's a longhouse?"

"It's a very long house," he said, smiling. "It's made of upright poles and covered with tight layers of bark to keep out the weather. Some are a hundred feet long and twenty feet high."

"These are Iroquois homes?"

"Yes. Inside, there's often two living levels. The lower level for gatherings and cooking, and a place for the fire to keep everyone warm. The upper floor is usually for sleeping."

"I guess I never thought about how they lived or

what they lived in. All you hear are tales of savagery and butchery."

"Makes it easier to take their land if they aren't seen as human."

She nodded her understanding.

"So on that day, we saw the village. A few days earlier, a farm a few miles away had been burned, and the occupants, a man, his wife, and three children had perished in the flames. Our lieutenant had no evidence that the people in this particular village of Iroquois were responsible, but he didn't care. He ordered us to open fire, and we did."

Nicholas quieted for a few moments and relived the sounds of the guns, the smells of the powder, the screams of the terrified women and children. "The men of the village must have been out hunting because there were less than a handful left there to oppose us when we opened our guns. They had only knives and hatchets, but they charged us anyway, giving their lives in the hope that some of the many women and children fleeing out the longhouse's doors and into the woods would survive our assault."

She tightened her lips and shook her head.

"In the midst of all the smoke, chaos, and death, someone in our unit put a torch to the houses and the four structures began to burn. By then, any Iroquois who could flee had done so and the men in our unit began to celebrate and cheer. Just as the last house became fully engulfed we heard a baby wailing. The cheering stopped and some of the men appeared concerned but it was just an Indian baby so . . ."

"So no one cared."

"It seemed that way. Yes, we were at war, but this was a baby. I told the lieutenant I couldn't stand by and let a child burn to death. He told me if I broke ranks, he'd have my fellows shoot me."

Faith's mouth dropped open.

"So I disobeyed orders, and by the time I reached the burning house, I had five balls in my back."

"No!"

"Yes. Somehow I still managed to find the child and when I did, I took him out of that burning building, put him inside my coat, and stumbled off into the forest in the direction the tribe had taken. I swore never to serve in the British Army again."

"So what happened next? You obviously lived."

"Barely. There was another longhouse village a day's walk away. I didn't know it at the time, I was just hoping to find the baby's people. By that point, I was delirious and in so much pain, I'd no idea where I was. The clan mothers said I walked into the village in the middle of the night and collapsed by a fire. They opened my coat to see if my heart was still beating and found the babe."

"And they nursed you back to health."

He nodded. "Eventually, yes."

"As you did me."

He nodded again.

"And the babe was well?"

"Yes. He turned out to be the grandson of the clan matriarch. She was very grateful that I'd saved his life."

"How long did you stay with them?"

"A year or so. Long enough to develop a fondness for sleeping on a pelt pallet and to learn their ways and myths."

"And after leaving them, where did you go?"

"North and west. Spent the next few years trapping, selling, and trading furs; guiding settlers; and accumulating enough wealth from the furs and the rest to call myself a very wealthy man."

"So that explains why you are so loose with your coin."

"I'm not loose. Since I can't take it with me, why not buy you new drawers."

She dropped her head and chuckled.

"In fact, the night I was shanghaied I was in a tavern celebrating having sold a load of furs to a Russian count. After vowing to never have anything to do with British military forces again, you can imagine my anger at finding myself impressed into their navy."

"That had to have been terribly upsetting."

"A polite way of stating it. I hate the British."

After hearing his story Faith understood why.

He looked at her and said, "This was supposed to have been a conversation about you and your life and I ended up talking about mine."

"That's quite all right. My life hasn't been nearly as exciting."

"I would have been happier with less, believe me."

Faith studied him silently for a long few moments. The two of them had needed this quiet together because now she knew more about him. He'd claimed to be half tamed and she understood a bit better what he'd meant. All that he'd experienced helped mold him into the man he'd become, and in a few more days he was going to become her husband. How would that mold them both?

"What are you thinking, Faith?" he asked quietly.

She shrugged. "Just how we are molded by our lives. Mine has been a life of frugalness and self-reliance, all the things a goodly raised woman should be, yet I've never seen the sun rise or set except here in Boston, while you've seen it all over the world. Parts of me envy you those experiences." She added, "Not the terrible ones though."

He smiled his understanding. "Then maybe we'll take a wedding trip when the weather warms. Since Philadelphia is the largest city in the colonies, we'll go there."

She brightened. "Truly?"

"Truly."

"We'll take the stagecoach and you can begin having your own experiences."

"I'd like that."

"Good." Nicholas thought about how simple it

seemed to please her. He'd known women in the past who would never have questioned the amount of money spent on them, but this little Tory-raised rose had fretted and nearly worried him to distraction. She was special; intelligent, bossy, beautiful, and blunt, but becoming even more special every moment they were together. Parts of Nicholas knew this was love, but he chose not to acknowledge it.

She had a question. "Will you be content to be a farmer after living life so freely?"

"I asked myself the very same thing a few days after my return, but I'm adjusting."

He paused a moment to look into her face and then said, "Besides, I have you around now, and that will probably be all the excitement I'll need."

"We'll see," she said, smiling. "We'll see."

Chapter 19

The day of the wedding, Faith awakened to dark clouds and rain. She supposed somewhere in the world such a downpour was greeted as a positive sign for a couple about to embark upon marriage, but in the colonies, it was just wet. With no alternative but to put a happy face on the situation, she got out of bed to start the day.

Two days had passed since their talk in the kitchen and she'd spent the time in between preparing the house for the wedding and the guests. Nicholas searched out Adeline's good china and found it packed away in tarp-lined crates in the cellar. The gold-edged plates had a single rose in the center, and their beauty outshone any other china Faith had seen. In the crates were every-thing from teacups to gravy boats, and she spent the remainder of the afternoon washing them and placing them in the dining room's highboy where Nicholas said they'd been kept when he was growing up. There were crystal goblets and silverware, some of it still in its original packaging, which made Faith wonder sadly if Adeline had died before she could use them. When passing through the parlor, Faith stopped and looked up at her portrait often, wondering what she'd been like, and what role she'd played in the feud between her father and Primus, but Adeline remained posed and silent, offering only the secretive smile in her eyes as her reply.

But now Faith was in the kitchen. It was still dark and she hoped the pounding rain would run its course before the pastor and the guests arrived later that afternoon. With breakfast on the fire and Nicholas's awful-tasting coffee ready to be poured, Faith was setting plates on the table when he walked in.

"Good morning," he said to her. "I'd hoped to come down and make breakfast for you today but as I can see, I'm late."

"Good morning, and yes, you are."

"After today, you are allowed to get up after sunrise."

"Why wait for sunrise when there are chores to do?" she asked, pausing to study his face.

He chuckled softly. "This isn't the Kingston Inn, sweet Faith. No one here but the two of us."

"And?"

He folded his arms and studied her. "You don't have to work so hard anymore, is what I'm trying to say to you."

She took that in for a moment and replied, "Oh." Getting up later wasn't anything Faith had ever considered. Rising before dawn so that she and her father could breakfast at six had been her routine since she was eight or nine years old. "I've never been a lazybones, Nicholas."

"And I'm not asking you to be. I'm just asking you to be human." And he added with an indulgent smile and voice, "If you can."

That touched her heart. "I will try. I'll get up at five tomorrow."

He raised an eyebrow.

"Six then," she said, amending her claim.

"Better."

Faith decided she liked this man, very much.

"And besides, tonight will be our wedding night. You may not want to get up tomorrow until noon."

"I've never stayed in bed that late."

"There's a first time for everything, Faith Kingston, and tonight will be one of those new experiences you've been seeking."

She blinked.

"Coffee ready?"

Tearing herself away from humor reflected in his eyes, she stammered, "Um. Yes."

Padding her hand with a cloth, she picked up the coffeepot and carried it to the table.

Charity showed up just as Faith was finishing the kitchen cleanup. She had the cake, her hair irons, the food she was providing for the wedding meal, a tarp-covered crate of unknown contents, and a tarp-covered garment on a hanger. Faith assumed the hanger held the dress Charity planned to change into later for the wedding. However, after they stowed the food and she and Charity went up to Faith's room, Faith found her assumption had been wrong.

After removing the tarp, Charity laid the dress on the bed, and when she drew away the layer of linen it was wrapped in, Faith stood gaping at the most beautiful ball gown in the world. "Mama said you are to wear this."

The bodice and overskirt were the palest yellow. The layers of tiered petticoats visible between the open panels of the over skirt were snow white, as was the lace on the square-cut décolletage and the cuffs of the long sleeves. The dress was breathtaking enough for a queen. "Charity, I can't wear this."

"We knew you'd say that so I'm simply going to ignore it."

Faith stared in amazement. "She couldn't have finished this in the time since I've seen her. Where did this come from?"

"Paris. Mama shipped it to a client last fall but the woman returned it with a note saying it didn't fit well. It arrived yesterday. We're hoping it'll fit you."

A few days ago, Faith had made the decision to wear her new gray suit as her wedding clothes, but this gorgeous confection would be unlike anything she'd ever worn before. "I will be very careful not to dirty it so that your mother may have it back."

Charity smiled and shook her head. "If it fits you are to keep it. Mama says it's her wedding gift. She'll be here in time for the ceremony."

Faith gaped.

"Close your mouth and sit so that I can start your hair."

Faith complied, but her eyes kept straying to the dress.

With her hair done and her dress on, Faith viewed herself in the mirror and felt tears wet her eyes.

Charity scolded, "Don't you dare cry. We'll both be downstairs with swollen eyes and that won't be a pretty sight. You look beautiful."

"Yes, I do," she whispered. The dress fit well. The square neckline offered only a tiniest hint of the rise of her breasts but to Faith's eyes it appeared very daring. "I'm not accustomed to showing my neck this way."

"It's only for a few hours, Faith. You can go back to being clothed to your ears tomorrow."

Both women grinned.

There was a knock on the door.

"Yes," Faith called.

"It's Bekkah Clegg. May I come in?"

"Yes, please," Faith replied earnestly.

Bekkah was tall and had hair the color of a bonfire. She also had a smile on her face. "You look so beautiful. Oh my word, what a gown."

Faith beamed.

"I came up to introduce myself and to see if you need any assistance." She nodded Charity's way. "Wonderful seeing you again, Charity."

"How are you, Bekkah?"

"You know each other then?"

Charity explained that they had worked on a church aid project together a few years ago.

Faith said, "I'd like to thank you for bringing over the food while I was sick, and for your helping out today."

"I'm glad to do it. I've known Nicholas since we were very young and I'm looking forward to the two of us knowing each other as well."

They spent a few minutes talking about the dishes she'd brought over, and once that was done, Bekkah turned to leave, but Faith stopped her. "Please stay. If we're going to be friends I'd like for you to enter the parlor with us."

Bekkah paused and met Faith's eyes, then she gave an almost imperceptible nod. "How can I turn down such a gracious request. Thank you, Faith."

"You're welcome."

Twenty-five minutes later, at precisely two o'clock, Faith entered the parlor to become Mrs. Nicholas Grey.

Dressed in his formal attire and with Arte by his side, Nick turned to watch her enter. At the sight of her his heart swelled with so much pride, he thought it might burst from his chest. He'd no idea where she'd gotten the stunning dress she was wearing, but she looked like a queen. From her gleaming hair to the faint paint on her lips, he could honestly say she was the most beautiful woman he'd ever laid eyes and he was humbled that she'd agreed to be his wife. She was followed in by a teary-eyed Charity and the smiling Bekkah, but he saw them only in passing. Faith, holding a small bouquet of red primroses, was his focus.

She seemed to glide as she walked over to stand at his side, and as she reached him she looked up into his face and smiled. Nick knew from that point on he would do everything humanly possible to keep that same smile on her face for the rest of their life together or die trying.

The ceremony conducted by Arte's uncle Absalom took only a few moments. Nick solemnly pledged his love and fidelity, and when her turn came, she pledged the same. Pastor Absalom then declared them man and wife and with a kind smile invited Nick to kiss his bride. Knowing that he couldn't kiss her with the passion he felt in his heart because of the guests looking on, he gifted her with a soft, gentle kiss, then stepped back.

The guests applauded. Charity cried. Bekkah cried. Mrs. Locke cried. The baby Peter cried in Ingram's arms. Faith glanced up at her husband through tears of joy, and Nick took her hand and kissed her fingers. "Thank you for marrying me," he said to her softly.

"You've made me very happy today, Nicholas. Thank you, too."

The wedding feast was held in the formal dining room. Faith sat at one end of the table and the pleased

Nicholas at the other. Even with everyone gathered around helping themselves to the food, offering toasts, and drinking ale, the newlyweds couldn't take their eyes off each other.

When the time came for the Cleggs and the Trotters to leave, Faith wondered if the rain had been a blessing after all. The day had been perfect. She and Nick walked their guests to the door, exchanged farewell hugs, and thanked them for their love and friendship.

Then Nick and Faith were alone. Standing with his back to the front door, Nick took in the sight of his lovely wife and wondered how long it might take him to get her out of that beautiful dress.

Faith could see the mischief in his eyes and so asked, "And what are you thinking, my handsome husband?"

He grinned. "How long it will take me to get you out of that dress."

She dropped her head. "What am I going to do with you?"

"I believe I can answer that as well."

Anticipation shot through Faith. Come morning she would know everything about the intimate mysteries of being a married woman and she was admittedly anxious to begin.

And so was Nick. With that in mind, he walked over and kissed her until the room spun. While Faith fought to recover from the sensual opening volley, he picked her up and carried her up the stairs.

He set her back down on her feet in the center of her bedroom and she asked, "Shouldn't we be in your room?"

He dropped a kiss onto her neck and his hands began to roam languidly. "You said this should be the room of my wife, remember."

And she had, but Faith was finding hard to think with the passion he was kindling in her with his kisses and hands.

"We'll initiate it . . . and you."

Faith moaned. His lips on the exposed expanse of her throat above the square neck of her dress were so hot, she thought her skin might catch fire. Her limbs were trembling, her lips were parted, and she reached for him to pull him close. It was all the incentive he needed. Running his hand up and down her silk-covered back while he licked at her lips set Faith on the road to desire. They fed on each other with humid kisses and slowly mating tongues, taking their time and prolonging the moments because they had all night.

"Let's get you out of this dress."

In the firelight from the grate, Nick played lady's maid and undid the buttons at the back, one by one. He paused between each opening to brush his worshipping lips against each patch of soft skin, then gently slid the silk down her shoulders. Holding the frothy dress against her waist, Faith, her eyes closed, felt the warmth of his fingers grazing her back, followed by the return of his lips. The familiar haze brought on by pleasure melted around her and encompassed her senses. He allowed her a moment to step out of the dress and laid it across a chair. She faced him wearing her snow white shift, drawers, white stockings, and shoes.

"You look ravishing."

Faith trembled in response to his husky voice and stepped out of her shoes. When he joined her again, he led her to the bed. And once he rid himself of his coat and breeches, he joined her there.

He looked into her eyes.

She confessed, "I'm a bit nervous, Nick."

"Don't worry. I know this is your first time and I'll make sure it's very special."

She whispered, "Thank you."

He smiled and traced a slow finger from her mouth and down her throat and then circled it over the small nook at the base. Leaning in, he flicked his tongue against it and moved his lips slowly across the bare spaces above her shift. She knew he could feel her small shakes, but his hands moving up and down the tense arms soon lulled her into ease and all she wanted to do was to feel what might come next.

The opening of the three small ribbons on her new shift followed. He eased the thin straps from her shoulders, then opened the fluttering halves to his admiring eyes. Faith didn't remember lying flat but somehow she was and he was above her looking down. Holding her eyes, he passed a strong hand over the dark nippled twins now free for him to explore, then dropped his head to reacquaint himself with their sweetness.

She groaned from the bliss in his loving of her. The erotic sucking and tugging from his lips made her hips rise. He moved a hand over her waist framed by the open shift, then down her legs encased in the silk hose and squeezed the flesh tenderly.

Nick wanted to spread her legs and take with all the fire he felt inside, but knew he had to keep the pace slow. She was his wife, a virgin, and he wanted her to look forward to their love play in the years they'd be together, not cower because he'd not been considerate of her needs this first time. In truth, however, he was enjoying hearing her sighs, watching her arch to his hands and croon as he filled her breasts with his hands and took the peaks into his mouth again, and his manhood, hard as it had ever been, was looking forward to the spirited release, but until then, he wanted her wet and ready as any man would want his wife to be.

To make certain she was, he teased the heat between her thighs through the opening of her drawers until she rose greedily for more. The urge to place his lips there and worship boldly at the shrine was strong but he'd save that for another time. Lovemaking was an adventure, too, but better if new experiences were doled out a bit at a time.

Faith pleaded soundlessly for mercy from the scandalous play of his long fingers between her legs. She opened for him and then opened wider. The dew flowing from her, the kisses he stole from her lips all conspired to make her feel shameless but she didn't care; she just didn't want it to stop.

Through the fog she watched him pull back, and heat and embarrassment filled her as he slid her drawers down her legs and off. Then his fingers returned and with her legs spread wide as the Boston Harbor she couldn't hold back the passion stacking up inside her like storm clouds converging in July. He slid a finger into the damp channel; her body exploded and she cried out as her hips rose from the bed in jubilation. The slow strokes that followed made her twist and call his name.

"What, darling? You want more . . ." Another finger went in filling the space, and she groaned and growled like a woman gone mad.

"This is what I'm going to do to you." The fingers sliding in and out enticed her hips into an age-old rhythm that Faith had no idea she knew and when the crisis passed and he withdrew from her body, she protested weakly.

"There'll be more."

Breathing as if she'd run a race, she looked up at her magnificent man. It never occurred to her that this was what lovemaking entailed, and then he was teasing her to open once more for the next part of the adventure and all thoughts fled.

Nick was a big man, so he eased the head of his manhood into her damp tightness a bit at a time. Feeling her taking him in and stretching to accommodate his size felt so incredibly good it made him want to push his way home, her virginity be damned, but he was better than that, he told himself as he gritted his teeth and held himself back.

"This hurts," she protested.

"Just hold on. It will get better. I promise."

After a few tense moments, her body took in all that he had and he held again, pulsing and aching, while waiting for her to accustom herself to the feel of their joining. When he felt her relax a bit he began to stroke her slowly. It came to him that he hadn't even come close to imagining how incredible making love to her would feel. Watching her begin to move beneath him with her nipples hard from his lips and her satin hips in his hands was far better than any dream.

He teased her invitingly to increase the pace, sliding himself in and out, bit by bit, and Faith's pain was replaced by a glowing brilliance that rose not from his worshipping hands or seductive lips but from the hard, enticing promise between her thighs. Soon they were moving as one. Nick felt her response radiating over him in much the same way as the firelight flickered over her partial nakedness, and the sights and sounds of her pushed him to the brink. Seconds later she cried out her release, and feeling her sheath clutch him so tightly, he couldn't hold back any longer. He'd been sensually toying with her for days and his own orgasm was rising and gathering steam. When it broke, the eruption threw his head back and possessively stroked her with all the fervor and passion he possessed. Sated, he rolled away and lay there pulsing.

They spent the remainder of the night enjoying their erotic adventure. Faith had no idea lovemaking could be done in so many explosive ways, but with Nick as her teacher, she became a very apt pupil. Finally they stripped the soiled sheets from the bed, and he pulled her close, covered with the quilts, and they slept.

The next morning, Faith awakened and found herself alone in the big four-poster. The sun was up and shining and her eyes widened when she saw the time on the clock on the wall. It was nine o'clock. She'd never been in bed so late, but rather than worry, she lay there and smiled. Nick had been right about their wedding night resulting in a late rising, and as her mind went back to last night, her smile broadened. What an experience. Her body felt sore but not in an angry way. There was also a bit of tenderness between her thighs and for good reason, she thought. She wondered where he was. Getting up, she quickly took care of her needs, dressed herself in one of the new day gowns, tied back her loose and all-over-her-head hair, and went downstairs to find Nicholas so she could give him a good morning kiss.

Chapter 20

When Faith entered the kitchen, a man she didn't know was cooking bacon on the grate. She stopped and stared.

"Morning," he said, turning to her with a friendly smile. "You must be Faith."

Wary, she nodded and asked, "Where's Nick?"

"Out back. He'll return in a moment. My name is Gaspar. Nick and I are old friends." He was built like a mountain, had arms the size of logs, and his skin was African dark.

"Have a seat," he invited. "Breakfast is almost ready."

Confused, Faith complied but hoped Nick would soon show himself so she could get an explanation as to what this man being in the kitchen meant. She'd come downstairs expecting to share an intimate morning with her new husband but was instead greeted by a huge stranger with a gold hoop hanging from one lobe.

A moment later Nick entered via the back door and

was accompanied by two more strange men. "Ah, you're awake," he said to her. "Good morning, sweetheart. I assume you've met Gaspar."

She nodded but was still very confused.

"This is Dominic LeVeq, and Esteban da Silva. Gentlemen, my wife, Faith."

"*Enchanté*," the one named Dominic said. His voice held an accent that made her think him French.

"My pleasure," da Silva added.

His voice sounded foreign to her ears as well, but being a country girl from Boston, Faith had no idea of his nationality. Both men were incredibly handsome, however, and were as tall and well built as Nick. Gaspar towered over them all, though. Their combined sizes and girth seemed to fill the large kitchen to the walls. Feeling quite small in comparison, Faith waited for an explanation.

"Breakfast is ready," Gaspar announced.

The men all took seats while Gaspar brought the food to the table.

Dominic said to Nick, "She's very beautiful. I see why you were doomed."

Faith was embarrassed by his comment but had no idea what the last part meant so she looked to Nick for explanation.

He told her, "Pay them no mind. They are even less tamed than I."

On the heels of that, Esteban asked her, "What does such a beautiful senorita see in a tick like Nick?"

Faith couldn't stop her smile.

"Again, ignore them." Nick chuckled over his coffee. "Especially him," he said, indicating Esteban.

As they helped themselves to the eggs, potatoes, and bacon, Faith asked, "Are you visiting the city?"

"We are," Dom said, "but the air here stinks with the scent of the British, so we'll be going back to our ship later today."

Faith found that surprising, "You came in by ship, but the blockade—"

"Is not a problem for men like us," da Silva explained.

She looked over at Nick questioningly but he said nothing in response. She'd never heard of anyone successfully breaking the British blockade, and again she wondered who the men were. She also wanted to know how and where Nick had made their acquaintance, but thought it best to save her questions for later when she and her husband were alone. Why they'd come and what they'd been doing outside added to the mystery. However, as soon as breakfast was done, they prepared to leave.

She and Nick walked them to the front door, and Dominic bowed gallantly to her in parting. "It has been a pleasure meeting you, Faith."

"For me as well."

Gaspar nodded and Esteban bowed, too.

"Thank you, my friends," Nicholas said.

"Let us know if you need anything else," Dom said.

"I will. Godspeed."

The three men climbed into a wagon parked out by the road. Esteban took the reins and the wagon rolled away. Nick and Faith stood on the porch until they disappeared from sight, and then reentered the house.

"Who are they?" Faith asked.

"Friends. They were members of the crew that saved me the night of the mutiny."

"Ah, and they just stopped by for breakfast?"

He took her into his arms. "Good morning, Mrs. Grey."

"Good morning, husband. I came downstairs to give you the first kiss of the day and found only Gaspar."

"You didn't give my kisses to him, did you?"

"No, and you didn't answer my question."

He gazed down into her eyes. Faith could see him thinking, so she prodded him a little. "Our adventure shouldn't hold secrets, Nick."

He nodded understandingly. "I asked them to bring in guns for the rebels."

She went still. If the patrols found them, they'd both hang.

He said seriously, "They are needed if we are to prevail. I don't want to live out our lives with England's boot on our necks."

"I knew you supported the rebels, but to bring in guns? Are your friends smugglers?"

"Among other things."

She thought that over for a moment. "And you?"

He shrugged. "I've been known to dabble here and there."

Her eyes went wide. "This truly is an adventure."

He chuckled.

She backed out of his arms and surveyed him for a moment. "I have a secret to share as well."

He raised a brow. "And it is?"

"You must promise me you won't get angry and shout, or make me leave you."

He looked perplexed. "What could you possibly say that would make me do that, Faith?"

"I'm Lady Midnight."

His eyes widened and he stared, shocked. "That's why I kept bumping into you in the middle of the night."

She nodded. "And I am so sorry about Primus. I got word to him as quickly as I could. Please don't be angry. I know you've been looking for her, but I truly don't know who betrayed him."

She watched him assess her for a silent few moments but couldn't discern his mood.

"You play the crone well, Mrs. Grey."

"Thank you," she whispered, still unsure.

He held her eyes. "In truth, part of me does want to be angry because you knew I'd been searching high and low, but the smuggler in me is very impressed, Faith. It takes balls to do what you've been doing."

"Balls?"

He chuckled. "I'll explain later." He held out his arms, "Come here, my lady."

Faith went to him and let him hold her close. His arms tightened, and when he placed a reverent kiss on her brow, she basked in all that he was, and what he meant to her. She was glad she'd finally told him the truth.

"No more secrets between us," he whispered.

She looked up through her tears and whispered in reply, "No more secrets.

He pulled her back against his heart and she never wanted him to let her go.

"Are you sore from last night?" he asked, looking down into her face.

"A bit."

"We'll let you recover today so it won't get worse."

The disappointment she showed in her face evoked his smile. "Liked your first night as a wife, did you?"

"Yes."

"So did I. You were the most passionate and beautiful bride any man could ask for."

Faith felt her feelings for him swell her heart. She wondered if what she was feeling was love. What she did know was that she wanted to wake up with him every morning for the rest of her life. She was enjoying what they were trying to build together and she wanted it to endure. "Thanks for a wonderful wedding night, Nick."

"You're welcome.

In the days that followed, when they weren't making love, Faith settled into managing her beautiful new home and Nick drilled with his fellows and went to secret meetings with the Sons. Now that the calendar had turned to mid April, the citizens of Boston were certain it wouldn't be long before Gage sent his troops out to crush the rebellion once and for all, so everyone waited and prepared. One of the directives from the colonial leaders was to keep a sharp eye on the road, especially after sunset, because the soldiers were more likely to move under the cover of darkness.

That night, Faith joined Nicholas on the porch where he was keeping watch. "Here's your coffee," she said, handing him the cup. "I still don't understand how you drink this foul brew."

"You are such a Tory," he teased.

She tossed back, "I'm a rebel Tory, Mr. Smuggler."

The weapons brought in by LeVeq and his crewmen were now in the hands of Prince Hall and Colonel Middleton's regiment, the Bucks of America. The debate as to whether men of color would be allowed to fight continued to swirl, but Nick and the others planned to add their numbers whether they were given approval or not.

"It's a nice night," she said, hooking her arm into his and looking up at the stars twinkling in the cloudless black sky. There was a chill in the air but she had on a cloak.

"That it is." He looked up at the sky and asked, "Do you know the names of the stars?"

"Just the dippers."

"The Iroquois call the big one *Nya-gwaheh*."

"Which means?"

"The Great Bear."

She listened as he told her the legend. It began with four hunters who were also brothers tracking a large bear that was terrorizing the Iroquois villages. One of the brothers was lazy and always wanting to stop and eat, and his antics during the story made her smile. In the end, the lazy brother finally killed the bear, but when it slowly came back to life the four braves realized that they'd tracked the bear so far that they and their dog were up in the sky. Nick finished the tale by saying, "The square bowl of the Big Dipper is the Great Bear. The brothers and the dog are the handle."

Faith found the story fascinating.

He added, "During autumn when the Big Dipper turns upside down, it means the lazy hunter has killed the bear, but in the spring when it's upright, the bear rises and the hunt begins all over again."

Faith smiled. "I like that. I'll see the dipper in a whole new way now."

"Good."

He leaned over and kissed her passionately, whispering, "Do you know what the Iroquois call a husband and wife who make love outside in weather like this?"

She grinned, "No, what?"

"Cold."

She laughed.

"Come on let's go inside."

They went in and he made love to her on the pelts by

the bedroom fire until they were both nice and warm.

The next morning while they were having breakfast, Arte came over bearing news from the Sons. "The leaders want everyone to report to Concord to help with the final preparations."

"When?"

"As soon as you can. I'm leaving this afternoon. Can you join us?"

"Yes. How long will we be needed?"

"As long as necessary, I was told." He then gave Nick directions to the Concord farm being used as the headquarters and added, "Bring any hand tools that you have. We'll be pounding out bayonets and the like."

Nick nodded approvingly. "I'll ride over this afternoon as well. Thank you."

Arte offered up his good-byes and hurried back to his home.

Nick spent the rest of the morning packing the clothing he thought he'd need and added some of the hand tools in the shed. As the time neared for him to go, they shared a quick lunch and Faith made sandwiches for him to carry along.

He had everything he planned to take with him in the parlor when they heard a knock at the door.

"Who could that be?" Faith wondered aloud.

Nicholas had no idea, but he left her and went to see. To his surprise, it was Stuart Kingston. The two men eyed each other silently until Kingston said finally, "I'm here to speak with my daughter."

The last thing Nick wanted was a serpent in the Eden he and Faith had made. "I'll see what she says."

From the hostility Nick saw on Kingston's face, it was clear the man didn't like being kept waiting, but Nick ignored it. Leaving him standing on the porch, Nick walked back into the parlor. "It's your father," he announced. "He says he'd like to see you."

"Whatever for?"

Nick shrugged and asked, "Should I invite him in?"

Faith didn't want to talk to him because she sensed no good would come out of it, but she said resignedly, "Let's see what he's after."

"Are you certain?"

"No, but have him come in anyway. Maybe afterwards he will get on with his life and we can get on with ours."

"All right."

When the two men returned, she slowly got to her feet. "Good afternoon, Father."

He offered her a terse nod of greeting, but as his eyes strayed around the room and he took in the large portrait of Adeline hanging above the fireplace, he stilled. As Faith watched him she saw myriad emotions cross his face: surprise, sadness, anger, and then resolve. His accusatory eyes swung to Nicholas for a moment and held, before he turned his back on the portrait and trained his attention Faith's way. "I'm here to take you home."

She sighed audibly before asking, "Why?"

"Because this is not your home."

"Yes, it is. Nicholas and I are married."

His eyes widened and he stared between the two of them before shouting at Faith, "How could you! Have you no shame!"

"You asked me to leave, remember."

"How dare you!" he shouted. "How dare you sully my blood with the blood of this"—he swung his eyes to Nicholas—"this bastard!"

"Father!"

"Don't *Father* me, you ungrateful chit! Have you no idea of the perfidy that runs through the Grey line! How traitorous and vile they are! His father stole Adeline from me! Impregnated with his foul sperm and that," he snarled, pointing with fury at Nicholas, "is the result!"

Faith was trying to hold on to her temper, but she was shaking with angry emotion. "You should leave, Father," she declared through gritted teeth.

"Not until you renounce this disastrous union and come home where you belong!"

"Leave us! Now!"

He slapped her.

The painful blow exploded in her cheek and rocked her off her feet. She covered her throbbing cheek.

Nick roared and threw a punch that exploded into Kingston's face. When the man staggered and went down, Nicholas followed him, landing blow after blow.

Alarmed, Faith screamed, "Nicholas! Stop!"

But Nicholas was in a blood rage. It was his intention to beat Kingston to death for his violent act, and he probably would have had not Faith's cries finally pierced the furious fog encasing him. Only then did he feel her frantic tugs on his arm, trying to pull him away.

"Nicholas! For me! Please! Please!"

His anger still ruling, he saw her tears and the terror in her eyes.

"Please," she whispered, sobbing. "If you kill him you will hang!"

She was right, of course, but his anger was white hot. Breathing harshly, his fists still balled, he backed off and looked malevolently down at the bloodied face of the man at his feet.

"You're still a bastard!" Kingston spat out as he wiped at the blood pouring from his nose and mouth. "And I hope Primus is rotting in hell! I'm proud to be the cause of his arrest and death. He deserved no better after what he did to me!"

Nicholas stared and roared, "You were the one!"

Kingston stumbled to his feet. "Yes! He called himself a friend. Said he'd look after Adeline until I returned from England, but by the time I did, they'd married and she was carrying you!"

Something inside Nicholas shattered. He grabbed Kingston by his collar and seethed, "Only my feelings for Faith are keeping me from killing you. Get out of my house! Never come back! Never!" He dragged Kingston to the door and threw him out.

When he returned Faith was dragging her palms over her wet eyes.

"Let me see your face."

She showed him her cheek throbbing from her father's blow. He touched it gently. "I want to kill him for putting his hands on you and then kill him again for my father!"

She had never seen him so angry. "I know. I'm so sorry. I never thought he could do something so vile. He boasted that Gage had Primus in his sights, but I didn't know it was because he'd betrayed him."

"God, I want to kill him!" he growled again and pulled her roughly into his arms.

She could feel his heart pounding.

"If he even looks at you after this, I'll hang."

She squeezed him tight. "He isn't worth your life, too."

"I don't know what to do with this anger, Faith. He's your father."

"I know."

Nick knew if he didn't do something with his murderous feelings he might wind up lashing out at Faith and he didn't want that. "I need to work this through, so it's good I'm going to Concord. I don't wish any of this to boil over onto you. I'm not accustomed to letting a man live after all he's done and I'm trying very hard not to go after him and slit his throat."

She stared up at him.

"I'm sorry but it's true. I've lived life by a very harsh

code, and a man like him doesn't deserve to see another sunrise."

Their eyes held.

He told her softly, "It's who I've been. Who I am. Remember the conversation we had about why I don't pray?"

She did.

"This is one of the reasons why."

She didn't know what to say.

"If I don't wish for our adventure to end with me on the end of a rope and your father in his grave, pounding out bayonets will help."

"You will come back to me."

"Always."

Tears filled her eyes. "Then go and help the rebels and slay your demons. I'll be here when you return."

He nodded.

Nick looked at this woman he'd made his wife and who held his heart. "I love you."

"And I you."

"If the war does begin, I may not be able to get back and tell you good-bye until it's done."

She nodded stoically. "I understand."

The last thing Nick wanted to do was to leave her, but he'd already given Arte his word and knew that his help was needed in Concord. If the war started he and the others had no alternative but to fight. However, the thought of being away from her for who knew how long made his heart ache.

Nick looked down and drank in her lovely presence so he'd have the memory to call upon in the days ahead. "If the fighting does break out before I return, go to Bekkah's, and the two of you hide in her woodlot if the soldiers march through. I wouldn't put it past them to ransack and plunder on their way and you shouldn't be in the house if that's what they do. Keep yourself as safe as you can."

"I will. Godspeed," she whispered, before adding pointedly, "and do not get yourself killed."

He smiled. "I won't. I promise."

They shared one last fervent embrace before she walked with him out to the porch. A few seconds later, she watched him ride away. He'd promised he would return and she would have to be content with that, but her heart ached as she went back inside and closed the door.

As she walked into the parlor, she looked up at Adeline's portrait and wondered if Adeline knew how her marriage to Primus had resonated through time. It was like a tragedy written by the Bard. Faith just wished she and Nicholas hadn't been written into the epilogue.

Chapter 21

The next morning Faith awakened to a silent house. There were no sounds of Nicholas outside chopping wood and the fire in her grate had died and gone cold. The room was freezing, so she got up and made her fire, then crawled back beneath the bedding to wait for the temperature to rise enough to cut the chill. With him away for who knew how long, she supposed she was on her own. It was not daunting but she already missed him very much. Having had him by her side since the day of the wedding, it was odd to have him gone. She needed to find something to occupy her until the sharp edges of his absence dulled a bit, so she decided to make it bread-baking day with the hopes that the task would keep her hands and troubled mind busy enough to prevent her from drowning in her woe.

As Faith set the first few loaves on the fire, Charity and the baby stopped on their way to Boston, and Faith was glad to see her friend. Charity set the basket holding the sleeping Peter down on the table. She took one look at Faith's swollen cheek and asked softly with concern, "What's happened?"

Faith told her about her father's visit and that he'd confessed to betraying Primus. When Faith finished, Charity shook her head sympathetically. "I can't believe your father would do something so awful. Did he and Nicholas fight?"

"Oh yes. I don't think he'll be visiting us ever again."

"Then that's good. Where's Nick now?"

"In Concord with the minutemen preparing for war. I'm not sure when he'll return."

Charity sighed. "I know the British have to be chased out, but you and Nick are newly married. This has to be difficult."

"It is."

"You both seemed so happy."

"And we were until the past rose up and sent us both to hell. I don't blame him for being angry at my father. Had someone I loved been betrayed that way, it would take me who knows how long to rid myself of the fury. However, I miss him, terribly. He's in my heart now, Charity, and there's no taking him out. I also told him about my being Lady Midnight."

Charity's mouth dropped. "And how did he react?"

"Said I had balls."

Charity's hand flew to her mouth and she laughed. "The man loves you. He'll return, you'll work out what to do about your father and make me an aunt before the year is out."

"I hope you're right."

"I know I am. The way he watches you makes me envious. I wish Ingram would look at me as if he wanted to eat me up." She paused, looked into Faith's eyes, and said with genuine feeling, "You're very lucky, Faith. Always remember that."

Faith knew she would value their friendship for the rest of her life. "I will, but I wish this war would go ahead and begin so that everyone can get on with their lives. Being on pins and needles is very wearing."

"Gage has been marching all four thousand of the troops day and night according to Mother. She thinks he'll send them out in the next day or so."

"Everyone keeps saying that but nothing happens. It's maddening. What of Ingram? Is he still supporting the King?"

Charity sighed. "Yes. In fact, he and some of the other Tories have signed up as auxiliary reserves. They won't be issued uniforms, but will help with the driving of munitions and supply wagons. He gets angry with me when I take the rebel side. He says that as his wife I should let him do my thinking. I scoffed at that, of course. He knew I had my own opinions when he married me. It's far too late for either of us to pretend otherwise."

"I'm sorry."

"His single-mindedness is worrisome because he knows nothing about war or weapons. He's a farmer. That innocence could get him killed, and, Faith, I would not survive if something happened to him."

"Seems like we both have woes."

"Yes, we do."

"As do most of the women around here with men in the fight. Nicholas says if the shooting starts before he returns, I should go to Bekkah's and hide with her in her woodlot. It's far enough away from the road for us to not be seen. You should think about joining us if Ingram leaves to help the British and you and Peter are alone."

"He keeps assuring me that the babe and I will come to no harm because we are a Tory household, but I'm not so certain. If there is shooting, I'll join you over at Bekkah's as soon as I am able. If the soldiers are using the road, I doubt I'll be able to make it to Boston and my parents."

Faith was glad they'd formed a plan but prayed it wouldn't have to be implemented.

Eighteen miles away in Concord, Nicholas and over a hundred men were making preparations. Blacksmiths were by their fires pounding bayonets out of white-hot metal while the smoke filled the skies. Donations from colonies up and down the coast were flowing in with everything from food and clothing, to wagons filled with old lead utensils and tools, to a herd of sheep. Everything except the lead was divided up and secreted away for use later. The lead was being melted down and turned into musket balls. Nicholas was on pouring detail, a task that involved ladling out the hot melted lead and pouring it into molds for musket balls. Once the metal cooled again, the balls of lead would harden and be given to the minutemen to use in their guns. Problem was, not only were the muskets so inaccurate as to be virtually useless in a battle situation, but not all the molds in use were of the same size. Some balls were larger than others, and some, depending on the quality of the lead, were not uniform in their density, which would only add to the ineffectiveness of the muskets, but it was all the minutemen had, so they worked feverishly in order to make enough.

Most of the men he was working with were from Concord and its surrounding towns but men from the Boston area were in attendance, too. Arte and his contingent were moving a cannon the last time he'd seen him. Nick had also seen a few of the men of color he'd helped train for Prince Hall. While he hoisted yet another steaming ladle of lead and dribbled it slowly into each round cup, the air rang with the sounds of the smithy's pounding, feet marching and drilling, and the comings and goings of messengers and other men on horseback. It was orderly chaos. They were in the field of one of the local farmers, and men were swarming over the place like ants, but were focused on one purpose, freeing themselves of the British.

When his shift was over, the weary Nicholas handed his heavy apron to the man who'd come to relieve him. Barrels of fresh water had been set about, so he ladled himself enough to quench his dry throat and walked over to trees where his bedding lay to try and get some rest. The chaotic atmosphere, coupled with the not knowing if Gage's men were on their way, made it next to impossible to sleep, even for a short while. However, Nick closed his eyes, and Faith's face shimmered into his mind. He wondered how she was faring and if she missed him as much as he was missing her. If he couldn't handle being away from her for a few days, he had no idea how he'd make it through when the war came, and it was coming. Being here and working so hard had cooled his anger a great deal. Instead of it consuming him as it had been immediately after he tossed Kingston out of the house, it was now only a simmer. Although he still wanted the man's head, Kingston was the father of the woman he loved, and killing him would affect his marriage no matter Faith's anger at her father and his deeds. Nick wasn't used to bridling his anger. He was more accustomed to handling his emotions on his own terms because there'd never been anyone in his life who cared enough about him to do it any other way. No one had ever wanted to help shoulder his burdens. To open himself up and show someone the depths of what he had inside was foreign. Being with Faith seemed to be altering that. However, now that he'd found her, married her, and fallen in love with her and found the answer to the questions surrounding his own father's arrest and death, could he find peace?

He thought back on her confession that she'd been

Lady Midnight. He still found that amazing. She had pulled the wool over the eyes of nearly everyone in the community. What was a man supposed to do with a woman like that? It never occurred to him that the stooped, gravel-voiced lady in black who'd visited him that night was the daughter of one of the area's staunchest Tories. Her father would probably keel over were he to learn the truth; first her marriage into the family of his nemesis, and now the revelation that she was working with the rebels against the crown would send him blithering to the nearest lunatic asylum. Nick allowed himself a tired smile. He needed to return to her because she was the peace he'd been searching for. As he drifted off into the twilight just before sleep, he vowed to ride back as soon as he could.

Faith spent the bulk of the next few days peddling her bread up and down the road but did not meet with much success. Of the twelve loaves she'd made she was returning home with eight. Many of the owners of the inns and taverns that she stopped in declined because they were already purchasing their bread from someone else. One owner did buy four loaves because he was running low and his regular baker had taken ill. He promised her that if his patrons liked the bread, he'd consider buying more on a regular basis, but he wasn't ready to commit just yet, and Faith had to be content with that. She'd avoided places that were known Tory gathering spots because she didn't have the requisite permits. Registering for a permit also meant her profits would be subjected to crown taxes and she had no intention of adding to the British coffers.

Frustrated by the lukewarm results but still determined to sell the remaining loaves, she'd driven all the way to Lexington, an eleven-mile journey, and now heading home on the eleven-mile return trip, she was so weary she could barely keep her seat on the wagon's bench. She had never driven such a long distance before or had to handle a animal who was not her own. He belonged to Nicholas. His name was Barney, and she spent most of the time trying to keep him under control. It was obvious that he was more accustomed to the strength of a man's hand, because he kept trying to gallop away at full speed, a pace that would crash the wagon and possibly throw her from the seat. Her arms were stiff from pulling back on the reins for so many miles, and the burning in her shoulders matched the fire feeding on her spine and lower back. More than anything she wanted to stop and let someone else drive but there was no someone else. It was up to her to hold on to the reins and make the balky horse take her home.

When the house finally came into view, she wanted to weep with relief. Her leaden arms were so numb and heavy, she wasn't sure she'd be able to move them when the time came to drop the reins. She made a mental note to work up to driving longer distances so that she could increase her stamina for the future.

Moving as if she was made of wood, she managed

to get the wagon unhitched and the horse in the barn. Shooting daggers Barney's way, she took care of his needs, then slowly trudged up to the house and entered by the back door. Her steps took her into the kitchen, where she stopped to bank the fire and add more wood. She then retrieved two large buckets and went back outdoors to the pump. She planned on taking a long, hot soak in the bathing tub. In a perfect world, Nicholas would be there to pump and then heat the water while she went up to her room to fall across her bed until he called and said everything was ready. It wasn't a perfect world, however, and she also wondered just when she'd become so pampered that pumping her own water had become something to whine about.

While the water heated atop the fire in the bathing room, she did indeed go and lie down across the bed. Too weary to move, she lay there and took in a deep breath. *Finally.* A knock sounded at the door, and she found herself growling at the inconvenient intrusion as Nicholas might have done. The knock sounded again, so she dragged herself up to see who it might be.

She opened the door to find Elizabeth Sutter, or more correctly Elizabeth Sutter Kingston, standing on the other side. Either way, it was the last person Faith expected to or wanted to see. "May I help you?"

"It's your father."

"What of him?"

"May I come in?"

Faith studied the seventeen-year-old for a moment,

taking in the perfectly painted face, the costly cape and black velvet slippers. She was fair enough to pass for White. According to the rumors, her older sister, Ellen, had indeed crossed over and was now the wife of a prominent tanner down in New Bedford. Both Sutter girls were fabled beauties but between them couldn't read a word.

"I'm very tired, Elizabeth, is this something that can wait until tomorrow?"

The dark eyes flashed anger for a second before she masked it. "I'm afraid not."

An unhappy Faith stepped aside to let her enter. "Let's go into the parlor."

As they both took seats, Elizabeth silently studied the portrait of Adeline. "Is that her? The woman who betrayed Stuart?"

"She is Nicholas's mother, if that's your meaning. We have only my father's side of the tale."

"He's been ranting about her for days."

Faith stayed silent.

"He's also becoming increasingly difficult to manage."

Faith thought her choice of the word *manage* an interesting one. "He's always been difficult to live with."

"More so than normal. He yells and threatens if his breakfast is not done on time, or if the table is not set correctly. He seems to think that in comparison to you I am lacking in all things."

Faith waited.

"Your man beat him very badly. His lips had to be sewn by a surgeon and he lost a few teeth."

"Nicholas didn't care for him striking me any more than I."

"He said you deserved it for being disrespectful and obstinate."

"Again, he's only given you his side of the matter."

Faith still had no idea what this visit was about, but her bath was waiting. She needed Elizabeth to get to the point. "Is there another reason you are here?"

"His wealth, or should I say his lack of it."

"Meaning?"

"Is he as penniless as he now claims?"

Faith met the question in Elizabeth's eyes. *So the fatted calf turned out to be straw.* Faith had nothing for her. "You will have to take that up with him." Hoping to intimate the end of the visit, Faith got to her feet.

Elizabeth ignored it. "He promised me new dresses, a home, a carriage."

"That's between you and your husband."

"Did he think I married him for his handsome appearance?"

"Why did you marry him?" Faith asked her bluntly.

Elizabeth turned away for moment as if to ponder that, and Faith saw a brief modicum of what appeared to be regret. But in the end, she flashed Faith a hostile look and stood. "Thank you for your time. You've been very helpful. I'll show myself out."

Faith watched her depart. Upon hearing the door close

she left the parlor to make certain the young woman was truly gone, and saw her being driven away by a young, blond-haired British soldier seated atop the wagon. The surprising sight made an interesting encounter even more so. However, Faith didn't have the time or the desire to dwell upon the new Mrs. Kingston's machinations; the water for her bath was probably good and hot, so she wearily ascended the staircase once more.

That evening as Faith lay in bed reading, she wondered how Nicholas might be faring. She missed him dearly. Was he still angry, or had the time away allowed his ire to drain? She'd prefer the latter, but had no way to determine whether it had or not, until he came home.

Her mind drifted to Elizabeth's surprising visit. Faith felt not a teaspoon of sympathy for the conniving young woman with her soldier driver. It was plain from the conversation that she was beginning to regret her marriage, but Faith felt nothing for her on that, either. Although the church encouraged people to take the high road, she couldn't help but enjoy learning that the bed her father and his bride had made was filled with rocks and nails.

Exhausted after the long day, she set her book aside, blew out the candles, and snuggled down into the bedding to sleep.

On the fourth morning that Nicholas was away, Faith was returning home from visiting Bekkah when Henri Giles rode up.

"Good morning, Henri," she said with as much cheer as she could manage. Both she and Bekkah were worried that they'd heard no news from their men.

"Good morning. Is Nicholas about?"

"He's away for a few days. Business."

Henri looked her in the eye. "Rebel business, no doubt."

Faith's face remained bland. "Is there something I may help you with?"

"I saw your father yesterday. He came to the general's office to show off the results of his fight with Nicholas."

"And?"

"I assume it was earned?"

"It was. He struck me again."

His lips thinned.

"What was the general's response?" she asked.

"Dismissed him summarily. Said with war imminent, he had no time to intervene into petty disputes."

The answer was a double-edged one. It was good to know that her father no longer had the general's ear but not good to hear that the war the colonies had been anticipating would really come to pass. "Thank you for letting me know."

"You're welcome. When will Nick return?"

"Soon" was all she would say.

"Then consider me at your service until he does."

She gave him a curtsy, then smiling winningly, asked, "How would you like to buy some bread?"

To her delight, he purchased what she had left, minus the two loaves she kept for herself. He also contracted with her for a future dozen loaves a week. The price they negotiated was fair in Faith's estimation and she couldn't have been more pleased.

As she walked with him back outdoors to where he'd tied his horse, he said, "You can count on me buying at least a dozen loves a week for as long as I'm deployed here. I'd prefer to come by and pick them up on Saturday afternoons so that the men can have fresh bread with their Sunday rations."

"Saturday afternoons it shall be. Thank you, Henri."

Astride his horse now, he bowed. "Thank you. When Nicholas returns please pass along my regards."

"I will."

Offering her a final nod and a smile, he rode back towards Boston. Faith reentered the house humming happily. In the kitchen she did a quick inventory of the ingredients she'd need to make more bread. There were enough dry goods like meal and flour but only enough molasses on hand to make Henri's initial twelve-loaf order and then she'd have to buy more. Because of the British blockade of Boston's harbor and the colonial boycott of slave owners in the Indies who'd gone along with the hated sugar tax imposed by Parliament, molasses, also a key ingredient in the making of rum, was increasingly difficult to come by. Any quantity that did make it to sale commanded extremely high prices. She remembered that there were two gallons back at her father's inn, not that that did her any good, but she would have to find more for purchase if she wanted to fill Henri's future orders.

That afternoon, an unfamiliar man came to the door. He said he had a delivery for her from Babette Locke. It was all the new clothing Nicholas had purchased and she was so eager to see what Mrs. Locke had created she could barely contain her excitement. The driver carried in first one trunk and then returned to the wagon to bring back a second. Faith tipped him for his service out of her bread profits, and once he took his leave to continue his other deliveries, she knelt and lifted the lid on the first trunk. It was filled with beautiful lace-trimmed shifts, satin drawers, and petticoats, and the exquisite design and needlework took her breath away. The second trunk held three well-tailored day dresses, a skirt, and a matching overblouse. Beneath those garments was a thin layer of linen and below it were three beautiful nightgowns. Faith held up the first one; it was made of lightweight snow white wool that weighed next to nothing. It lacked any ornamentation and had a curious split in the back that began at the top of her spine and veed down to the base. She guessed it was meant to be worn in that way, but she'd have to put it on to be sure. Gently setting it aside, she investigated the two remaining. They were obviously designed to please a husband's eyes. There was lace, and tiny buttons she could already imagine Nicholas slowly undoing. They both weighed less than a cloud, and she was certain they'd feel that way once she put them on. She wondered how Nicholas might react to her wearing them, but in order to gauge his response he'd have to come home first, she reminded herself. However, she found Mrs. Locke's creations quite dazzling, and so emptied the trunks and carried the bounty up to her room.

Faith had dinner at Bekkah's. They'd taken to eating together the past few days, and this evening Charity and the baby joined them. Ingram had left earlier in the day to be trained in his duties and Charity had needed cheering up. Peter never failed to put a smile on Bekkah's face. She and Arte had been married for over a decade but had yet to have any children. She always made a fuss over Peter whenever he was around and the look on her face when she held him was touching to see. Holding Peter often made Faith wonder about the possibilities of her and Nicholas having little ones as well.

When they ended their evening, they shared hugs, and Charity and Faith went back to their respective homes.

Faith had decided even if Nicholas never came home again, she was never moving away unless she could take the bathing tub with her. Washing up and then soaking herself in a hot tub of rose-scented water had become an evening ritual.

She was lying in the chest-high water with her head cushioned by one of the house's fat towels and daydreaming when she heard a few familiar footfalls on the stairs. Sitting straight up, she listened, hoping it hadn't been a tub-fed fantasy, and then she heard his voice. "Faith? Where are you?"

The part of herself that was still modest around him wanted to jump from the tub and cover herself, but the part of herself that loved the touch of his hands and kiss wanted to catch his eye and show him just what he'd been missing by staying away for so many days. With that in mind, Faith decided she was going to seduce her husband whether he was still angry or not. "I'm in the bathing room, Nicholas," she called out.

A second or so later, the sound of his boots neared, followed by a knock on the closed door.

"Come in."

Opening the door, Nicholas took a look at her in the tub and had to close his eyes for a moment to steady himself.

"Close the door please, so the heat will stay in."

His eyes riveted on the picture she made sitting in the tub with her wet shift transparent enough to show off the dark nipples beneath, he reached back blindly to comply with the request.

"Welcome home," she offered quietly.

Nicholas closed his eyes again and took in a deep breath as his manhood rose in silent appreciation.

"How are you?" she asked, but he couldn't answer because he was too busy staring at her as she rose slowly to her feet, letting the water cascade down her breasts to her thighs. Only then did she step out and take up a towel. To further torture him, she paused for a moment to slowly draw the wet shift over her head to remove it, showing off the taut muscles of her belly and waist, while her breasts revealed themselves in all their shimmering glory. He thought he might fall over.

She smiled and slowly dried herself, languidly moving the towel over all the places he longed to touch and kiss. "Cat got your tongue?" she asked softly.

"You're aware that you're killing me."

"Am I?"

To add more heat to the fire, she took down the small tub of creamlike lotion and gently smoothed it over her limbs while he watched with glowing eyes. Done, she picked up a long white gown he'd not seen before and slid it on over her nudity. The gown covered her from neck to toes and clung to her curves in a way that was both seductive and demure, but when she turned from him to pick up the towel and her discarded clothing, the slit up the back of the gown fanned open just enough to offer an enticing slice of her beautiful back, and he uttered a groan.

She looked his way. "Do you like the gown?"

"Very much."

"It's one of the things Mrs. Locke sent over."

"Remind me to give her a larger bonus. I came home to find out how you were faring and to tell you how much I love you, but I'm finding it difficult to remember the speech I'd been rehearsing on the ride."

"You can tell me in the morning. Right now I'd rather you show me how glad you are to be home."

"That I can do."

And to prove his point, he crossed the room, took her into his arms, and kissed her until they were both breathless. Then he picked her up and carried her to her bedroom.

Nicholas spent an inordinate amount of time on the bared path of back revealed by the sultry white gown. She was lying on the bed on her stomach and he couldn't ever remember being so aroused by a woman's spine before. He brushed his hand down the velvet-soft skin peeking through the space and then lower over her shrouded hips. It took all he had not to rip the garment at the seams and take her from behind. "I missed you," he whispered while he slid the gown up her legs. When he raised it over the curve of her sultry behind, his fingers played wantonly between her thighs. Uttering a pleased moan, Faith parted them in welcome invitation and he smiled.

"Turn over for me, sweetheart."

She complied, shuddering and trembling in response to the familiar feel of his hands. "I missed you, too."

"How much?" he asked, his voice hot. He moved his fingers over the swollen damp gate of her soul, enjoying the slickness there and the way her legs parted even farther, before dropping his head and using his tongue on the tiny kernel of flesh.

Her eyes popped open with surprise. "What are you—"

With a gentle hand on her waist, he kept her where

she was. "Just showing you how much I missed you." He slid a finger inside. Her growl of pleasure coupled with the feel of her sheath tightening as he possessively stroked in and then out caused his manhood to surge in lusty response. He lowered his mouth again, and this time she was filled with so much fire, she let him have his way.

"Oh my," she breathed as he dallied and lingered. He'd loved her in many soul-exciting ways since their memorable wedding night, but this was new and raw and so very very scandalous, her legs flew wide and she soon exploded, screaming his name.

Only then did he take what he'd been dreaming of while he'd been away, and they spent the rest of the day and most of night savoring what they'd missed while apart.

Chapter 22

Faith awakened the next morning to sunlight pouring through the windows and her husband leaning on an elbow watching her. When he smiled, she gave him a soft one in reply. He gave her a soft kiss.

"Good morning."

"Good morning." Faith always enjoyed waking up with him beside her and it was especially wonderful this morning because he was back.

"I missed you."

"I noticed. Are you here to stay?"

He shrugged. "Depends on Gage."

She turned on her side to face him. "And all that anger?"

"Better."

"Good," she answered sincerely. "What my father did to Primus was heartbreaking."

"Yes it was. I've come to grips with it, though. Having you in my life helped."

Faith looked at the man she loved with all her heart, and knew without question that he meant each word.

"You've helped me as well," she replied.

"How so?"

"I've not had someone to love me since my mother died."

He peered into her eyes, and upon seeing the emotion reflected in them pulled her into his arms. "And now you have. Plan on being loved until death do us part, my Faith."

Their smiles met.

"I will." Faith didn't know what she'd done to earn such happiness but it radiated inside like the sunbeams filling the room.

"So, tell me what has been happening with you while I've been away."

She began by telling him about her lack of success with selling her bread. "And then Henri Giles stopped by and purchased all that I had left."

"To sell to his smuggler friends, and at a profit, no doubt."

Faith turned to him with surprise on her face. "Smuggler friends? Henri isn't a smuggler."

"Yes, he is."

"No," she said, awed.

He nodded.

"Should I not sell to him then?"

"Oh, by all means do. War's coming and the price of bread will probably rise high as the moon. You stand to make a good profit, too."

She lay back. "Henri is a smuggler. He asked if you

were out on rebel business but I didn't reply. Does he know you support the Sons of Liberty?"

"He does. Being a soldier is just his way of making extra coin. He has no love of the King, either."

He looked at the continued surprise in her eyes and grinned. "I'm sorry to be the one to tell you he has feet of clay."

"You'd never know to look at him."

"Which only adds to his success, no doubt."

Faith shook her head in wonder. "And here I thought myself to be a good judge of character."

"You judged me fairly well."

"I know you lie. I didn't expect that he did, as well."

He chuckled and asked, "Anything else I missed?"

She then told him about the odd visit from Elizabeth, her blond soldier driver, and General Gage's rebuff of her father and his woes.

Like Faith, he was glad to hear that Gage had better things to do than go chasing after Kingston's enemies, but also like Faith, he hadn't liked hearing why Gage sent him packing.

"There were over a hundred men working with us in Concord. I'm told there are more than ten thousand men who've volunteered to fight."

"Are the rebels ready?"

"No, but then no one is ever ready for war. Everyone has been instructed to keep watching the road."

"Are the rebels still sure the general will strike at night?"

"If he's the tactical commander everyone thinks he is, yes."

Faith thought about the death and bloodshed that would follow. "Ingram is training with the British and Charity is afraid he will be hurt. She's promised to come here and stay with Bekkah and me if the fighting starts. Ingram is convinced she and the baby will be safe because they are a Tory household but she's not convinced."

"Neither am I, but I'm glad you ladies will be in one place."

"So am I. Is it wrong to wish the war would hurry and start so that it can be over?"

"No, but sometimes you must be careful about what you wish for."

"Then right now, I wish for my husband to make love to me, so I can forget what is ahead for the moment."

"A wish I will willingly grant. Come here."

At ten P.M. on April 18, General Gage made his move. He sent a thousand soldiers on a mission to Lexington to capture the rebel leaders John Hancock and Samuel Adams. From there they were to proceed to Concord to destroy the large rebel arsenal that was hidden there. The plans were so secret that not even the soldiers knew where they were going, but secrets were made to be exposed, and rebel patriots Paul Revere and William Dawes rode quickly to Lexington to warn Hancock and Adams while rousing minutemen along the way.

All over the countryside, from Boston to Lexington to Concord, minutemen jumped to the ready. Church bells rang, men frantically knocked on the doors of their neighbors, and little by little word spread that the British were on their way.

Nicholas was up and drinking coffee when Arte knocked on his door. Nicholas knew by the tense set of his old friend's features that the time had come.

Nick said, "Let me go up and say good-bye to Faith and I'll be ready to ride with you."

Arte nodded and headed back across the road to say his own good-byes.

Nicholas walked into her room holding a candle boat to lighten the darkness. The last thing he wanted was to leave her but it couldn't be helped. "Faith," he called softly.

Rousing her gently, he said, "Sweetheart, wake up."

Her eyes slowly opened. "What's the matter?" she asked sleepily.

"The British have marched out of Boston. I must go."

She sat up and wrapped him in her arms. He put down the candle and held her close to his heart. Nicholas had no words for how holding her made him feel, nor were there words for how much he loved her. "Keep yourself safe," he whispered.

"You do the same. I'll be very angry if you get yourself killed, Nicholas Grey."

"And we don't want you angry, do we?"

Her reply was soft. "No, we don't."

He smiled against her fragrant, midnight black hair. "If you have to hide, do so. I don't want you risking your life, either."

"I won't."

He pulled back so he could see her face. "Do you have any idea how much I love you?"

"I believe so, but you can tell me the depths of it when you return, and I promise to do the same."

He smiled. "You have a deal. Now give me the best kiss ever so that I will have something to sustain me while I'm away."

The kiss they shared was a tender, poignant reaffirmation of the feelings that bound them together. And when he reluctantly ended it, he felt compelled to give her yet another. "Good-bye, my love. I'll come to you just as soon as I can."

"Godspeed."

Her sitting on the bed and framed by the candlelight was his last look before he turned and hurried away to meet Arte.

Because the British soldiers had to be rowed across to Cambridge and had to wait for their supplies to do the same it was a long four hours before they began their march to Lexington to capture Hancock and Adams. Although both Revere and Dawes had been captured by the advance mounted patrols Gage had sent out to ambush or intercept anyone attempting to spread word of the British advance, the four-hour wait had cost the

British precious time, and gave the rebels enough time to spread the word. By the time the soldiers began to march towards their targets in earnest, thousands of minutemen of all ages, sizes, and races were following and trailing them under the cover of the trees.

Captain John Parker was the leader of the rebel contingent in Lexington and although his men had been alerted, it was a cold night, and when the British didn't show up in a timely fashion he sent his men home. As fate would have it the soldiers made their appearance shortly after, and although the rebel drummer sounded the alarm, many of Parker's men by that time were too far away to return to add their support, so Parker, a veteran of the French and Indian War, met the British force with the small number of men who'd stayed behind.

They were laughably outnumbered, but he and his men walked out to meet the King's regulars hoping the troops would see their displeasure but pass them by as the British had done at other close confrontations in the past. He instructed his men not to fire and supposedly the soldiers had been told the same. However, a few moments later shots rang out. The British said the patriots fired the first shot; the patriots said it was the British. It didn't much matter. In the chaos that resulted, the rebels ran in the face of the withering fire, forgetting their training and abandoning their posts for the trees, much to Parker's anger and dismay. The fight didn't last long, and after the British celebrated with a cheer, they marched on to Concord leaving the dead bodies of the patriots behind.

A bit after dawn, Nicholas and Arte, along with the men from Concord and Lincoln, stood on a ridge and watched the soldiers completely fill the Great Road with their superior numbers. The soldiers, after having met with success in Lexington, were moving confidently in their scarlet coats and snow white stockings. Nicholas had to admit they did make a handsome sight but he wondered, as he looked around at the minutemen wearing the earth colors of green and brown, why anyone would send their soldiers out in so distinctive a color that not even a misfiring musket could miss. It spoke to the arrogance of the crown, but he wondered if they knew that there were now a good fifteen thousand rebels armed and ready to meet them. As long as the rebels held on to their training, they'd give the King's regulars a fight to remember.

But they waited.

While Nicholas and the other rebel commanders waited outside the town of Concord, the British marched into the town's center and began their search for the weapons. Because the arsenal had been moved, they found little, but what they did find they piled up and set afire. Outside the town, the minutemen seeing the smoke thought the redcoats were torching the city. They rallied, lined up the way they'd been taught, and the war officially began.

Nick and the minutemen fired on the British for over

two hours and the British fired back. Men died on both sides, but the firing continued. Unprepared for the sheer force of the rebels' displeasure, the British commanders, Lieutenant Colonel Francis Smith and Major John Pitcairn, prepared to withdraw for the return to Boston. They'd been hoping for reinforcements but they'd never arrived. Leaving their dead behind but taking their wounded, they set out on a forced march back to the safety of their barracks.

The rebels gave them hell every step of the way. The British were angered that the patriots weren't following the rules of war. Instead of meeting the soldiers head-on and in a line, the colonials were shooting at them from the trees and from behind the stone walls erected on parts of the road, and then running down to the next ambush point and pounding them with their gunfire again and again. The British might have had more discipline, training, and skill but the rebels had the advantage of numbers, and they were fighting on land they knew well, and by dawn the soldiers of the King were all but running in retreat.

The rebels also broke another rule and used their marksmen to target the British officers, who fell one by one.

By the time the British made it out of the area surrounding Concord and into Lincoln, they hoped to have put the bulk of the rebel firing behind them but it continued. Even the citizenry, many of them women and men too old to fight, were shooting at them. The patriots had lost all discipline and every man was out to get to as many soldiers as he could. The soldiers, tired, exhausted, terrified, and angry, began torching the homes that held snipers as they continued their fast-paced retreat.

Hiding in the woodlot on the Cleggs' land, Bekkah, Faith, Charity, and the baby did their best to stay out of sight. They had seen the thousands of troops pass by on the way to the fight and were relieved that there'd been no looting, plundering, or shots fired. Now hearing the sounds of gunfire and seeing minutemen swarming the trees, the women ran back to Bekkah's house to get themselves out of the line of fire. It was a good thing because the redcoats' cavalry arrived shortly after chasing the rebels and being chased in turn by rebels on horseback.

Inside the house Faith and her friends barricaded the door with the heaviest pieces of furniture they could find, then went upstairs to peer from the windows to view the spectacle before them. A sea of soldiers flowed by them. The wounded lay across saddles. The red coats of the foot soldiers that had sparkled in the sun earlier were now covered with gunpowder and mud. Their white stockings were white no more but bore the stains of fresh blood.

The rebels chased the British all the way back to Boston, and once there the rebels made camp outside the city.

Nicholas and Arte came home later that evening

exhausted but, to their wives' relief and delight, un-injured. A joyous Faith ran to Nicholas before he even reached the gate. Grinning at the whirlwind approaching him, Nick picked her up, swung her around, and kissed her with newfound energy. Content, they draped arms around each other's waists and walked into the house.

Faith dearly wanted to know everything that had happened but he was too exhausted. After eating a bit of what she had left over from her dinner, he dragged himself outside to take a plunge into the cold swollen creek to rid himself of the stink and dirt of war. When he came back in, he gave her another kiss, then went to bed and slept like a dead man for a day and a half.

Down the road, Charity's worst fears had come true. While driving one of the munitions wagons sent out by Gage in the early dawn on the day of the fight at Concord, Ingram and the small escort of soldiers accompanying him for protection were fired upon. In the ensuing chaos he slapped down the reins to get the horses moving at a faster speed. One of the wagon's wheels hit a boulder and he was thrown from the seat. In the fall, his neck was broken.

Mrs. Locke stopped by to give Faith the terrible news. Nicholas was still sleeping, so Faith quickly penned him a note and left with her to go and offer what solace she could to her grieving friend.

While Mr. and Mrs. Locke kept an eye on their

grandson, Faith sat in the kitchen with the devastated Charity.

"What am I going to do without him?"

The sadness in Faith's own heart welled up. She had no answer. Faith was sitting, but Charity was on her feet pacing. Her face was tearstained and her eyes were filled with pain.

Charity whispered hoarsely, "I loved him so much."

"I know." Faith had loved him, too, in her own way. Being with Nicholas she now understood that what she felt for Ingram wasn't a lover's love, but it didn't diminish her grief.

"I'm carrying. How am I going to raise two children without their father?" She broke down into sobs.

Faith got up and held her while tears streamed down her own face. "You have me, and Nicholas, and your parents. We'll help you through this."

Faith knew that were she to lose Nicholas in such an abrupt way, no one would be able to help her through, so she held on to Charity even tighter.

"What do you need me to do?" Faith asked. "Whatever it is, I'm here."

They moved apart and both fished handkerchiefs out of their pockets to blow their noses. Charity spoke. "I need someone to dig his grave. I want to bury him by his mother and father."

Ingram had lost both of his parents to last year's smallpox epidemic. "We'll do that. What else?"

"Someone to say the words over his grave."

"I'll make the arrangements for that as well." Faith waited to hear if there were any other tasks needing attention.

Charity whispered brokenly, "I know there's more but I can't think."

"That's all right," Faith said reassuringly. She wanted to soothe Charity's pain but knew nothing could at the moment.

Mrs. Locke walked in. "Faith's man is here. He wants to offer condolences, Chary. Shall I send him in?"

Charity nodded.

When Nicholas entered, the tiredness in his unshaven face was plain. "I'm sorry for your loss, Charity."

Her emotions rose in response and she whispered, "Thank you, Nicholas."

He held out his arms to her and she went to him and let him hold her while she cried. Faith cried silently as well. The future was going to be hard on Charity, even with the help of friends and family, but she was a strong, smart, resilient woman. She might bend but she wouldn't break.

Once she and Nicholas parted he asked, "Do you know where he'll be buried?"

"Yes. Here."

"Do you have someone to dig his grave?"

She shook head.

"Then I shall. I'll come back in the morning and you can show me where you'd like it to be."

Faith could see relief course through Charity, who

responded to the gracious offer by saying, "Thank you, Nicholas. You have set a part of me at rest."

"You're more than welcome."

He looked over at Faith, and she nodded her silent and grateful thanks as well.

Charity said, "You two go on home. Nicholas, you look dead—" She paused and brought her hands to her mouth. "Dead on your feet," she said, finishing the sentence in a whispered voice.

Faith walked over and gave her another strong hug. After a few moments, Faith offered, "I can stay the night if you wish."

"No, you go on home. Mother and Father are here. I'll see you in the morning."

"Are you certain?"

"I am. They'll look after me and Peter."

Faith knew that they would, so she said, "I'll be back bright and early." She walked over and stood by Nicholas, who gave her waist a sympathetic squeeze.

He said to Charity, "Again, my condolences."

"Thank you."

"Try and rest," Faith said in parting. "We'll see you tomorrow."

After bidding farewell to the Lockes, Faith and Nicholas drove home.

Ingram Trotter was buried the next night. He'd been an only child, and since he'd lost his parents, Charity, Peter, and their unborn child were the sum of the family

he left behind. To his credit, families both Tory and patriot came out to pay their respects. Even her father and
Elizabeth were at the graveside. Faith ignored her father,
as did Nicholas, but the Kingstons seemed intent upon
ignoring them as well, so the short service performed
by Arte's kind uncle Absalom was as reverent as it was
supposed to be. Dressed in her black widow's weeds,
Charity held Peter, who at such a young age would probably never remember his father, but Charity would and
so would Faith. As Nicholas and some of the other men
began to throw shovels of dirt upon the wooden casket
holding Ingram's body, many of the mourners drifted
away, including her father and his tight-lipped bride.
But Faith, Charity holding her son, and the Lockes stood
silent until the grave was filled. Once Nicholas placed
the temporary wooden headstone in place, they all pro-
cessed back to the house.

Chapter 23

Faith spent the next few days letting Nicholas get his rest, checking on Charity, and dealing with her own grief. At breakfast one morning, in an effort to lift her mood, Nicholas proposed they do something special.

"Such as?" she asked with interest.

"A day-long fishing adventure."

"But aren't you supposed to be on call just in case the British march again?"

"Everyone is, but no official word has come down yet."

The colonial leaders were meeting in secret to formulate a plan to blockade Gage's soldiers inside the city. The British general was reportedly furious at the drubbing his men had taken at Concord, and the rebels and their supporters were holding their collective breath in anticipation of him unleashing that rage by sending his troops back out into the countryside to burn and kill.

"So let's make some fun while we can."

"Where are we going to go?"

"Just down to the creek. In the event an alarm sounds I need to be where I can be found."

The weather had warmed considerably over the past few days and Faith could certainly use an idyllic day, so she agreed. An hour later, carrying their fishing gear and everything else they needed to spend the day outdoors, they walked down to the creek, found a likely spot, and set up camp. They had a wonderful time. They fished, talked, cooked their catch over a fire, shared kisses, and talked about the future.

"What do you want to do once the war's over?" she asked.

"Fill the house with daughters that look like their beautiful mother . . ." Nick was seated with his back against a tree and she was being held tenderly in his lap.

Faith felt that was a lovely thought.

"What about you?" he asked.

"When I'm not selling bread, have a passel of sons who are all brave and as handsome as their father."

He hugged her against his heart and they were both content.

As night fell, they stretched out on the quilt and looked up at the stars. They were moved by the grand time they'd had together and although it was far past the time when they should have gathered up their things and headed back to the house, Nick treated his wife to her first taste of outdoor lovemaking.

"No screaming," he warned her with a grin.

Although it was difficult, Faith somehow managed

to keep from bringing the British down on their heads with her vocal responses to Nick's uninhibited caresses. She had no idea that being nude under the night sky could be so arousing.

When they were sated and finally able to move again, they dressed and gathered up their belongings. Reeling from the experience, the two returned to the house and fell into bed.

Chapter 24

Faith!"

When she heard Nicholas call her name there was something in his tone that led her to believe something was terribly wrong. Running to the parlor where she knew him to be, she entered hastily and found him standing beneath the portrait of his mother. The pain in his eyes stopped her. "What's the matter?"

He directed her eyes up and when hers came to rest, her hand went to her mouth in horror. The painting had been damaged; no, destroyed. The large canvas had been slashed in so many places pieces of it hung in long curling strips that resembled the peelings from an apple. The violence had rendered it so irreparable, Adeline Grey would never smile down from the walls of parlor again.

As if in a trance Faith walked closer. In its present state it was almost impossible to tell the frame had held a portrait at all. "Oh, Nick."

There was a deadly chill in his eyes. "We both know there's only one person angry enough to do this."

She agreed. "But when? It hadn't been this way yesterday. I distinctly remember the portrait being fine before we left to go fishing."

"As do I, so it must have taken place while we were out. We were far enough away from the house not to have seen anyone wanting to visit. Why he'd come isn't important but he took advantage of our absence to do this. First Primus and now—"

Tight-lipped, Faith realized there was nothing she could say. Why was her father bent on tormenting them this way? His actions were hateful, ugly, and in her mind quite irrational. Was he so filled with malice at the past that he wanted to destroy everything connected to it? What would it take for him to move past his anger and the need for revenge and cease this awful campaign? "This has to end."

Nick nodded. "Get your cloak. If we can't talk some sense into him, I'm not sure what I may have to do."

She nodded understandingly and hurried out to get her cloak.

It was Faith's first return to the inn since her marriage, and when she and Nicholas entered, memories both good and sad flooded her mind. She wondered how the life she'd had there would have been different had her mother not died so long ago.

Her father was seated at one of the tables. At their entrance he glanced up and then smiled smugly. On the heels of their entrance, Elizabeth entered from the kitchen, looking weary and small. Upon seeing Faith and Nicholas, her eyes went wide with surprise. She quickly looked to her husband but he had his gloating attention fixed on Nick.

"Found what I did to your whore of a mother, did you?" he asked Nicholas.

To Nick's credit he didn't react.

"Should have done it when I first learned she'd spread her legs for that bastard father of yours."

"Is that the only word you know?" Nick drawled, sounding bored. "I might be more insulted if your vocabulary weren't so limited. I've heard parrots with a better stock of curses."

Kingston's eyes bulged.

Faith glanced up at Nick approvingly. He was taking the high road in a way that she applauded. If her father wouldn't be reasonable, at least Nick wasn't allowing himself to sink to his level. A quick look over at Elizabeth showed her smile at the tactic before she hid it away.

Nick continued, "It occurred to me that you are a sick old man, worthy of my pity and nothing more."

Kingston jumped to his feet angrily and began a soliloquy of curses, threats, and hate that made Faith eye him as Nick had, with pity. Neither she nor Nick tried reasoning, or reacted or challenged him. They simply stood there and waited. Their lack of reaction only served to infuriate him further, and soon he was screaming like a man gone mad, hurling curses as if they were weapons.

The unholy glitter in his eyes wasn't anything Faith

had ever witnessed before and that concerned her. Had he really become unhinged? Would Elizabeth have to see about putting him away in a place where he could be watched and cared for so he wouldn't harm anyone or himself?

Foam could be seen pooling at the corners of his lips. Sweat poured from his brow and shone on his face. Nothing he was saying was comprehensible anymore and Faith's concern for his sanity increased.

Nick had seen all he could stomach. He placed a comforting hand on Faith's waist. "Come. Let's leave him to his madness. There's nothing for us here."

Faith agreed, and the part of her that had loved him was saddened. However, before they could take a step, her father clutched at his chest. His body went rigid and she watched in horror as his eyes rolled back and he sank to the floor.

She and Nick ran to him. Nick knelt over the unmoving man and placed his fingers against his neck. To Faith it didn't appear as if he was breathing and Nick confirmed her fears in a quiet tone.

"He's dead."

Faith dropped her head into her hands.

"I'm sorry," Nick said.

But before she could acknowledge his sympathy, Elizabeth declared in a loud, satisfied-sounding voice, "Thank God!"

Faith stared.

"Don't look at me that way," she snapped in response.

"My life has been a living hell. I'm glad he's dead, and deep down inside, so are you."

Faith couldn't believe her callousness. Yes, Faith had suffered much at his hands during their life together, but her father's death still saddened her very much.

"And," Elizabeth added as she headed towards the stairs that led to the living quarters on the upper floor, "since you are so moved by his demise you can handle the funeral arrangements. I'll not be attending." She hurried up the steps and disappeared.

"What a hateful girl," Faith stated once she and Nicholas were alone.

"I agree."

Faith went to the linen closet to fetch a tablecloth and gently draped the white fabric over the lifeless remains. "Rest well, Father," she voiced quietly.

She glanced up at Nick, who drew her into his arms and held her tenderly.

"I'm so sorry."

She savored his sheltering embrace. "He was quite mad at the end, I think. Maybe now he'll find peace."

"We'll hope. Will you handle the arrangements? I can hire someone if you prefer not to."

"No. I'm the only blood he has left. I'll do it."

Elizabeth reappeared carrying a cloth valise. "I've taken nothing that wasn't mine. If there's anything coming to me from his estate, give it to my parents. They'll know how to contact me."

Faith couldn't believe her ears, but there was something she had to know. "It's rumored that you are with child. Is the baby my father's?"

Elizabeth laughed. "Don't be ridiculous. Stuart couldn't sire a fly. He was too old and soft, if you get my meaning." On that, she sailed out.

Faith sighed.

Stuart Kingston was laid to rest in Copp's Hill Burying Ground the next day. The entire community both Tory and patriot came to the graveside to listen to the words and to pay their respects. Even General Gage sent a soldier bearing a handwritten note expressing his condolences. The gesture filled Faith with mixed emotions but she put it with the other missives she'd received and decided to sort out her feelings about it at a later time.

When the grave was closed and only she and Nick remained, she shed her first tears. He held her while she wept for the man she'd once loved, but who'd given her so little in return. When her grief had run its course, he placed a solemn kiss on her brow and whispered, "Let's go home."

In reality Nick had no feelings for Stuart Kingston. The only reason he felt anything was because of the pain he saw in his wife's eyes. Kingston was dead, and now maybe Nick could find some peace of his own.

That night at home in bed, Nick glanced over at Faith lying so silent beside him. "How are you?"

She shrugged. "Sad. Even though he might not deserve it, it's there."

"You buried him with all the dignity due a parent. That should count for something."

"I know."

She rolled her head over and held his eyes. "I don't ever want to have that kind of hate and anger touch our lives again, so in a way it is good that he's gone."

"I know. I feel the same. Eventually it may have affected what we have and that would have been a shame." He pulled her back against him and held her tightly. "I love you, Faith."

"I love you, too."

A short few days later, the word came down from the Continental Congress to begin the blockade of Boston. Gage and his troops hadn't left the city since taking the licking at Lexington earlier that month, and the Congress wanted to institute the blockade to ensure they never did. The idea was to rally minutemen from across the colonies to encamp on the city's perimeter, thus preventing the troops from marching back out into the countryside.

Once again, Nick was heavy-hearted as he told his wife good-bye.

"I'm already weary of war," she said to him. She was once again making sandwiches for him to take along.

"So am I but it can't be helped. I just wish I knew how long this might take. According to Arte, men are pouring in from as far away as Virginia. The successes at Lexington have been a big boost for the cause."

"I know, but I wish it would hurry and end so that

you and I can have a continuous adventure instead of this disjointed and fragmented one."

He smiled and tenderly raised her chin so he could memorize her midnight black eyes. "We will survive this challenge as well."

Faith knew he was talking about the mess with her father. "Thanks for settling the inn's debts so that it will stay in the family."

"That was easy. With the help we've hired, all you'll have to worry about is keeping the ledgers balanced, and I applaud your idea of running a bakery on the premises. I'll feel better knowing you are there and safe and not peddling bread up and down the road during wartime."

"I do, too."

They fed on each other visually, because it would have to sustain them until they were together again.

"I must go," he said.

They walked together out to the porch.

"Do not get yourself killed," she scolded, as had become her habit at moments like this.

"Keep telling me that so I will remember," he said with a soft smile.

Their final parting kiss was filled with such bittersweet tenderness it nearly broke their hearts, but he had a job to do and she had to let him go so that he could.

"Take care of yourself," he told her.

"I will."

A few moments later he rode away. Waving, she

watched him through her tears until he vanished from sight, but she had no idea that it would be summer before he held her again.

Time passed slowly for Faith. She devoted her time to getting her bakery up and running, and because Bekkah and the pregnant Charity needed a way to occupy their time, Faith hired them to help with the baking.

The days turned into weeks. Although Bekkah had gotten word that Arte and his regiment were still camped outside Boston, Faith heard nothing about or from her own husband.

At the beginning of June, Bekkah entered the inn with happiness filling her face.

"What's happened?" Faith asked. "Is the war over?"

Charity had been to the blockade to sell bread to the rebels. "Arte sent this to you. It's from Nick!"

Faith all but snatched it out of her hand.

Charity smiled. "Go sit outside and read it. Hopefully it's good news."

Faith did exactly that and as she excitedly unwrapped the twine, she saw that it had been dated on the tenth of May and it read:

My dearest Faith,

My apologies for not corresponding sooner but there was no time. As I pen this I am in the wilds of Canada under the leadership of patriot commanders Ethan

Allen and Benedict Arnold. We are only eighty-three
men strong but have successfully taken the British
stronghold Fort Ticonderoga. I am aware of how slow
the posts are, and that I may already be back in Boston
by the time this reaches your hand. If not, rest assured
that I am on my way. I've missed you sorely and am
eager to hold you in my arms and resume our adven-
ture. I hope you are well. My heart beats with yours.

Your loving husband, Nick

Faith raised her eyes to the sunshine and whispered
through her happy tears, "My heart beats with yours
as well, my Nick."

Chapter 25

On the last day of June, Faith was outside sweeping the porch when she looked up and saw a familiar man riding down the road in her direction.

"Nicholas!" she screamed. Throwing the broom aside, she launched herself to meet him.

Crying and waving she screamed again. "Nicholas!" Tears were streaming down her face and she was running as fast as a carrying woman could. When she reached him, he snatched her up onto Hades' back and held her so tightly she thought her back would crack but she didn't care. The kisses they shared went on forever as they laughed and wept and she ran her hands over his tired, bearded face to make certain it was really he.

He pulled her tightly against him again. "It's so wonderful to see you," he breathed. Nick felt like a thirsty a man finding an oasis. "So wonderful." All the cold and death and terrible conditions he'd been forced to endure on the march to Canada and back melted under the heart-filling feel of having her in his arms again.

Hades skittered in response to all the activity on his back but Nick kept him under control. "How are you, my love?"

"I was so worried," she breathed. "And then I got your letter." She was so overwhelmed with joy. *He was home! He was really and truly home!* "We're having a baby."

He stilled and searched her face looking for the jest. "Really?"

"Yes. I'm due around the new year."

With a laugh, he pulled her back into his arms and couldn't have imagined happier news. "Are you well?"

"Yes, and our baby, too."

Nick looked back into her tearstained face and grinned. "I want a daughter."

"I'll see what I can do."

Nick and Faith rode the short distance back to the house and they both swore they were the happiest couple in the world.

Later, although Nick was so road weary he planned to sleep until autumn, he forced himself to stay awake long enough to bathe, eat, and make love to his wife. Afterwards as they lay sated and filled with their love, she asked, "How long can you stay?"

When he didn't give a ready response, Faith turned so she could see his face. "Nick. What's wrong?"

"From what I've been told, General Washington and the Congress are going to forbid men of color from participating in the rest of the fight."

"No! Black men have died for this cause."

He shrugged. "I know, but Washington and the rest are slave owners, so it isn't as if we haven't been expecting this."

"Maybe saner minds will prevail."

"Maybe."

Faith now understood his mood. "Is it awful of me to be a bit glad to know you may be here to see your daughter born?"

He grinned and traced a finger down her cheek. "Not in the least. I'd like to be here for the big event, too."

"Then Washington can change his mind anytime after that."

He chuckled. "Come here."

She snuggled close.

"Do you know how much I love you?"

"Yes, but I never tire of hearing you tell me or show me," she added slyly.

"No more loving tonight, greedy woman, unless you wish to wake up with a corpse."

She chuckled. "Can't have that."

Nick kissed the top of her head. "I think I'm going to sleep now."

"You're allowed." She turned and gave him a kiss, whispering, "Sleep well and I'll be here when you wake up."

"Promise?"

"With all my heart."

His lids fluttered closed and he drifted away.

Faith lay in the dark listening to the rise and fall of his breathing and knew that she would never lack love again. With her husband by her side and their baby on the way, life was perfect. Smiling with contentment, she drifted off to sleep as well.

Epilogue

Nick got his wish. On January 1, 1776, Morna
Adeline Grey came into the world weighing a
healthy eight pounds, three ounces, and yelling loud
enough to be heard in Lexington. The slave owner generals and congressional representatives in charge of
the rebellion realized they needed the men of color in
order to chase the British from the American shores
and rescinded the ban.

A month after his daughter was born, Nicholas Grey,
former smuggler and now father, marched back to war
with the hopes of making the new country a safe and
secure place for the two women he loved. He'd found
his peace.

Author Note

Dear Readers,

Writing Faith and Nick's story was entertaining and educational. I knew very little about the true role played by people of African descent in the nation's battle for freedom, and after my research I was blown away, not only by the facts, stories, and statistics, but by the knowledge of how strong and politically active the nation's Black communities were in the eighteenth century. When the Revolutionary War began, there were five hundred thousand Blacks living in the thirteen original colonies. Most of them were slaves, but many of the larger cities like Boston, New York City, and Philadelphia were home to small free Black communities where men like Prince Hall led protests and presented petitions calling for equal rights and the abolishment of the slave trade. After the war ended in 1783, these communities would continue to grow in both numbers and influence, reaching their political zenith during the Abolitionist era of the 1850s.

Doing the research for *Midnight* also led me to the stories of men like William Lee, a slave who was General Washington's valet and man servant before, during, and after the war. Lee can be seen in some of the paintings of the general, the most notable being the portrait done by John Trumbull. Others who caught my attention during this era were Peter Salem, Salem Poor, and the young James Forten. Search out these names as a way to increase your knowledge of American History.

Women also played a vital role in the conflict with the British. One of the most celebrated was a female patriot spy known only as 355. She is said to have supplied vital information to the rebel forces, but her true identity remains a mystery. Because of the accurate intelligence she passed along, it was assumed that she had access to the upper echelons of the British military. When I read about her, I said, why not, and the fictional Faith Kingston was born. If you would like to know more about the race's role in the founding of our nation, here are some of the sources I consulted.

Eggerton, Douglas E. *African Americans and the Revolutionary War.* New York: Oxford University Press, 2009.

Fleming, Thomas. *Liberty! The American Revolution.* New York: Viking Press, 1997.

Greene, Lorenzo Johnston. *The Negro in Colonial New England.* New York: Athenum Books, 1968.

Lanning, Michael Lee. *African Americans in the Revolutionary War*. New York: Citadel Press, 2005.

Malcolm, Joyce Lee. *Peter's War: A New England Slave Boy and the American Revolution*. New Haven: Yale University Press, 2009.

Knowledge is power but shared knowledge empowers us all.

In closing I'd like to thank my readers. For the past sixteen years you've followed me all over the literary landscape, whether it be historical, contemporary suspense, or faith-based women's fiction, and I do appreciate your love and support.

Until next time,
B.